LA REINA

LA REINA

A Novel

J.D. YANEZ

BOWL BOOKS
PUBLISHING

Published in Partnership with:
Bowl Books Publishing LLC
King City, California

Cover Design: Tyler Evelyn Rood
Editing: Kat Howard , kathowardbooks.com and Julie K. @yarnwyvern IG/TikTok
Interior Design: Bowl Books Publishing LLC

First Edition
Paperback ISBN: 979-8-9864287-5-8
eBook ISBN: 979-8-9864287-6-5

Printed in the United States of America

For my real-life Tommy,

Thank you for taking me away and holding my hand through every stage of life. Without you, I would have wondered far and without purpose.

To my sister,

We made it. We're allowed to be happy.

NOTE FROM THE AUTHOR

I know that by all accounts, I am white. My skin is white, and the average person who sees me will see me as a white person. Though I am of Mexican descent (my mother and stepfather who raised me), and I grew up in the throes of 1990 Chicano culture, it does not mean this story is representative of everyone's experience. The Chicano experience is wide-ranging, our stories are varied, gorgeous, and full of life.

And they are all different.

If something is corny or too "cholo" to you, it is because that was my experience. Almost every scene where characters interact in a Mexican-American/ Chicano setting as a family is a version of events that have already happened once upon a time in 1997. This does not mean that every Mexican-American family you meet is going to have a similar familiarity. In fact, it is hurtful to assume so.

Additionally, my Spanish is weak, and so was my family's growing up. How it is used here, interchangeably between English, was and is commonplace because it was the only thing we knew. It was all we were taught. I know to some it will feel like baiting to a demographic by throwing in random words but consider the very specific culture of the characters first.

Lastly, any similarities between the cities of Casa Grande/Coolidge/Florence/Eloy, Mesa, and 11-Mile-Corner are coincidental. The setting is completely fictional, and these locations are meant to be only inspirational.

Thank you, from the bottom of my heart.

TRIGGER WARNINGS

First and foremost, although there is a romance subplot, none of the below-listed triggers are due to any romanticization. **THIS IS NOT A DARK ROMANCE,** this is a horror/paranormal thriller, with a small romance subplot.

If any of the subjects listed below are something you struggle with, please be mindful when reading or forego reading altogether. Not all subjects are discussed in length, many are only alluded to, but I felt it necessary to mention them.

<u>THE TRIGGERS ARE AS FOLLOWS:</u>

Murder, PTSD, war, military sexual trauma (MST), rape, childhood sexual trauma, childhood sexual/physical/emotional abuse, intense nightmares, generational trauma, blood, murder, unwanted advances, violence, severe mental health disorders including depression, anxiety, and bipolar disorder, animal cruelty, alcoholism, religious trauma, drugs, satan/devils/demons, desecration of bones, and any variation or inherent sub-category of the aforementioned.

"The companions of our childhood always possess a certain power over our minds which hardly any later friend can obtain."

-Mary Shelley, Frankenstein

PROLOGUE
JULY 7, 2019

I wish I could return to the exact moment as a child when I was forced to learn that my no's had become synonymous with yes. Maybe then, I wouldn't be in this cell with my body and restraints doused in cold, musty sweat. Maybe then I wouldn't have grown to become a liar, a fake, a murderer.

The air is cold in this psychological prison, causing shivers to snake down my spine, and still, I sweat because of my nerves. Rattled, fear-fueled nerves from the horror that lives and breathes in my dreams each night.

The uniformed staff saturates my bloodstream with every mind-fog medicine they can, subduing the voices and keeping him at bay. I don't think they've used these restraints since the 1960s, but it's the only way to keep him from acting out through my feeble hands. It's all the same to me. I can't stand the thought of anyone touching me anymore, the thought repulses me. The long-sleeved clothing helps.

They can't keep him away at night, though, and he knows it.

I've been in this ivory-padded hell for 99 days by my unreliable count. Ever since he tried to force my hands around the neck of the nurse injecting me with tranquilizers—they haven't let me out of this jacket.

They wipe me down and give me the fastest bird bath known to man, but it's so quick I can't help but see the insignificance of it. They sprint as a team to tie me back up when they're done, depositing me back onto the built-in bed against the wall. The smell of grease lingers in my long, black tresses, and the stench of body odor never quite leaves me.

It's taken all my will to keep myself from falling asleep over what I presume to be several days, and blinking feels as though sandpaper scratches my corneas.

He makes no residual noise in my mind so long as I am awake. He's scurried off into a far corner I cannot reach. I wonder if the meds help or if he is only biding his time, fooling me into a sense of complacency. After all, he has more fun in my dreams.

The last time I remember sleeping was a particular cruelty. I'd been up for five days, and I couldn't resist the pull of the drugs to a heavy reluctant sleep. I was a child again, five years old at most, and my small child body lay in a crooked and sunken bed.

Watching myself in that dream was surreal. She didn't look like me, not like how I saw myself now. She was at peace, happy even, in the way only a small child could accomplish before their fear of the world around them takes root, embedding itself in their being. I've had first-hand experience with the darkest fear living on Arizona soil. It lives in me now, and so, I don't recognize that contented girl. I lost her long ago.

Melodic sounds interrupt her deep sleep, and it keeps the real me in my own to watch and observe. Rising from the derelict bed, she walks through the decrepit house. Her feet move with unhurried steps down a hallway, through the kitchen, and onto the sliding glass door leading to the backyard.

Before she slides the door open, exposing herself to the harsh heat of an Arizona summer night, she glances down at the long braid on her shoulder. A frown forms on her lips as she takes in the bright red bow holding it together.

"Strange...," she whispers.

That it is. I never braided my hair as a child. Ephraim always did.

You look too grown up with your hair all messy. A braid keeps you young.

I cringe at the reminder of his words, and the little version of me in this dream does too. Every syllable that forms our stepfather's words worms its way into our thoughts like a parasite, refusing to leave. She pushes her lips together, and a small tear forms at the edge of her brown eyes. It threatens to glide down her cheek to serve as penance for every time she could not say no. An outloud claim to her objection.

Distracted by the melody ringing around her once more, she shoves the braid to the side. Chlorine invades her sense of smell when she finally steps into the backyard, but she ignores the pool. Ignores the call of the cool water in the heat of the night. Something much stronger draws her to the corner of the yard once more. Small feet shuffle all the way there to meet her personal devil. A pet dog in the yard growls behind her, snarling, foaming at the mouth at the devil it can't see. But it knows what comes next because it's the same as every night, in every nightmare.

Five-year-old Raina bends before our devil, nuestro duende. Her knees fall to the hard earth, and she ignores the pain that greets them. Instead, her eyes lock on the boots before her—curved, curling in on themselves at the toe, in solid black leather. Dragging her gaze with fierce reluctance, she takes in the sight of the long black coat, leather gloves, and pointy hat atop its head.

Digging her hands into the dirt, her knuckles go white with fear when her line-of-sight lands on his face. Or rather, what should be his face. The all-black blank space where features should reside holds nothing but glowing red eyes.

The silver-strummed melodies from an invisible guitar ring louder, egging her on. Impossible words leave the devil's nonexistent mouth; they sound inside our heads because that's where he resides and lives and breathes.

Eat the dirt, Raina. Take back what's yours, dear child.

His instructions are clear, but her head shakes back and forth, refusing to follow orders.

"Please don't make me," she whispers, the tears freefalling now.

How do you expect to know the answers to your questions without becoming one with the earth that was stolen from you? Your ancestors still live in this native soil. It is a part of you. Eat. The. Dirt. Raina. Or you'll never sleep soundly again.

With a cry, she does. Gagging with horrendous fervor, she continues shoving fistfuls of dirt until the world fades to black, and I am once again waking to the bright fluorescent lights of my cell. Highlight reel of a nightmare over.

Garbled screams left my mouth when I woke the last time, causing a stir of panic from my captors. They feared I'd found a way to end it as they rushed through the door to find that in a perfectly normal cell, I'd managed to lay in a bed of grass and piles of dirt, covered in sweat, tears, and vomit.

The second nurse to discover the anomaly, sank to

her knees in zealous prayer at the very sight of me.

"Dios te salve, María,
Llena eres de gracia,
el Señor es contigo.
Bendita tú eres entre todas las mujeres,
y bendito es el fruto de tu vientre, Jesús.
Santa María, Madre de Dios,
ruega por nosotros, pecadores, ahora y en la hora
de nuestra Muerte.
Amen."

She fears me and has since refused to come into my room.

I think I am on day five of no sleep now. I can't hear him, but I can feel him lingering. Pacing in a dark crevice, waiting to strike. I roll my head full of grimy braided hair to the side and stare at the outline of him that has begun to live in the corner. I wonder, is this my mind playing tricks on me, convincing me of something that isn't real because of my fear? Or has he grown stronger? Am I unable to resist his pull without mind-debilitating pharmaceuticals?

I do know one thing, at least. A distant memory floats in my thoughts, forcing me to remember a time before I was invaded by this demon from the seven circles of hell. My mother, drunk, repeating lines to me over and over and over. Ensuring I never forgot.

I understand my mother's fear of the dirt now. Her unwillingness to accept that she would spend any second of eternity buried in the ground.

You never know what's waiting for you there.

I. PLOT HOLES
APRIL 1, 2019

Death won its battle with my grandfather because there wasn't anyone left for him to fight for. At the ripe age of 94, when all eight of his kids were dead and buried, he said goodbye, too. They were nothing but bones when he finally realized he could choose himself and rest. Decades spent giving every ounce of himself to children who never bothered to consider how their actions hurt him, or their mother. He wanted to be at peace with his dead wife and children for who knows how long, and when death came knocking, lying down in the cold dark earth with Nana Isabel somehow now seemed acceptable.

Unlike my mother. Lenny didn't want anything to do with burials, Catholic or otherwise.

Burn me to ash, or so help me God, Raina, if I end up in the earth, I'll come back and haunt the shit out of you.

Those words tumbled like a waterfall from Lenny's lips when she was three wine bottles deep or coming down from a high, paranoid, and fidgeting. An incessant warning that she would not let go of.

You're being unreasonable, Mom, knock it off.

She'd swat a drunken hand at me and scold me.

Your precious Nana Isabel would agree. She al-

ways said I needed to act right and be mindful of where I ended up. As if me having a good time means I'm destined to go to hell.

If you're not worried about your actions damning you, then why do you care where you're buried? I asked.

She would grace me with a careless shrug.

Sometimes the superstitious ones get it right. I'd rather be careful than be wrong.

When she died in a heap of sickness derived from her own self-indulgences five years ago, I was thrust into a situation I was not prepared to deal with. Every expense, emotional and financial, rested on me and my sister's hands. I was 21 and still fresh into adulthood when my mother died. In my mind, it was unfair to expect such a burden to land in my hands, an unfair judgement of the universe that reckless, know-nothing-me was in charge of funeral processions.

My grandpa's dying wishes were a stark contrast to what Lenny wanted, from what she begged for in her most pathetic moments. I'm reminded of her with every decision I help make for his services. The simplicity of my grandfather's death wish, the absolute predictability of it, feels like a move in the opposite direction of one of his eldest daughters.

He wanted a Catholic mass. She couldn't and wouldn't have one.

He wanted to be buried next to his wife. She wanted to be fried, and her ashes spread across the northern Arizona mountains.

At every turn, it feels more and more like Lenny was this wild freak of nature compared to the rest of the family. As troubled as they all were, Lenny seemed to take the cake.

Her inability to walk away from recreational activities overshadowed most of my childhood, too. She never could stay away from a good time or a shot of whiskey with her pills. I don't know if it was the pills, the alcohol, or the brujeria running in her veins that made her crazy enough to drink herself to death. There always seemed to be something about the fear of death that pushed her to tempt it more than others.

The Medina family called me insane when I said she wouldn't be buried in the plot my grandparents paid and reserved for her. Their harsh words fell on deaf ears because I knew it was ridiculous, and I knew I had to do it anyway. The church practically laughed in my face when I asked for a funeral mass for someone who was to be cremated. At the time, I supposed it was unconventional for a "good Catholic woman" to take the cremation road in place of a proper burial. But Lenny was nothing if not determined to always be the center of attention, and her death cloaked me in doubt, absurdity, and annoying grandeur worthy of an outstanding embarrassing proportion.

In the end, she turned me into the bad guy so she wouldn't have to be.

Lenny wanted her cremation to act as a form of art, too. She used it as a war against the traditions she was bound to on top of ensuring there was nothing that could find her in the dirt of the afterlife.

But she used me to get it, knowing of the two sisters, I would comply with her wishes, which pisses me off the more I think about it.

Lenny could be loving and caring, and she was always artistic and beautiful. Despite her many faults, my memories are full to the brim of happy and joyful times with me and my mother. But for every good memory, there are more terrible ones. They stain the good, diming their light. Those are the ones I can't seem to walk away from.

I know that if I do not carefully monitor myself, I'll be Lenny 2.0.

"So, she ruined her liver, then? And you're afraid you'll do the same?"

My therapist offers me a look of fake empathy. I can tell it's fake because her lips pout too much, but her eyes squint just enough that I can see the annoyance in them. She isn't genuine in her compassion, but Doctor Ingrid Leslie is nice enough. I've been going to her since moving home after being forcibly medically retired from the army. My options for a therapist were shit to none, and I was left with Doctor Ingrid from the Veterans Affairs office for therapy sessions instead of paying to go out of network with my health insurance.

Ingrid wasn't my first or last choice. She was the only choice. My dealings with her are to help with my sanity, or rather, the lack of it. And because the VA says I have to. That shiny bipolar diagnosis requires it.

I shrug and decide to word vomit on her, giving her perceived golden nuggets of information she has probably read in my file. Maybe we've discussed it once or twice, but I regurgitate it anyway to waste the hour.

Sometimes I forget what I tell her because I feel like I'm just here for entertainment purposes, an animal to be examined and researched for veteran statistics.

"Around the time I turned 10, she had such a scare with her liver, it terrified her into sobriety." I laugh as the words leave my mouth. At the joke of her being sober for those years. "The funny thing about the liver is that it can take a beating. You can go hard, honestly. Beat it with a baseball bat every weekend until it's black and blue. By Monday, it'll be ripe and pink and ready for a new day. Isn't that the beauty of the human body? Always willing to fix what we destroy in ourselves, willing itself to be better the next day. But when you take a rock to it, and you curb stomp that motherfucker every day until it couldn't recognize a toxin if it tried? It's going to have some difficulty with the rebound."

Ingrid's lips form a thin, frustrated line at my lack of acknowledgment of her question. She scribbles a note with a crease etched deeply between her brows.

She returns her focus to me, saying, "Raina, I must be honest here. I'm not sure what one has to do with the other. Can you connect what your mother's liver has to do with all this anxiety surrounding your grandfather's death?"

I cross my legs and lean on one arm of the couch, casual and relaxed.

"Just a moment, Doc. I'm getting there. You see, Lenny was nothing if not persistent. She kicked and kicked and kicked. Eventually, that liver of hers gave in, and it stopped performing all of its neat tricks. It gave up, much like she did. I wonder if my grandpa is like her liver. His kids gave him such a beating, always taking and never giving, that he simply...gave up."

"I see," Doctor Ingrid says with sympathetic ease and this time the concern reaches her eyes. "But do you see her actions as something you yourself need to be afraid of repeating? You don't drink, and your grandpa was a casual drinker. As long as you stay sober, you are not doomed to repeat your family's mistakes."

"I don't know," I say, another shrug. "She was bipolar, too. She struggled to be touched and struggled to differentiate between reality and what she was imagining. And yet, she was sober for several years before the first sign of trouble sent her spiraling into full-blown addiction again. I mean, I came home from Afghanistan eight years ago. I fought in a whole war, and my mom said she was so stressed that she couldn't calm herself without drinking, as if she was the one overseas."

Ingrid objects, "You didn't begin drinking because you went to war."

"No, but I had my first manic episode because I went to war."

"That's why we are here. To help monitor you and work through those episodes. What is your worry, then?"

"That eventually I'll have that first sign of trouble like Lenny and begin to drink myself to death," I blurt out. I don't regret the words, though. They are the truth.

She hums in response, barely audible except I can see that thin line forming on her mouth again. "Do you feel like drinking now?" she asks.

"No." Yes.

"Okay. That's good. That's where we want to be. What else do you worry about?"

I have several moments of silence here to decide what I'm willing to be forthcoming about. The more truthful I am, the more she will expect of me, which is not inherently bad, but I don't know if I'm ready to face it head-on.

"What are you thinking?" She asks after a moment.

"I think everything happening now feels a lot like

what happened before when Lenny died. I'm thinking that I know my mother loved me. It just wasn't the way I needed her to. She couldn't bother to be sober for more than a few years at a time anyway. As creative, charming, and wild as Lenny had once been, she did not handle change well. She wilted at the thought of it, especially if the change didn't benefit her."

"You are quite the opposite. The military thrives on change, constantly evolving. You learned from that and grew from it. Maybe Lenny's inability to handle some of that change, especially stress-induced, made it hard for her to maintain relationships. Even with you and your sister. You can accept that your mother was extremely flawed and still did her best. You can accept that she was human and made mistakes. You can accept that you deserved better because you did. Raina, you are not your mother. You're allowed to feel all these feelings," Ingrid suggests, tilting her head in a very patronizing way that I can't stand, as if I hadn't considered any of this before.

I grit my teeth at the fake niceties. I'd rather be at home reading, but the VA says this is a necessary part of my disability compensation. Routine two-week check-ins confirm my stability and ensure I am monitored during manic episodes. I kick myself for saying too much already.

I cough, reluctant to continue now that we are narrowing down the real problem. Avoidance is the name of the game. It's why I'm in therapy to begin with.

Sometimes it's fun just to watch Ingrid get aggravated at my avoidance; she thinks I'm avoiding as a defense mechanism, and sure, sometimes I am. But when I'm in this chair, I also like to piss her off as compensation for her lack of compassion when it comes to me. She thinks she is good at pretending, but I know the truth. I see it every time I shake her hand.

Humans start to sweat when they get mad sometimes, and their faces flush with a hint of red. Ingrid is no exception, and I've found her an easy toy to play with.

"So, why does your grandfather's funeral bring you so much anxiety?"

I am ripped from my stream of thoughts by her line of interrogation.

"I think I know why this feels so similar. Can we skip the fine-tooth comb?" I ask, hoping to nip it in the bud now that we've gone too far. Ingrid is experienced with veterans like me, though–veterans who would prefer to say we are fine and move on once we touch a subject that burns.

I should be grateful for the support, but I feel trapped here with her.

She nods again, paired with more tapping of her pen. She will wait me out and force an answer out of me by simply being patient.

I relent in answering. "When Lenny died, it felt like I could breathe. She wanted to be done with everything, and I couldn't help her anymore. I didn't want to help her, so she left. My grandpa...it sort of feels that way, too. Like his death brings me a small sense of relief now that I don't have to do what I don't know how to."

"Mhmm," she hums, scribbling in her notebook. "And what is that? That you don't know how to do."

"Care."

She stops scribbling and looks up at me. A small flash of shock sits on her features, but she is quick to wipe it away. I shake my head, talking her down from her presumption that I'm probably a psychopath, and giggle a little.

"Chill, Doctor Ingrid. Don't throw yourself into a panic. I do care. Don't misunderstand me. I loved my mother. Maybe I only loved the idea of her, but still. My inclination is to say that I loved Lenny.

But I loved my grandpa even more. My Tata José was...he was everything to me. But loving someone who doesn't want to be here is exhausting. Besides, he was so old and so sick. It's better for him anyway. Still, everyone else is upset, fighting over each other about what needs to happen and who makes the decisions. I'm just relieved he's gone. That is what reminds me of Lenny the most. It's not just their differences. It is glaringly obvious similarity for me. The relief."

Ingrid contemplates my words with a few taps of her pen against her lips. "You made a lot of the decisions for Lenny's services. This could be a trigger if it's happening again. Do you feel they expect the same authority level from you with your grandpa's arrangements?"

Ingrid is strategic in her questioning. We're getting the other parts of the meat now.

"Maybe. People like them...they need someone to be the boss. They need someone to take charge and tell them what to do and when because if you don't, they fall apart. They don't have it in them to be the deciding factor because responsibility is like an allergy to them. Whenever a decision needed to be made, they all looked at me.

I just came home last month. This neighborhood has been the same for my entire life, and somehow, everything changed once I left. I can see sky-high apartments behind his house when I stand in the front yard. They weren't there the last time I set foot in that house five years ago when Lenny died. That's how much has changed in the world around us. Why am I, the one who ran away, the go-to for decisions? I don't even know his parents' names."

It's more word vomit, but she seems satisfied when she glances up at me with softer eyes than before. Sometimes she wins at our very own game of chess by getting me to spill more words from my lips than intended, even though she doesn't know we are playing.

"When you say people like them, do you mean drug addicts?"

I stare at her for a beat, second-guessing what I meant when I opened the floodgates. Contemplating what I want her to believe when I leave this session.

"Yes. Maybe. No." I twist my fingers. "I don't think someone acts like that just because they have an addiction. I think it might just be those I share DNA with."

"Everyone you share DNA with?"

"Just the ones who live in that house."

She hums again. She does that when she's dissecting my words, trying to find the plot hole in my story and make me face it instead of ignoring it for later.

"Is it possible that, because you've been gone, no one actually expects anything from you? Have you considered that maybe you are projecting your fears onto them? They live in your grandfather's home, but it doesn't mean that requires anything of you."

"It's crossed my mind," I snap, my words laced with a hint of wariness.

"Maybe you're so worried about being responsible you've convinced yourself they have these expectations when they don't. How much of this do you think stems from the position you were put in after Lenny's death?"

She earns a nod from me. "I mean, anything's possible."

I hate when I'm the problem.

"Maybe they understand this isn't an appropriate time to ask you to make all the decisions, but you seem to be hyper-focused on this. Have you been under a lot of stress lately?"

"No." Yes.

"Have you been keeping up with any of your hobbies to relieve any stress you do experience?"

"Reading." Obsessively so.

Her eyebrows perk up, interest written in every line on her forehead. "Anything good?"

"It's all good when I'm not here anymore," I mumble. Escapism has never been something I struggle with.

The humming again. It's grating on my nerves. She scribbles notes on her pad as she says, "We've talked about that before, too."

She sets the pen and pad on her lap, looking up at me again with intention as she continues, "The reading is a wonderful tool, a hobby you can rely on for stress relief. But it might be an issue to consider if you are not leaving the house, not showering, and foregoing some of your hygiene to read instead. You should be enjoying it in moderation, making sure to take care of basic needs first and foremost. Otherwise, when we obsess over one thing to avoid doing another, we haven't cleaned up our act at all. We traded one vice for another, and the addiction repeats itself. Have you been keeping up with your hygiene?"

She looks me up and down in that way she does. Appraising me for cleanliness, looking for tangled hair, discreetly trying to see if she can smell me. I nod because I am showering, combing my hair, and brushing my teeth. I am doing all the things she says I'm supposed to do, the things I know are normal, healthy human functions.

I'm not sure I would do them if I weren't constantly reminded that this was normal. Most people learn this healthy habit from their parents, and so did I; I was taught to be clean. Lenny got that part right. Lenny's few moments of clarity regarding her parenting doesn't make things okay, though.

With all the things Lenny got wrong, my brain managed to hardwire itself into a disorder I couldn't avoid anymore. Sometimes, I didn't care to do any of those normal, healthy human functions.

"I'm clean, Doc. Painfully so. I took a scalding shower this morning."

"And the reading? Are you leaving the house and getting some sunshine? I don't want you spending all day in bed."

"Ah, well," I start, avoiding her eyes. I need to make a joke, take the pressure off, somehow make this funny, but I can't think of anything. "You know what they say, keep your nose in the books and out of the pills, and you'll make it out of here."

I wink.

With a blank stare, she asks, "Who says that?"

"Lenny said that." I laugh, though her lack of a chuckle indicates my joke was far too underwhelming.

"Your mother told you that if you kept reading and

stayed away from the pills, you'd...?"

"I'd make it. I'd make it out of here." I gesture to the window and the city outside. The projects where I grew up aren't far from here. Ingrid knows that.

"Mmm." More humming, dammit. "Well, let's dissect that, but another time. We're out of it today."

She's right. The hour is up. We haven't made any progress or resolutions. We've simply tossed ideas back and forth, but that's fine. No one wants to examine their problems too closely anyway.

Rising from her large executive chair, she crosses the room to lead me to the door. "It sounds like you've identified some triggers regarding the funeral and such. You know what to do to work through them until next week. Remember –"

"Yup, small wins every day. Got it."

The cliché might as well be tattooed onto my brain matter. Small tasks done one right after the other are easier to manage, and it's something I do every day. Overwhelming myself with too much at once will guarantee I do none of them.

If I'm given the choice, I will absolutely do nothing.

If given half the chance, I will choose the demons inside me.

But society says those demons need to stay out of reach, hidden where the light doesn't touch. They want them tucked away. For once, I wish someone would allow me to let them out to play.

Maybe therapy was a small win for the day. It does its best to keep those demons locked up.

Ingrid shakes my hand and bids me farewell, promising to touch on all these chaffed and sensitive subjects later. When her hand touches me, though, I see the truth of it. Ingrid doesn't really give a shit about me. She never has. Ingrid loved her job years ago; she truly and honestly gave it her all when she first started. But patients like me, or worse, took a toll on her. Now, she's going through the motions.

The thing about having the Sight is that it takes physical contact, and it's brief, minute. A sense of feelings, emotions, and flashes of thoughts. It's nothing concrete because humans are far too complex for that. We're fickle, too, and our internal monologue reflects that whether we know it or not.

My Sight: mi malcición. Another unfortunate family curse that is driving me insane. There were no gifts passed down to me, and there will be none after me. No chains to be broken, only curses.

Just like Lenny. And if I'm not careful, I'll end up dead like her, too.

2. MATCHING HEADSTONES & DISRESPECT
APRIL 1, 2019

This cemetery is the only place in Arizona besides golf courses where the dirt is soft, and your shoes sink a little when you walk through it. It's one of few places where the ground seems more forgiving than the heat. Everywhere else in the Sonoran Desert, you will find that the land is hard and difficult to sink shovels into without human intervention.

But the groundskeepers in the Mesa Cemetery have no such difficulty. They sank their shovels and backhoes in with no issues, and a large hole now sits gaping open, ready for my grandfather's casket to be laid to rest. Right next to Nana Isabel's matching headstone.

I donned dark sunglasses before I came out here and after leaving my therapy session. I won't cry, unlike everyone else, but this way, I can avoid people's eyes and their need to wish me well. They will think the glasses are to cover the tears, but it's really to fight off interactions. Distant relatives are less likely to approach me with sympathy if they have to get my attention first, unsure if I'm looking at them.

I covered myself in a long-sleeved leather jacket and ripped black jeans to ensure additional protection from unwanted interaction. I look like an asshole, an outfit that does not befit a funeral, and judging by the long-held side glances from old Tía Maria, I would wager I fit the bill.

I'm perfectly happy to fill that role if I am left alone.

As the casket begins its journey six feet below, the soft crank the only sound among the sobs, a soft, inappropriate chuckle tumbles from my lips. Lenny would have damned me to hell herself if I'd put her in the ground just as my Tata José is going right now.

"*Callate la boca*," Tío Henry says to the right of me. I offer him a small, apologetic smile before I inch away from him and closer to my sister, Lilliana.

"Get me out of here. Soon," I whisper to her as the priest laments more Hail Mary's and Father Full of Grace, hooking my arm to her tighter. Physical touch is how she shows her love. She is the only person I allow to be so close even though it's not skin-to-skin with our long sleeves.

A half-assed elbow gets me on the side, a hand placed on mine, and she whispers back, "Can you pretend to give a shit?"

I am flooded with emotions too strong for me; her feelings have always run deep and fast, like an endless canyon with an unnaturally fast river running through it. No end in sight.

I see all the small flashes of tears shed in bathrooms, fighting with cousins and distant relatives, and an overwhelming ache takes over in the pit of my stomach. These are her experiences. It's what she's feeling now, and her heart shatters with Tata's death. This flash of Sight flows through every vein and pore in my body without restraint. She looks at me, disappointment living in the soft set of her eyes.

"Don't touch me," I hiss, yanking my hand away.

"You're wearing your heart on your skin. It's too much."

She locks eyes with me and purses her lips. Her only response is a deep breath to calm her nerves as she turns away to look back at the service.

My sister doesn't believe in this Sight. Not really. She entertains my delusions—her words, not mine. Because the alternative is to not have me around. The alternative is that I have no relationship with her kids and my brother-in-law, who's been around since I was nine, because I refuse to have people in my life who think I'm just crazy.

She would rather pretend she accepts my Sight than risk my absence.

I am the only one of us to inherit this particular curse from our mother, and though she is willing to entertain me, I know she thinks I've inherited much more than some gift she doesn't believe in. She thinks, maybe, I've inherited Lenny's need to always be the center of attention, to be special.

But the truth is that I tried to end myself in order to not feel special anymore. I wanted the memories of others' feelings and touches to go away because they refused to leave the crevice of my brain that they lived in. I couldn't make it stop, so I tried to make me stop.

I would never tell her that, so I offer an apologetic grimace instead and return to the funeral activities before me.

I should feel more than I do about my grandfather's death.

I do feel.

I feel what I'm supposed to feel, I think; a hint of sadness, regret, and even loneliness because my grandfather was everything to me growing up when Lenny and her men were off ruling the world, leaving me and a dozen or so grandkids at my grandparents' house. I couldn't count on two hands how many of us lived there at any given time, but we loved it. We loved him.

He is the standard I would grow to hold all men up against and the one Lenny was determined to find the opposite of. Where he was kind, her men were spiteful and mean. Where he was gentle, they were violent.

But the relief is driving home my guilt with a hammer on top.

I think I'm the only one of the dozen-plus grandkids to feel this way.

I morph my face into obedient sadness as my sister and I walk to the coffin when the prayers are over, and the coffin has been laid into the ground. My inability to outwardly show genuine emotion right now is concerning but not surprising. I'm not sure it has anything to do with my bipolar disorder. I worry there may be other things wrong with me too.

Why else would I play with my therapist like a puppet?

Maybe I am a sociopath, unable to feel and express emotions appropriately, and I don't even know it.

Of the fifteen grandkids still alive, only seven are in attendance. The rest have buried themselves in back rooms with hot spoons, lighters, and dilated eyes, terrified to face this tragedy else they fall into deeper holes. Others sit behind cold metal bars, unable to say their goodbyes though they want to.

That makes one sociopath, six semi-normal, five with meth pipes in their mouths and needles in their arms, and two behind bars. What a line-up.

Arm in arm, some hand in hand or shoulder over the other, the seven of us reach down together, circled around Tata José's hole in the ground, fistfuls of dirt at the ready. More prayers, more cries of mourning as we hold our hands above his mahogany casket and release. The sound of falling dirt greets us as we each reach over to the stunning flower display and each take a flower of our own.

Eddie, my cowardly Irish twin of a cousin, lingers at the end of the line. He is the last to take a flower and has been the only one to avoid my eyes since I've noticed him.

Eddie The Coward, his not-so-loving title, managed to remain a loner all the way through into adulthood, it seems. He hasn't spoken to anyone during the funeral, and those around him do not acknowledge his presence. He is a ghost amongst the crowd, and his movements are slow and calculated. Careful not to draw attention to himself.

I drag my eyes away from him, and we all continue the ceremonious movements without further ado. One by one, with dutiful sadness, we toss our various miserable and pitiful gifts, flowers, old photographs, his favorite cigars, and a single shot of whiskey down on top. He will rest with all his favorite things in the world with my Nana and their seven children beside them, minus Lenny.

Many of our relatives are buried here. After decades of raising families side by side, you're bound to share dirt space in the end. Sitting on the edge of town, the bright lights from the neighboring town shine like a beacon on one side of the cemetery and the dim barren desert on the other. The ghost town I avoid, 12-Mile-Corner, also sits a few miles from here. Its closeness to me and to Eddie, who shares with me the secrets it harbors in the earth, is disconcerting to me.

I do my best to ignore the anxiety humming within me because of it.

As the last of us toss our gifts down, the prayers end, and the funeral is over. Various distant relatives crowd the grave, eager to offer their condolences and feel important as if they haven't ignored our part of the family and our problems for years. As if there weren't years of drugs, violence, and abuse happening when my Tata was too old to help anyone but himself, and they never bothered to see if he was still around or if we were okay.

In their defense, I wasn't around either. I ran as far away as the army would take me in the ten years I've been gone. But I was running away for safety, desperate for a life that resembled anything but my own. What was their excuse?

Before anyone can corner me and force conversation out of me, I nod at my car and leave my sister to be the receiver of well-wishes and apologetic hugs. For a moment, I think Eddie might stay, too, ready to step out of his social anxiety box. But his foot hesitates just a second before he moves towards me.

I hold up a finger with a straight arm in his direction. The gesture says **No** without needing any additional recourse, and it works. He halts, takes a deep regretful breath, and crosses his arms across his chest as he stands rooted to the ground next to our grandmother's grave.

I don't bother to say or do anything else, and when I make my way to my remodeled Bronco, I snatch the lighter and cigarettes from the front seat with uneasy hurriedness. I feel like I need the long drag of the cigarette like I need air. I need to feel the burn of the smoke in my throat, the pleasure neurons firing in my brain at first inhale.

He's still watching me, standing on our grandmother's bones. Lenny always said we had a different grandmother than she had a mother, implying that Isabel was cruel or spiteful in some way or another to her own children. I often wonder if that was the case or if Lenny only thought her mother didn't love her because Isabel didn't love her choices or her path in life.

Isabel's judgment of her daughter rings in a distant part of my memory.

"Your mother is reckless; she has no care for what happens to her mortal body because she is not worried about what will happen to it once it's gone. This is why she has such foolish notions of cremation. Her soul will never rest!"

"*¿Qué quieres decir Nana?*" I asked her.

"Be mindful of where you are buried, *mijita*. This is important. We cannot be buried just anywhere. Our spirits lay there after we do, and sometimes, things are waiting there for us."

Tata Joe, as well called him, believed no such thing, and as far as Nana Isabel was concerned, this ground was sacred and, therefore, safe. Growing up, Lenny was always at war with being a pious woman and a rogue spiritual one. That indecisiveness may have irritated such a convicted woman as Isabel, who refused to believe there was any other way but confessions on Fridays and mass on Sundays.

Eddie leans on the grave, which I find out of character but then again, I don't know anything about him anymore. Having not seen him since I was eighteen, he may have grown into a man who dared to be disrespectful and not someone who withered at the thought. It was very un-Mexican of him. And a lot like Lenny of him.

We'd spent most of our memorable teenage moments with our other two best friends. Eddie and I always sitting at two different ends of the stick. Related by blood and friends by choice.

After all these years, maybe we'd ended up more alike than different. I begin to think that I won't lay eyes on either of the two other members of The Four, an unsavory and not at all catchy name for the four of us growing up. Always glued together like perfectly matched four corners.

Maybe the other two ran away and never returned, unlike Eddie and I.

However, the thought that it would be so convenient to never see them again is fleeting. My eyes catch sight of one Dolores Serrano, arm leaning on top of Eddie's shoulder. It's very casual. Intimate, even.

Lola.

My first best friend, childhood bully, and biggest fan wrapped into one.

Her eyes flash to mine, and it holds for long, crawling seconds. An unspoken bond ruminating between us as the world moves around our frozen feet.

"You didn't have to drive yourself. You, too, fall into the dreaded category of immediate family."

My sisters' words break the trance, and I am forced to tear my gaze away from Lola.

"We're both aware of why I'm not riding in those things," I tell her.

"They're limousines, not a prison cell."

"Not to me."

She takes a deep breath with a smile that says I

give up. "I'll see you at the house," she mumbles. I nod and light another cigarette as she walks away towards her sad kids and sadder husband.

I'm still leaning against my vintage Ford Bronco, and I refuse to smoke in it. But much like my mother, I am a fiend for nicotine, and I can't leave mildly stressful situations without lighting one.

Amidst the chaos of leaving patrons Lola and Eddie talk briefly. Both take a moment to focus their attention on me. I avoid their gaze now, determined to act as if they do not exist. The sensation of their lingering eyes on me is uncomfortable. I wish they would go away.

One second.

Ten seconds.

Neither step in my direction. But again, our eyes unwillingly meet, and there's an unspoken message there.

We remember. Do you?

I turn away, averting my eyes from them, and I am struck with the sensation of...other. It's an intense feeling, like when you know someone is staring at you from a distance. But when I turn back towards them, Lola and Eddie are walking away, and a lone figure stands in their stead.

Broken. Burnt. Dirt. Fire.

My whole body begins to shake horrifically. Fear is one emotion I've never been able to shut out, no matter what grounding techniques I learn in therapy. Now, I am unraveling with it at the sight of the thing before me. A monstrosity of a man, smoke rippling from his overcooked body and gasping for air, limping towards me. The charred lips on his face open and close, with wild eyes pinning me to the spot. He reaches his black, scorched fingers in my direction, desperately trying to get words out. Instead, terrible sounds come from its mouth. Every step is a dramatic limp, his shoulders jerking unnaturally.

In a rush, I shove myself into my car, and with trembling fingers, I turn the engine over. Seconds later, I'm driving down the road, and I'm smoking in the dream car I swore I'd never smoke in.

3. BOOKS AND ALL THAT ...

The house fills up so fast that it quickly becomes stifling to be inside it.

Thirty minutes ago, everyone was in tears, hugging each other tight and praying that my grandfather was at peace. But as I pour myself a bowl of pozole, various forms of nineties music now play at a horrific level instead, with whoops and yells of excitement from numerous people in the house. I consume the bowl of soup at lightning speed and wander to the phone someone has left out, controlling the music.

I hear the excited shouts of, 'SHOTS FOR EVERYONE!' and I mentally note where the tequila bottles are. I'll need more of that if I'm to survive this outing.

Taking a glance around, I slide the phone into my hand, searching for the appropriate music instead of whatever Eazy-E album is playing. This is the music of my childhood, and I don't have anything against Eazy-E. I remember this song blasting loudly in an older cousin's bedroom when I was about six or seven, the smell of weed leaking through the cracks. It isn't a great memory, but it isn't a bad one. It just is.

Tata would have yelled at us to turn that crap off,

though, so I am.

No one notices that I've got the phone in my hand. Whoever it belongs to clearly lacks situational awareness because I walk away from the speaker just enough to be out of sight. Moving to the side of the crowd weaving in and out of the walkway leading from the kitchen to the dining room, I change the song. The growing groups of people in the house are instantly on high alert, stunned by the sudden change.

There is a small but monumental moment where the house goes still, where the masses cannot tell if they're okay with the change that's being forced on them or if they want to riot instead. And then drunken shouts of joy from all around follow suit.

I hit shuffle on the screen before I slide the phone onto a random kitchen counter. I smile, grab a beer from an unguarded ice chest at the sound of my grandpa's favorite music, and head outside before anyone can find a reason to talk to me and play catch up. The mighty baritone of Vicente Fernández makes my heart sing back, and a tiny hum escapes my lips. I put the beer to my lips to stop myself immediately, hoping no one noticed. But maybe wherever Tata José is, he's singing and humming with me.

Before I can escape, my feet falter at the large entertainment center that takes up residence by the front door. Its large figure is the first thing you see when you come in, and it is still decorated with memories of all of us as kids. There are plenty of me, kindergarten recitals with Eddie and Andrés, and sleepovers with my sister and cousin Lydia. There are high school graduation pictures for Mark and Polaroid printouts of Enzo and Marcus during one of their many extended stays in the Arizona state prison.

I see Lenny and her sisters and brother smiling by the lake before the taste of illicit drugs tempted them to be different people than they were meant to be. I see my grandparents before they had to bury any of their children.

I see me. Wild, free, begging to be loved. Eyes frantically searching for something safe in every frame.

"Everyone was so happy once," Mark says beside me, the noise from his feet scraping the tile startling me. He's staring at the same pictures; all I can do is nod. "Why couldn't things have stayed that way?"

I shrug, offering no answer or solace because I don't know how, and I'm not the right person for the job anyways. I leave him to his feelings of regret and grief before he can think to hug me or throw an arm around me.

Touching means feeling things I don't want to because, somehow skin to skin-to-skin always happens. It's shaking my hand, large hugs where they rest their head against mine, kisses on the cheek, what have you. The end result is me being blinded by flashes of things I have no business knowing, and it's always taken the wrong way when I shrug them off.

Another cigarette graces my lips as soon as my feet hit the cold concrete of the front porch, the door swinging shut behind me. A few steps into the yard, and I am standing in a bed full of yellow grass, clearly on its last leg of life, judging by the crunch beneath my shoes. I drag on that cigarette and watch as my feet take slow, calculated steps toward the yard's edge. I lean against the concrete and metal combination of a fence, a staple style of fencing in this neighborhood and easy to sit on, and I face my grandfather's house.

It sags a bit now. It's exhausted from time and generations of abuse from this family's lack of care. The grand cinder blocks that used to be decorated with vibrant grays and blues from my Tata's paintbrush are now dull, full of scuff marks and chips. The barred windows my grandpa used to keep people out have been ripped off, leaving deep holes where they used to be. The right side of the house features an add-on my grandpa built sometime during my childhood. Unlike the brick, it is made of wood that is now dilapidated and crippling at the bottom. There's mold growing.

My eyes find purchase with the concrete on the front porch from where I sit. I can just make out where we etched our names into the wet pour when we were kids. Liliana, Raina, Mark, Jonathan, and Eddie, all our names are memorialized here forever.

When this house is gone, our names will still be in the hard concrete for some construction workers to smash to pieces when it comes tumbling down. When this house is gone, our trauma will still be around to tell the tale.

Once, I loved this family with every inch of me. I think I still do if love is something I am capable of. But at 28, I am not capable of looking past the transgressions they refuse to take responsibility for, and so, I find it increasingly difficult to tolerate something as simple as their presence. I am bitter that my name sits next to theirs, and though I will try to make something of myself, the stain of everyone else and their failures will be attached to me. Just like our names in the concrete.

Enzo bursts through the front door, overly tall and loud with boisterous laughter. Almost excessively so, like he's compensating for some unknown self-internalized inadequacy. He spots me and makes a beeline in my direction because I am the only one out here.

He nods at the cigarette hanging from my mouth. "Can I bum one?"

I nod and hand him one with the lighter, but I don't say anything. I look him up and down as inconspicuously as possible, surveying which Enzo I am in the presence of today. I know he's not clean. He hasn't been clean for years. But I'm curious whether he's hurting for another high or fresh off one. I'm no expert, so I can't really tell, but by the gentle bob of his head as he lights the cigarette, and the overall relaxed demeanor, I'd say he's not hurting for anything now.

"How are you doing, *prima*?" He asks, head still bobbing like he can feel the beat of the music from inside all the way out here.

He throws the word prima in there because it's one of maybe ten phrases he knows in Spanish, and I think it makes him feel better about his identity crisis. Most of us have it. We all lost parts of ourselves, our roots, and our history, to our parents' attempts to perfect their whiteness.

In my completely unqualified opinion, being able to speak Spanish is not an indicator of whether someone is Mexican enough. But it is a flex commonly used to make us no sabo kids feel bad when we can't. No sabo is just another way of telling us Mexican-American kids that no matter what we do, we'll never be enough and if I'm honest, it works.

Kids from the hood, original gangsters from the nineties especially, compensate for this pit in our souls by learning specific sets of language and throwing them around with their English. Words and phrases like prima, mijita, ese, andale wey, carnal, and pinche puto are tossed here and there, adding color to every conversation.

Lenny and her sisters were ridiculed for speaking Spanish as children, locked in closets during recess, and spanked with paddles if they didn't speak English clearly enough. It left us nineties kids with hardly anything to learn but English. Their refusal to teach us is partly rooted in safety and lack of care. This was reiterated when they only spoke it around us to disguise what they were saying. No authentic Mexican accents here, aside from the slight Chicano accent you might pick up from growing up in the projects and limited access to the language.

Our ancestry, our culture, lived and breathed with our grandparents. It blossomed with every instance of my grandmother's hands forming around the dough for tortillas, around my grandfather's boots moving to the beat of a mariachi's trumpet.

But it died with our parents.

I tried for so many years to revive it in myself, to reconnect with a part of me that still exists in my blood. I can feel it flowing in every molecule, but the resistance to it, the pushback from Lenny's adolescence spent trying to speak more American, to act white enough, classy enough...beat it out of me.

I have a hard time taking back what she pushed away, too.

"I'm alright," I say with a small, quiet delivery. Short answers and he may go away.

"Just alright? No heartbreak? Tata just died. Can you believe it?" He laughs awkwardly.

It should be offensive, but it's not. We both know why.

It's not a wonder he's gone. It's simply hard to believe sometimes that he finally said, 'fuck it'. We all thought he might be here forever, waiting in the winds to catch those of us who needed him when we stopped flying on our own.

"He was too stubborn. Afraid to leave people, I guess. But yes, I'm just alright."

Another cigarette drag and I'm contemplating my escape, maybe even leaving this house alto-gether. Who would notice I was gone?

"You know, we're super proud of you. The army, the book, and all that. "

Book and all that. The tension would be more uncomfortable if the awkwardness of his attempt wasn't even worse.

Sometimes I wish I'd never released the damned book on my shelf. When I was active duty, I suc-cessfully published a novel from a large publishing house. The book, La Reina, is simultaneously the root of my faith that I am not entirely useless while also serving as the root of my shame. It is a nod to my nickname, a journal entry reimagining, and an ode to the processing of my trauma. Its original draft, a cracked leather-bound journal where the original words on paper were recorded, sits next to the printed version on that shelf, and I've never let anyone look at it.

I swallow down the regret. The story needed to be told. It doesn't matter that they saw the worst of themselves on paper.

"Thanks," I say softly.

"Did you mean everything you said in it?" He asks, turning this conversation in a direction I didn't want it to go.

Sadness bleeds through, telling me some of my ink on paper hurt him. I would feel bad, except I have a core memory of him chasing his girlfriend throughout this house and eventually forcing her to the ground right next to me while he tried to choke her to death. I'm not Doctor Ingrid, but I'd take a guess that fucked me up one way or another.

"Some of it," I say.

"Which some?"

I freeze and just stare at him. "I'm not having this conversation."

"Why? You had no problem writing it, no problem putting us all on blast like you didn't grow up here like the rest of us." He gestures to the house and all its painful memories stacked up with the good ones like the bricks that hold it up.

I don't say anything because he doesn't really want my answer. He wants to tell me how he feels. I inch further away because I have a feeling I know what's coming next.

"Why did you have to do that, *mijita*?"

Mijita. I hate that word. It's condescending as if I am a child, someone he must instill the rules in, not a 27-year-old woman.

He's older than me by a significant amount. Thirteen years. He could be seen as an uncle, but the sheer size of our family means he's just a first cousin. I was one of the baby cousins my whole life, which may be why my book hurt them so much. The older cousins, aunts, and uncles who molded me were being called out by the baby of the family.

They cared enough to be offended now but not enough to take care of me back then.

And now the baby was resentful, and mean, and scornful.

He inches closer. I take another step back and look up at him with defiance. Caution resting in every joint in my body, ready to fight if I have to.

"Don't call me that," I snap. Everyone is hurting, and I'd rather not be the cause, but I've had enough condescension today.

His eyes have a glaze to them, hazy and red. He's probably a little drunk, but there's something else stirring behind it, morphing his features into something...wicked. It lives behind his mask. Something that makes my senses go off like it did when I saw that thing at the funeral.

But I blink, and when I open my eyes, he is his normal drunk self again.

"I don't mean anything by it, *prima*, you know I love you," he says in that thick homie accent.

A deep voice grumbles from beside of us, "Last I checked, Raina doesn't like being touched, esé. She also really hates that word. Why don't you head inside?"

"Tommy...," I whisper, startled by his presence

now.

Tommy The Jock has arrived. All members of The Four have now made their re-entrance back into my life.

Enzo laughs his awkward laugh again as his head whips towards Tommy's general direction. He doesn't acknowledge Tommy. He barely glances at him, looking as if my old friend's presence makes him as nervous as I am. He returns his focus to my face.

A light tilt of Enzo's head in my direction. He stares at me with quiet concern for one beat, two beats. Then says, "Yeah, okay, *prima*. I got you."

He almost twitches, like he is fearful. But he says nothing else as he places a gentle hand on my shoulder, careful not to touch skin as he composes himself. He squeezes lightly before he walks away, and I am left with Tommy.

I soak in the view that is Tommy's large figure. He looks a lot like me in dark, fitted jeans, a black t-shirt, and a black leather jacket, albeit much more conservative and less flashy than mine. The only real difference between our attire is the love for Vans that he acquired during our high school emo phase, where I firmly attached myself to Chuck Taylor's and never walked away.

And unfortunately for me, he looks good.

Tommy doesn't speak. Shoving his hands in his pocket the way he does, all suavemente and perfect, he leans against the concrete post I was up against moments before.

He's taller now, with a full perfect beard and perfect dark hair and perfect curls. High perfect cheekbones to compliment his perfectly brown skin, perfectly strong legs, and perfectly muscled body that I can see peeking through his shirt.

Perfect, perfect, perfect.

As he always was. Older now. More mature. Grown in a way I had not imagined I would ever see him.

He holds my gaze as I drag on the cigarette I've been gripping with such force that I'm surprised it didn't break in half. His dark eyes burn with a knowing sensation I can't pin down like he can read me and hear every internalized anxious thought.

As if his demons know mine.

For a fleeting moment, I am seventeen again, and we are standing on opposite sides of the fire in the middle of an Arizona desert, eyes locked on one another. Music is blasting, and a dozen or more teenagers drinking, dancing, and falling all over the place, but I only see Tommy. I can only think of Tommy, and I swear I can smell the scent that is so distinctly him over the haze of the fire.

The reminder of fire breaks me from my traveling thoughts, and I'm the first to break eye contact. When I look at him again, he's no longer looking at me but staring at his feet as if relieved not to be entranced anymore.

I don't speak either. I wait. I wait for a reason. Why he's shown up here. Why the three of them are returning to haunt me when I thought I had compartmentalized them into a carefully put-together box. I've circumvented them at every turn in this town, avoiding certain hangouts, staying at home, not attending family events. I haven't stepped foot inside a grocery store, instead opting for grocery pick up, to make sure not to run into them.

Or be reminded that they ever existed here.

He waits me out, testing me to see if I'll be the first to break. His hand moves in my direction, and I flinch. He doesn't seem real, and the movement is startling. Suspended in the air, he freezes with his fingers angled just so towards me. A signature Tommy move, one that I should have recognized right away for what it was.

Time slows as he waits patiently for me to fish a cigarette out for him. When we were teens, it was an endearing, silent communication only we had, and I loved it. Now, it floods me with memories I was quick to disregard when I left.

Blood rushes to my head, a woozy feeling almost causes a stumble in me. My heart pumps with wild fervor. None of these things are concerning, though they should be.

They're a reaction to what I thought I'd forgotten. A physical response to the reality that my feelings for him, the ones I'd shoved away and stomped out, are ripping through that fucking box I made.

A small part of me wants to resist. Tell him to go back to wherever he's been living these days and stay away from me. Another part of me, maybe even smaller than the first, begs me to act on what he's requesting of me. This tiny sliver is taking up space in the cracks of my heart that I believed to be filled. The hollow cracks in my heart that no longer beg for his presence like it did for so many years after leaving. I moved on.

Now, they've wiggled their way out of the box and back to where they were as a teen. That's what's making it pump so hard.

A split second goes by, and all my small internal

objections disintegrate. I don't fight it; I don't bite in vocal retaliation. I complete the ritual and I slide a cigarette between his fingers.

Stepping away from his resting place against the post, he puts the cigarette to his lips with quiet, slow movement, and leans toward me. His cigarette makes contact with mine and our eyes lock as he inhales. Both light up as his catches and smoke plumes between us.

Another ceremonial act I never could quite forget.

My blood alights at the thought of what almost was, that rapidly beating snare drum of a heart pumping it wildly in my veins. I feel like a teen again in his presence, and certainly not like the woman I proclaimed to be when Enzo was taunting me.

In Tommy's presence, I would always be a puddle of feelings—no matter my delusional reservations that he meant nothing. Or that I haven't missed him since I saw him last, when he was covered in dirt and blood.

No.

I force those thoughts away. I can't think of them now. The nausea it induces at the mere mention of it threatens to bubble into more.

He breaks the silence, his voice a deep, velvety texture. "Were you planning on acting like we didn't exist forever?"

Without hesitation, I let out a resounding, "Yes."

He rolls his eyes in response. Maybe he's unamused at my willingness to ignore them completely for the last month that I've been home. No phone calls. No reaching out.

Radio silence.

"They're inside, you know," he offers, like it's a fact I was unaware of and would want to know.

"I'm aware."

As if their ears were burning, 'they' come walking outside. Lola first, as always, and a sheepish Eddie close behind.

Lola puts her arms out to the side in a theatrical display as she says, "The Four back together again. The Jock, The Cheerleader, The Artist, and The Coward. What a time!"

I let out a groan and this time, it's my turn to roll my eyes. "*Que dramática*," How dramatic, I say at the notice of our titles.

The names were given in high school by those who generally disliked us as individuals and even more as a group. Vague titles that could apply to anyone but stuck to us so they could knock us down a few levels. A reminder of how completely and utterly average we were to them.

"*Buenas tardes, la Reina*, our Queen of Art," she taunts in response.

Another title given. This one instead was given by the three who stand before me, a play on my own name and one meant to somehow signify that I, in one way or another, led this group.

I didn't. I was just the oddest. The freak who didn't like to be touched. The bitch who would bite back, and bite hard in defense of her friends. I suppose being angry all the time and frustrated with the goings-on at home, I took it out on everyone else. I'm much calmer now with the bit of safety I've given myself.

Unfortunately, I've also become a hermit because of it.

Lola put up a good front, but she didn't like confrontation. She was the people pleaser, able to smooth talk anyone into anything with barely more than a smile. She had a charisma you couldn't say no to.

In striking commonality with each other, Eddie and Tommy were both mild boys, quiet and reserved. Tommy avoided trouble not because he was afraid of it, like Eddie, but because he was holding out hope that he would make it out of here. It was unyielding optimism that he would make something more of himself than those around him. The fact that he's standing before me implies he may have never accomplished it. I make a quiet wish to myself that he did leave and that he's only here to visit.

Eddie on the other hand was terrified of everything in the world. Always frightened of what lurked in the dark, assuming something or someone would come snatch him in the night if he were not constantly vigilant and cautious. If he ever had to the strength to leave though, I know he couldn't have made it far. Tío Leon, Eddie's dad, would only let him be gone for so long without pressuring him into coming home to help with this or that. The leash made of parental guilt was still strong. Now that all our parents are dead, maybe he will leave again.

So, that just left me. The hot head, the fireball. The giant steaming pile of dog crap as far as other parents were concerned. Constantly fighting, I was the girl they told their kids not to play with. But I was only readily preparing to run away from here.

Lola reaches us, eyebrow high and mocks, "Sorry to interrupt."

"No, you're not," I respond, because we all know she isn't. She's been waiting in the crowd to corner me, and we all know it.

Eddie nods at me and quietly acknowledges, "Hey, Raina."

I greet him with a smooth, "Hi, Eddie the Coward."

Only a few months younger than me but deemed my baby cousin, he takes his turn to roll his eyes.

"We are full-grown adults. How long are these stupid names going to stick?"

"Until the day you are dirt in the ground, baby," Lola quips, and the silence that follows is stifling.

Dirt. Ground. Buried.

Everyone's expression seems to dawn a visible cringe, like we're all replaying a sequence of events in our heads.

Lola playfully taps me, careful not to touch my skin, and says, "Weird how we all ended up single huh?"

I flash her a look that says, 'are you fucking for real?' Instead I ask, "Is that a real question? How old are we?"

"Yes!" She laughs like the answer is obvious. "Statistically speaking, at least one of us should be in a relationship, maybe even married. What are the odds that not one of us has gotten married? Hhhmm? It's slim, I'll tell you that."

"I see you haven't given up on your love of numbers," Tommy smiles and tousles her hair. She swats him away, but the smile remains.

"Not for a second," Eddie replies, and I'm a little startled by his comment. How much time have they been spending together for him to know this?

Chewing on her nails, Lola mumbles through her teeth, "I've always had a thing for numbers, especially statistics. It's my career now. Full-time data analyst." Lola shrugs off this fact, making it seem like it's a lesser deal than it is, but I'm impressed. Not because I never thought of her as smart, only that she used to struggle with what her parents assumed was ADHD. It made certain things, learning in particular, hard for her to complete.

I always assumed she was somewhere on the spectrum; a colorful rainbow made of people that society deemed a little too much for their tastes. But I would have never told her parents that, even if I'd known what the spectrum was back then. The fact they considered the possibility of treating her for ADHD was a miracle in and of itself. These are things Hispanic parents struggle with, especially mental health. There is no such thing as depression or anxiety in a Mexican household.

Depressed? Go clean. Oh, you have anxiety? Get better grades then!

The spectrum thing might have made her awkward and uncomfortable, but instead it made her charming. And maybe a little inappropriate too. Lola laughs again, breaking me from my thoughts, seemingly oblivious to the unease beginning to rise in all of us and continues rambling.

"I'm just saying. It's been, what? 10 years? And yet, we're all home, single again, just the four of us."

Four sets of eyes bounce between each other, the truth lingering there among the tension; how could we move on to people who weren't there that night? Whoever we decided to stay with, it would never be quite right with this secret hidden in the closet like a proverbial fucking skeleton.

Eddie lets out a nervous cough. "It's good we're all here, actually."

"Actually, I was hoping to avoid you," I counter.

"I'm your cousin. It makes sense for me to be here, Raina. You aren't the only one allowed to be in attendance."

"Maybe, but I was hoping the thought of death would make your feet tremble enough to stay away from it," I snap.

He scoffs, "I am not a teen boy anymore. Not everything sends me scurrying to safety."

"Debatable." I arch an eyebrow, silently urging him to continue this argument. There is a small bit of resentment here, it lingers like an itch I can't scratch when I reach for it. I can't seem to scratch why I harbor the resentment at all.

Lola interrupts, "Enough. What is your deal, Raina? Why are you being so hostile?"

"Because I didn't want to see you three ever again," I blurt out, a breath releasing fast and flustered from my lips. "I'm aware that a funeral like this would bring the neighborhood and family back together. But fuck. I just thought...I guess I thought this secret would stay dead. You three being here feels like I'm forced to relieve it again. Like it's bringing it all back to life, and as far as I was concerned, it died in that desert."

Eddie pins me with his eyes, his persona is different now than who he was at seventeen. "Nothing ever really stays dead," he says as a grim offering. His hands twist together like the ball of nerves he used to be. This is the Eddie my brain remembers. Not the tall, confident man before me. "There's more, though. More to talk about."

Tommy slaps Eddie on the back, shoving Eddie forward a step as he loses his balance. "Go ahead, man, spit it out," he urges.

We all know Tommy is being playful. It isn't his nature to bully Eddie or make him uncomfortable. That same playfulness is what made Tommy so attractive as a teen and what is working for him still. But Eddie sometimes needs motivation to tell the story, or to finish his thoughts, especially when he's worried. It's like a twitch. Tommy is patient but good-humored.

I, on the other hand, chuckle at Eddie's nerves. It is a direct result of my own gracelessness when I notice the exchanges between the three of them. I am out of the loop. My mood sours a little at the realization.

They may have left our Podunk town, but they didn't leave the state like I did. In a sense, their connections are still here. Connections I severed when I got on a plane 10 years ago.

Eddie coughs again, and I do not miss the way his eyes linger on Lola for just a moment. Waiting for permission.

Once granted with a small nod from Lola, he mutters, "We need to talk about what happened in that desert."

4. STRAINED AND WEIRD RELATIONSHIPS ...

Standing there together, our feet shift side to side avoiding each other's gazes as the silence weighs heavy. No one wants to continue this conversation with extra sets of ears hanging around, so we wait for random guests who come and go from the front yard to move on and head back inside.

Being here with the three of them again brings back memories of running barefoot on the hot concrete of these streets. We were never inside. Always trying to as get far away from our decrepit homes as fast as we could. Always chasing reprieve from the horrors on the inside.

My thoughts wander back to Enzo and all the cousins, brothers, and sisters who never made it out the way we did. They didn't do anything wrong. They only existed in a world meant to keep them flat on the floor instead of high in the blue sky. I, we, are the exception to this rule–the odd ones out. It hurts because I wish more than anything we had all been able to get out of the hole.

When a lingering group by the door eventually decides to head back inside, I muster the determination to ask in willful ignorance, "What about the desert?"

"Don't play stupid, Raina," Lola taunts, shooting

daggers at my hands with her vibrant and animated eyes.

"I'm not sure how you think this works," I lift my hands, a gesture to the Sight living in my skin. "But it's not all-knowing. I'm not some omnipresent being, Lola. What the fuck is going on?"

Her face morphs and turns into something dangerous. Her eyes narrow as she responds in kind, "Who have you told, huh? Who knows about that night?"

I grimace at the accusation and stutter back a moment. "I haven't told anyone. Why would I do that?"

She scoffs, "Yeah, okay. And your therapist?"

I blanch. "How do you know about my therapist?"

"Everybody knows, Raina," Eddie interjects. "The army sent you packing for your crazy. We put the pieces together. And also, your sister has something of a big mouth. Liliana told my mom, who we know lives for the chisme."

I groan at the word chisme. What he means is that they live for the gossip. "Your mom talks too much."

"Maybe. But living like a hermit hasn't made your life any more private. It's made it worse because everyone wants a piece of the drama. They want in on the secret, something that will make them feel better about their pathetic lives. As long you're unhappy, and as long as you look like the odd one out, they sleep better with their decisions."

His eyes flick to my wrist where the scars are and then immediately to my face, like he's embarrassed to have noticed like everyone else. The scars are jagged and ugly because I was too manic to care about appearances when I did it. All I'd wanted then was to keep stabbing until I couldn't feel any of it anymore.

Spoiler: it didn't work.

I pull the sleeve of my jacket down to cover my insecurities and out of habit. If I focus hard, I may be able to ignore people's images when they rush through me as their skin touches mine. But if I'm not intentional, I'll see it all even if I don't want to.

I look at each of their faces, one by one. What I want to do despite myself is reach for one of them and hope to get glimpses. Sights, ideas, feelings, anything to put this puzzle together faster. But I know that if I take one step towards any of them, what little trust remains will evaporate into thin air quicker than a drop of water in the Arizona heat, and I will be shut out. No answers.

Then again, I'm not sure how much trust there ever was in me.

I look at Tommy, stone-faced and unusually quiet even for him. When he catches my eye, he sighs and says, "There's been quite a bit of unexplained activity. Things that can't happen unless someone outside the four of us knows what happened out in that abandoned desert town. And since everyone here swears we haven't said anything, and the only other person to know is dead–it's fair to assume this is paranormal."

"The shit getting moved around, the dreams. All of it. All the scary movie stuff you think could never happen in real life? It's happening time now. The second your feet touched the dirt here." Lola finishes for him.

"I've been back a month. This has been happening all month?"

"To the day," Eddie answers matter-of-factly. He would know when I got here since apparently word travels at lightning speed in the Medina family. I'm annoyed that I'm such a popular subject, but even more so that these three are using the family chisme pipeline for access to me. "It was small things at first. Small notes here and there, dreams every so often. It seemed like maybe it was just our imagination and worry running wild. Over the last week though, it's really picked up. I assume it's because of the anniversary."

Now, I'm sweating. "No, it's not that time."

"Yes, it is," Tommy says gently like he's urging me to remember something I don't want to. But I do remember, we all do, so why is he trying to convince me of some revisionist history I remember perfectly?

"No, it happened in March of senior year. It's April, smack in the middle of Arizona's pathetic excuse of a spring. Your timeline is jacked."

Three members of The Four assume a silent conversation among themselves, full of wary glimpses and worry set into their grim expressions. A conversation I am excluded from.

Unsure of what to say or do, I go with honesty because although the relationships are strained and weird now, they are the only ones on this earth who know exactly who and what I am. And what I did.

"I saw him," I admit instead of arguing the semantics of dates. "Maybe it's more about relative location than timeline. I moved back a month ago, I closed on my house almost right away. It's oddly close to Twelve Mile Corner. I closed sight unseen, so I wasn't paying attention to the proximity I guess."

An audible gasp escapes Lola's mouth in true dramatic fashion, Tommy's face whips to mine and Eddie freezes.

"Ww-what?" Eddie stutters.

Nodding in confirmation as I continue, "At the funeral. He was there, right where the two of you were standing. He looks...how, uh, how we left him..."

"What the hell does that mean?" Tommy hisses. I am taken aback by the out-of-character move on his part, and as if he can read me, he dutifully morphs himself back into a calm and easy state.

"How am I supposed to know that Tomás? Huh?" I bite back.

"Alright, let's keep the government names at a minimum," Lola gests, forever the jokester trying to lighten the mood when things are tense.

"He's dead," Eddie blurts out. We all stare at him in shocked horror.

No shit, I tell myself. But who says that out loud?

He looks timid as he glances between us, "What? It's the truth. I'm just telling the truth."

"Yes, congrats Coward you win. You've outgrown your fear of death. Any other bite-sized bits of helpful information you'd like to provide the group?" I ask him rhetorically, but of course, he answers anyway.

"Not at the moment."

"Fuck me, what is happening?" I ask, exasperated. My hands shake as I run them over my face in exhaustion.

When did I sleep last?

No one answers for a few tense moments, and then, Tommy's eyebrows scrunch together as he asks quietly, "What do you mean, 'looks how we left him'?"

I blink at him. "You know."

"Be specific."

"He looked like a giant charred piece of fucking barbecue, Tomás. Okay?"

Eddie looks like he's about to throw up, and Lola has begun to breathe rapidly next to me.

"He's dead," Eddie says again as if trying to convince himself of what happened that night. Maybe we all are. "He can't be alive. There's no possible way on God's green earth he could be alive. It's impossible."

"I think God is going to sit this one out, homie," I respond, dripping with sarcasm and irony. Although my faith has been rocky, in some ways it has always existed. However, Eddie has never, in his entire life, been considered a homie. I'm sure there's something more fitting I could have said, and the looks on their faces tell me they expected maybe something more eloquent, but I'm jumpy, and I can't think of anything. It seems fear and nervousness are two emotions I'm capable of today in gold.

"Every single one of you is experiencing...something?" I ask. They all nod in silent agreeance, and I'm taking inventory because, yes, I have been too, and I've refused to acknowledge anything.

"The notes say-," Eddie starts.

"Remember." I finish, and all eyes are on me again as I remember the note firmly placed on the stand by my front door written in blood, slightly burnt at the edges. It still sits there, taunting me as I come and go from my home. A silent threat to my existence and yet I haven't managed to get rid of it either.

Lola's brows crunch together as she snarls, "Have you been getting shit like us and just conveniently keeping quiet about it?"

My arms fold across my chest. The move is defensive and an immediate threat to her. She recoils from me as I say, "I didn't realize it was a relevant piece of information I needed to share with a group of people I hadn't spoken to in ten years, Lola. I thought it was, you know, my mind playing tricks on me. Being back hasn't exactly been easy, so I figured the constant reminders were making my subconscious act wild, too. Maybe."

She sulks and releases a long sigh. "Spare me the boo-hoo me, Raina. All of this?" She gestures around with her finger in a circle, signifying all the signs we're being given. "It's because of what we did. Together. All four of us. You're not special, no matter what your freak hands can do."

I cringe on the inside at her weaponized insult, but I keep a flat, disinterested face. "I'm aware, it's the reason I left."

"Is it?" Tommy breaks his silence, asking the question he seems to have been waiting for the opportunity to ask. The words are tinged with a hint of regret, like he's pissed he ever felt anything for me at all, and I am a shitty enough person to answer wrong.

"Yes. I couldn't take it anymore. And then boom—you didn't have to deal with me anymore. No more walking reminders of that night. So, you're welcome," I snap, cutting my hand through the air like a knife to demonstrate. My voice is rising as I lose patience, but it's Lola who is unraveling. She snatches my leather-covered arm and yanks my arm towards herself with a firm grip on my leather jacket. The jokester has gone away. I wonder how far below she has buried her over the years, only letting her out to play when necessary.

"Then why the fuck did you come back? Why couldn't you just stay gone?" she hisses, angry, eyes burning with hate. She is resentful that I'm here. I feel the vague sensation of it coursing through me. She may not be touching skin, but I can see it in the lines of her face and the shape of her eyes. It seems there is no love lost here. Not anymore.

I look down at the hand touching me, and with a slow drag, my eyes lift to meet hers. The animosity in her eyes is met with the malice and hazard of mine; I do not like being touched, and she seems to have forgotten. Her eyes flutter with uncertainty for only a moment, and she releases me.

"Good girl," I mutter. She flashes me a dirty look and says nothing more.

"I don't think your leaving will solve anything anyways," Tommy interrupts.

"I have no intention of leaving. This is my home."

"I hate to say this, Raina, but this hasn't been your home in years. We did what we did for you–" Eddie starts but is cut off.

"Because of her. Not for her," Lola snaps. "I did nothing of my own free will that night."

Tommy fires back in my defense, taking up an all too familiar role, "Speak for yourself. Magic hands or not, it fucking happened. And he isn't letting us forget it."

Tommy is holding my gaze as he speaks, and although I don't know what he feels or what is happening between us any longer, I know that he means what he says. Through snapping at her, he is trying to tell me this isn't your fault.

"How is this possible?" Eddie whispers to himself, staring at his hands. I imagine he sees what I see when I think about that night; blood soaked, tinged with the blackness of a fire.

I sigh and, after a few moments, say, "I'm not an expert or anything, but like Eddie said, he's dead. He can't hurt us. Whatever is happening, it's bullshit. It's a jacked-up fantasy land but is not real."

"You don't think someone knows? You think maybe someone is messing with us?" Eddie's voice trembles, like a reversion of his old self.

"Well, that depends, Eddie The Coward. Did you tell anyone? Because aside from us, Lenny was the only one to ever know, and she took that secret to the grave. She owed me that, and she made do. So, did you tell anyone?" I ask again.

He shakes his head, and the rest of us look at each other. We all shake our heads, too. No one has said a word like we promised all those years ago. "Look, I got enough shit to deal with. I'm not fucking with a dead guy. He's dead. Six feet under, rotting with the damn worms. He may even be bones by now. I have no idea. Either way, I'm dealing with my Tata's funeral tonight, and what I'm not about to do is deal with Ephraim's ghost. He can go to hell and stay there."

I leave them to their theories, worries, and ghost stories and head inside for more liquor. If I have to deal with my stepdad's ghost, I might as well be drunk for it.

———————

I make a beeline for the kitchen counter that I know is littered with various foods and liquor bottles. I can feel Tommy's presence behind me. I ignore it with the will strength that rivals my mother's ability to ignore my cries for help growing up. Absolute solid steel.

I snatch the closest tequila bottle from the counter and take two deep drinks. I don't grimace, but I have to hold it back because it has to be the worst tasting tequila I've ever had in my life. I follow it with a lime popped to my lips, and I revel in the sourness of it. I find Tommy still beside me, sitting on a kitchen barstool, watching. I arch an eyebrow and look behind him. Lola and Eddie did not follow.

I stare him dead in the eye, refusing to back down. "Go home, Tommy."

"No, do not go home, Tommy! What are you on, Raina? You must be drunk, too if Tommy is around."

She looks only at me as she speaks like I'm the drunk one and not her. My sister's words come out in long, run together slurs. She is overly friendly with everyone as they pass. Happy smiles, squeezes of the arms, long hugs. There is friendly, and then there is whatever this is. Where the hell is her husband?

She used to always say that Tommy made her feel stupid, like anything she said in his presence was not worth hearing. I'm not sure that was ever the case. Tommy was only quiet around those he didn't know. Besides, she was six years older than us. We were kids, and she was already an adult, heading off into the world to leave this place behind. Leave me behind.

So, I am not surprised when she all but ignores his presence. She acts as if he is only a figment of my imagination and not worth addressing. She's probably seeing two of him when she manages to look towards his stool.

When he smiles at her, she says nothing. I squint at him in suspicion.

"You okay? You're looking a little top-heavy," he laughs as he reaches an arm out to steady her, but I catch her before he does. He doesn't think this is funny. He's being polite. Liliana sways on her feet, and her face plasters itself with a greenish tint that rivals the Grinch in color. She's going to throw up, and Tommy and I both realize it at the same time.

We rush her to the door behind Tommy, which

conveniently leads to a bedroom and a small bathroom. It's one of the many opportune additions my grandfather made when he built this house.

I'm holding my sister's hair back as she lets go of every emotion she's shoved down her throat in the form of alcohol, and it reeks. When I turn my face away, I see Tommy standing surely in the middle of the room, hands in his pockets as he watches, concern making his eyes look harder than usual. Liliana may think Tommy doesn't like her, but the truth is that Tommy doesn't like most people, and she isn't that special in that regard. If anything, she is the only person from this cursed family he can stand the presence of.

He looks out of place in this room. It's filthy and uncared for; the bed is a sickening shade of yellow with a barrage of blankets thrown about it, and the carpet looks like it hasn't been run over with a vacuum in years. The mangled dresser in the corner is plagued with random cups filled with cigarettes and old lipstick stains. The ashtrays on top overflow like when you leave the sink running too long. No end in sight.

This is a junkie's room, and I'm not sure which one, but he shouldn't be standing in it. Tommy is the kind of man who deserves all the good things in the world after dealing with a childhood like ours, thick with hostility, drugs, alcoholism, and abuse. And I feel guilty that he is somehow being forced to be around it again. I can see it in his eyes that he is uncomfortable, even if he's putting forth confidence and concern. I feel bad that he is unlucky enough to be thrust back into my presence and all its inconveniences.

My sister moans and leans her face against the toilet seat, and I grimace. The bathroom is even worse than the bedroom, with yellow stains everywhere and mold growing in every corner. I pull her up and say, "Yeah, let's get you out of here."

"Can I take you guys home?" Tommy mutters from behind me as I help my sister stand.

"Please," I say as she moans again, and I mean it. I want out of here. I'm using Liliana as a scapegoat and pretending to be raging against Tommy's presence–but I want to be around him.

There are various calls from all manner of cousins, uncles, and whoever asking where we're going. Tommy says something noncommittal, and they accept it, because it's Tommy, and it saves me from having to say anything at all. It's a small thing that someone may not notice, but it's another gentle nudge in his direction. The side in which he takes care of everything. Takes care of me like he used to when we were kids and I wanted to run and hide. The pull between us has existed for too many years to count. I put distance to stomp it down into the ground and tried to bury it along with that incident years ago.

Now, with him so close and being so truly Tommy - I feel that tug again and I am swallowed up by my need to be near him still.

5. A HOME FOR MY SOUL

The drive is painful, long, and quiet. After an intense debate on my ability to function with heavy machinery, I win and drive us anyway. He should be driving, but since I wouldn't let him, he stews in the passenger seat. Every once and a while he runs a hand over his face as he stares out the window, his large chest rising and falling with his long, strong breaths.

The deafening silence starts to bury me in memories and mistakes, and I fiddle with my radio to mask my urge to play twenty-one questions with him. I didn't expect him to talk much. He seems to be over the need to converse. But I hadn't expected such dead silence either.

With the wide expanse of my car, I'm not suffocating underneath layers of small talk. Instead, I'm drowning in the waves of silence. It's so silent it's agonizingly loud. I swear I can hear the words he wants to say but won't.

Lili moans quietly off and on a few times here and there during the drive but manages not to throw up before we get her home. My brother-in-law, his stern face full of love, meets me out front so that I may pass her off with gentle care from my arms to his. My niece and nephew wave with excitement from the window when I hop back into my car.

Knowing she's no longer in that cesspool of a room at my grandfather's house is a calm relief. Her kids, as always, are ready to dote and love on her, and I relax minutely at the sight of it. I believe they will do this with every ounce of me, and not just because I can see through the window that one is grabbing her a large glass of water and the other is laying a blanket on her. But because Lili, despite our upbringing, is the best mom on this earth. I mean that genuinely–she is everything I wish I could be when it comes to how to love people.

I will never have a heart the size of oceans or be so fully committed to those around me, but my sister always has and does. It's a gift I'm still amazed she managed to walk away with after everything we've seen. We have our bit of contention, but she loves me such ferocity and without question, I can't help but do what I can to support her. Including looking like the asshole at the funeral who leaves too early and doesn't talk to anyone, so she can get drunk and sneak away. It wasn't my exact intention, but the rumor mill will start, and they will blame me for leaving early and not her. I'm okay with that.

I peel my eyes away from them and me and Tommy slowly start the journey to my house when he offers no other alternatives. I'm not drunk, but I am not sober. The drive is risky, but I am Lenny's daughter.

It doesn't take but two seconds of rolling down the road and "Bad Omens" is playing so loud, it forces Tommy to tear his eyes away from the window. He gives me the side eye in response but says nothing.

"Really? Nothing to say about my radio choices?" I tease, hoping to get something, anything out of him.

I didn't like his prodding, but silence is worse. It feels like a punishment even when it's not.

He sighs again. "You have taken over every radio in every vehicle we've ever been in together. I am not surprised."

"Mmm," I say. I don't have any witty comebacks. He glances back at me once. Twice. By the third time, I see that he's taking some sort of issue with me. Assessing me like a cat does his prey, checking to see if it's edible.

"What?" I snap.

"You look like shit," he says, no judgement in his tone, just a matter of fact.

"Thanks," is all I can say. Because I do, in fact, look like a steaming pile of shit.

"When was the last time you slept?"

I shrug. "It's been a few days."

"You should sleep more, you'll go–,"

"Crazy? I know."

"I didn't mean to offend you."

"You haven't."

Silence ensues again, and at some point, between my snipping at him and my wandering thoughts of how and why he's here at all, we've pulled up to my small house on the outskirts of town. I don't know where I expected to drop him off. Should I have taken him back to my grandpa's?

We aren't far from the Twelve-Mile-Corner, and the reminder that I bought a house so close to our biggest mistake suddenly causes nauseates me. I've realized that I brought him here. I have to swallow hard to push the feeling away.

"I'm sorry we bombarded you," Tommy says before

he opens his door.

"No, you're not."

"I missed you."

My head whips to him at the surprising confession. "What?"

"I missed you," he repeats, holding my gaze as he continues, "I didn't plan to go to the funeral. I wasn't going to come around because I knew you wouldn't want to see me. That maybe you weren't...ready. But when Lola and Eddie mentioned what was happening to them, it...it kind of gave me the excuse I needed."

I freeze like a deer caught between sprinting and fighting.

He missed me.

It's not an absurd idea when you spent as much time as we did growing up together, side by side through everything. I think, maybe, I missed him, too. I always assumed he hadn't thought of me once I'd left.

"You didn't miss me five years ago when Lenny died. You were nowhere to be found."

"I'm sorry about that. I was still...upset."

"Over what I made you do?" I ask as though the answer is obvious. I would be upset, too, if the person I trusted most in this world could force my emotions to sway one way or another and kill a man.

"No," he says firmly, and he grabs my hand. Skin to skin. I am slammed with everything he wants to express but cannot say out loud. The longing for me, dreaming of me, missing me, and the confidence in his decision of that night. The absolute lack of regret. "I would have done it anyway, Raina. You didn't need to do anything. I would have done it anyway."

I rip my hand away. It's too much, too quick.

Too much, too much, too much.

I nod a silent acknowledgment instead of pitiful useless words. As usual, he is patient in return. I see kindness, patience, and unyielding understanding in the soft set of his eyes. But I avoid them and do not return the sentiment. I look at my hands instead, studying the matte black of my coffin-style nails, relishing the harsh color.

Dramatic. Avoid. Stupid. Leather. Heat. Want. Hate. Fear. Like the rapid fire of an automatic weapon, these words go off in my head repeatedly as I refuse to look at his face.

"You left," he continues.

"And?"

"And you left me here, alone. It's like everything that happened, everything we all went through was for nothing. You didn't even bother to leave flowers when you caught that bus out of here. You walked away and left us to rot as if we didn't have your back through every single thing that went on as kids. You know I waited for you every night? I waited for your clumsy ass to stumble through that window every night, hopeful you'd come back to us. You never did, and eventually, I stopped seeing your footprints around my window. So now, I want you to stop insulting me by acting like this was nothing, like we were nothing." His finger points back and forth between us as he leans casually over the middle console. He throws my own words back at me when he continues, eyes locked tight on mine, "I feel that...that tug. No calls, no contact, nothing. Just disappeared off the planet like you and I never existed."

"The phone works both ways." But I'd blocked him, and we both know that. So he looks at me sardonically in response. "I'm an asshole," I admit. That hurts to say out loud, and I know it won't soften any blows because I am a giant shithead. But I can't go back in time and change what I did.

"I know it's not what you want to hear, but-"

"Then don't say it, Tomás."

"It's you," he confesses, ignoring my plea. "It always has been, and it always will be. Lola was right. This isn't a coincidence."

Simple, quiet, but loaded words.

I am silent, taking them in. Chewing them, attempting to digest them better if I go one word at a time. If I could feel love, if I truly understood the weight of it, I imagine it would feel like this—steady calm that somehow simultaneously makes my body come to life. But I worry I've been gone too long to salvage this into anything worth it for him. The notion that he could still love me after ten years apart sounds silly, even to me, who consistently sees and hears what is not there. Of all the people in the world, he is the only one whose words give my body a visceral reaction.

Distance and time have separated us, but it didn't change who we are at our core. The reality is that my soul never left his. It's been away, traveling, avoiding, and being a jerk to everyone around me, including myself. But my heart has known where its home is—right here in his strong arms and stupid caring face that never falters for me.

I am stupid, though, and I don't say any of that. Instead, I say the wrong thing.

"It wasn't me when your tongue was down Ana's throat, and you dated her after...after it."

I wait for the blow to land, for him to cringe and get annoyed. I wait for the move to strike me like many have before. That is the type of action I'm used to. It's what I was raised with because it's the sort of thing you do to keep your abused under control.

It was a cheap shot, but I can still see his tongue in her mouth, holding her in ways I wished he would have held me. So, I decided to do the same. My retaliation was swift and awful, with lavish displays of affection with anyone who would give it back then.

We were both mean.

He doesn't respond like I assume he will. Instead, his mouth hooks into a half smile, revealing the dimple on that side as he says, "I was a boy, then, mi reina. Angry and unable to process my emotions or convey what I needed to say. I am no longer a child."

Great. I am now a puddle.

Without fanfare, he exits the vehicle and comes to my side, grabbing something from his back pocket. Opening my door, he offers a hand–with a glove on it. I stare at it, frozen. So he takes mine in his and gently leads me out of the Bronco. I sway on my feet from the tequila still playing games in my bloodstream, and he balances me, all with no skin touch.

"You should not have driven, *reina*."

I respond with a look that screams, say another word, I dare you.

A soft smile is my reward, and he shakes his head as he leads me to the front door. I am acutely aware of his closeness and how my body vibrates when my eyes meet his.

Deep black eyes to match my soul.

Because it's Tommy, I unlock my door and walk in without regard for anything, leaving the invitation open and waiting. If he wants to leave, he will close the door. But he doesn't. He walks in and takes more assessments of who I am now—this time of my living space. I let the leather jacket fall from my shoulders and throw my Chucks in a far corner.

My black cat Salem meows at me once I'm threw the door. I give her a small smile and a pat, happy I chose a stunning feline to match my brujera vibes. She ignores the affection and saunters off to Tommy when I throw myself on the couch. She moves and twists between his legs and feet, rubbing against him flirtatiously, hoping for an ounce of attention. I smile because that brat doesn't like anyone in this world, including me usually. But she's throwing herself at my long-lost love like he is what she's been waiting for her whole life. Like he's what we've been waiting for.

Traitor.

He bends down and gives her the affection she so desperately craves, and now I'm the one to take a full accounting. He's so tall now like he grew an intense amount since I last saw him. He did the typical homeboy thing, and he covered himself in tattoos. Every single one I can see is immaculate. A persistent desire to see what the rest of them look like is shoved away as quick as it comes.

He isn't anything like the men from home who wear hair nets and Dickie pants, however. He only plays one when necessary. It's false, but it keeps the neighborhood off his back when he's there, I suppose.

His hair is long, much longer than I'd seen it as kids. Not since we were small, and he refused to get a haircut, telling his mom it was "precious". Our parents did a lot wrong, but those are the type of memories I think we've held on to. The ones where they were gentle instead of cold or abrasive.

His dark curls are pulled into a small half-bun thing in the back, and maybe this is an example of him living out what he wanted as a child. At some point, his dad had enough and cut all of it off. Now there was no one who could tell him anything, and so it's long. It's great hair.

This is the first lack of stereotype I see in him. It's as if he himself has raged against everything homeboy culture has told him he should be, aside from the tattoos. His face is full of sharp, hard angles and the easy lines of a man just beginning to age gracefully. The youth of his teens is gone, replaced with something much more primal and leaner. A man.

I swallow and it's audible because his gaze snatches mine up with quick finality. When he walks over to me, he sits with a gentle ease only he could muster at the end of the couch near my feet. The position reminds me of how we would hang out as teens–I would scribble in his notebook, drawing small pieces of art for him to write off of, with my feet in his lap while he read a book.

Another typecast he always broke into tiny pieces. Homeboys don't read, and neither do jocks. He must hear my thoughts because he shifts, grabs my feet, and sets them on his lap again. He eyes the coffee table and the side table next to him. He is precise in his consideration of every book his gaze lands on, considering each one individually.

Settling on the random horror novel full of dark evils and questionable behaviors, his large hand gently scoops it from the pile. I think he'll read the back and then toss it away, convinced I am insane for reading this nonsense. But he only makes himself comfortable, pulling my feet closer as he cracks it open and begins to read.

Every once in a while, I see him eye the plaque on the wall. It serves as proof of my unceremonious retirement.

"You can ask, you know."

"Mmm?" He lifts his head but doesn't look at me.

"About the plaque, the retirement. Why I'm home. You can ask."

"Okay," he says and turns a page. One hand massages my sock-covered foot as he holds his book with the other.

"Okay?"

"Okay."

"No questions? No musings on what set off a range of varying events that culminated in me not sleeping for five days straight and trying to unalive myself so I wouldn't have to hear the damn voices anymore?"

He sets the book down slowly, tilts his head, and looks over at me. "No, Raina."

"And why not?"

He arches an eyebrow, "Do you actually want to tell me?"

"Not really."

"Okay."

"Okay," I say quietly, relieved I don't have to relive the catalyst of how unwanted hands touched where they did not receive permission.

Societal norms dictate I should feel weird talking about my attempt at not existing anymore, but I don't. I don't even feel guilty. And when I'm low, I'm more annoyed that it didn't work and too depressed to do anything about it.

I breathe, and I stare. He breathes, and he goes back to reading.

"Raina," he says softly, letting go of my foot to turn another page. "You can tell me whichever version of the story you need to. You can tell me it all or none of it. Parts of it. Whatever you need. But now that you are home…" he pauses and looks up at me. "You need to know that there is no version of events you can tell me to send me away. No recounting of actions or motivations that will turn me against you. I am here until the end. You can't force me away this time."

I snort. "Just like that? You're moving in or what?"

I can feel his deep laugh rumble in his stomach where my feet rest. "Just like that."

He returns to his book as if the matter is solved and there are no more details to decide. And me, so very tired, so overly exerted and exhausted from all the hours I've spent on this couch, that I can't fight it. I spend hours upon hours obsessing over morally gray fictional characters that I resemble more than I don't, and I don't sleep. Or I don't sleep well. But in the here and now, lulled by the exhaustion and the warmth of his body, I can't stop myself as I pass out.

6. FEVER DREAMS

I wake an undetermined amount of time later and find that Tommy has fallen asleep too. The book hangs from his loose grip, resting on his knee with a thumb strategically positioned to hold his spot. One of his hands is placed on my feet, sock to glove. I like it. I nudge at him with my foot, carefully trying to prod him awake.

I know what I want, and I'm sure he will give it to me.

He rustles awake, and his eyes search the unfamiliar and dimly lit space for me. When they settle on my form, they relax, and I swear they dilate just a little. There are three long and intense breaths where we both hold the stare, waiting for permission. He grants it immediately when I reach for him, moving swiftly and to the point.

The kiss is a burst of love and trust so intense that I feel like I might cry. It's the missing piece of a song I've been trying to sing since I left this town. Two halves of a soul find their missing piece, taking a sigh of relief to be complete. I let everything he feels rush through me, no bars held. I let every good thing that he is, and I am not, fill me from the tips of my hair to the bottoms of my feet.

This time, unlike all the others after and before him, I don't resist; I don't try to shut them out when they touch me. I let him in, every single ounce of him. I place my hands strategically all over him, in any space where the skin is exposed, so I can feel what he does.

It's magic.

What I can do is magic. It must be. Just like his utter and pure faith in me. I feel it through those same fingertips, and I now know that I was never someone he feared.

I was a safe place for him, too.

His eyes drift upwards reluctantly, and he freezes. A rock of a man is now hovering above me, staring with fierce precision at a spot behind my dumb fucking head. He leans over and climbs off me, rushing to the bathroom. How he has any idea where it's at is beyond me, but I hear vomiting to confirm he found the toilet. Confused, I stand and turn.

I am faced with a sight so overpowering, pungent, and disturbing; I think I might throw up, too.

Salem is pinned to the wall with what looks like long, crude nails, her back flush with the wall itself. All four of her paws lay limp in front of her as her eyes stare out vacantly. The once vibrant green of her cat eyes are now dim and unseeing. Blood is pouring from her lifeless body, and it streaks down my wall, pooling on my hardwood floor like thick and murky oil. A giant, red, disgusting puddle. I notice then that the smell is off. I don't know how long she's been there, but she doesn't smell dead.

She smells like fire and smoke.

It isn't her smell that makes me recoil though. It isn't even the blood or the way her eyes sort of stare off into the nothingness. No, it's the writing on the wall, drawn perfectly in the distinguishable block letters of Ephraim's handwriting.

FOR THE ARTIST...DO YOU LIKE IT?
...SAY YOU LIKE IT...

Now it's my turn to throw up.

7. PLATONIC BLISS

We carefully unpin Salem's body from the wall, and Tommy is gracious enough to handle the rest as far as her body is concerned. He buries her in my tiny backyard, tossing cold dirt over her losing warmth of her body as the minutes drag by.

I'm left with the task of the blood message on the wall. I try every variation of cleaning products to remove the stain, but it doesn't budge. The words carefully printed on the walls scream at me, and by the end, I am in a puddle of tears on the ground, staring at them.

They are so loud, and I can't quiet them.

Sitting before the wall, I'm paralyzed with a sense of dread that I can't escape. A steady stream of hot tears rolls down my too-thin cheeks when Tommy comes inside and sits beside me on the hardwood floor. I'm hungry too, I realize, but I can't fathom putting food in my mouth right now.

"What do you want to do?" Tommy asks, and I tear my swollen eyes away from the painful stain to look at him.

I ignore his question and say, "He used to do this, you know. With the animals, he would snatch up from the alley. It's why the shed behind that run-down

"

house on the west side always smelled so horribly."

Tommy turns in a slow and deliberate swivel to face me. "Are you for real?" He sounds surprised like it isn't something his brain is capable of associating Ephraim with. "You never told me that."

"I didn't tell you a lot of things."

His lips thin with a sharp inhale as he says, "You could have, though."

"What would I have said, Tommy? 'Oh, by the way, my stepdad captures stray animals and tortures them in the backyard, and sometimes, when he's really drunk, he makes me watch.' Is that what you wanted me to say?"

An exasperated-like noise escapes him. "Stop being so defensive, Raina. Yes, that is exactly what you should have said because it would have been the truth. You act like you had this huge burden to bear on your own, but we were there. You were never alone. Even now, you're not alone. We're always here. We are here because you need us to be. End of story."

"Right," I snort.

"I don't understand what is happening to us," he says, exhausted, moving on from the topic I am unwilling to fully discuss. He rises from the ground and leaves me to stare at the bookshelf where the leather-bound first draft of La Reina rests.

"He's coming for us. I think," I say in defeat.

"How can you be so sure it's him? He's -"

"Dead, yeah, yeah, we know. But something is coming after us with him in mind. I knew we weren't going to be able to get away with it."

A slow trickle of his fingers lingers on the spine of the leather copy. "We did, though. He's dead in the ground, and no one has found him. I refuse to accept that we're haunted by some rogue demon ghost thing."

I gesture to the wall. "And this? You think we just happened to magically sleep through someone sneaking into my home, torturing my cat, and then pinning her to the wall? That isn't possible unless something supernatural is in play."

"This is insanity, Raina," he argues, his features falling as he gradually loses his grasp on what he believes to be his reality.

"Look, I know you're the calm, logical one, and I'm the batshit, lost her fucking mind one, but you can't explain this with logic. You can't explain this away with anything other than something dark. Something wrong."

He grabs the book now, changing subjects. "This what Enzo was giving you all that grief about?"

I nod. "I guess he saw himself in there somewhere between the lines. I didn't think any of them would ever read it, honestly. It's not their type of hobby."

He turns to smile at me. "I thought I was the poet back in the day. You're getting good with your words."

"You were The Jock, Tommy. With a pension for journaling and a smooth smile. I drew shit that no one cared about. I was never as good at drawing as you were with writing. That should have been your passion, not mine."

He glances back at the book and sets it back on the shelf. "You made it into something people could resonate with. I never got that chance. So, it's good that it's you. You're the right one to share that story."

My heart warms. Aside from a few glowing reviews when it was first published, no one has ever given me such praise when it comes to my debut novel. I am equally pleased by his praises and disappointed. "Why did you give this dream up? You wrote every day. Your pen was always on paper. You had a journal just like this," I gesture to the first draft. "And yet, you're a..."

I pause. I don't know what he is anymore. I don't know anything about this man really except the image I've decided on. How very immature of me.

What I do know runs in a list something like this.

17-year-old Tommy wrote every chance he could.

17-year-old Tommy dreamed of poetry.

17-year-old Tommy never wanted the jock title.

He wanted expression. Art. Love.

He wanted out of this town more than I did and doesn't seem to have left.

I have no idea what 27-year-old Tommy wants or needs in life, except for maybe me, apparently.

"A mechanic," he replies, pinning me with a stare. "Is that okay with you?"

"That you're a mechanic?" I look down at his hands, taking note of the callouses. He catches me. "Rough hands are a sign of work. They're a sign of dedication and the ability to look past your own discomfort in order to achieve a goal."

He raises his eyebrows. "Is that right?"

I nod. "Calloused hands are a good sign. It means you're devoted. Committed."

"What if I had smooth ones?"

I shrug. "I would like those, too. Because it doesn't matter if they're calloused or smooth."

"Then why bring it up?" He leans against the bookshelf, arms crossed with a playful smile.

"Because you saw me notice. I don't care whether they're rough or not, Tomás. You are who you are. I am who I am. Both of which are not who we were at seventeen. If I'm making you feel like it's important somehow, I'm saying now that it's not. I don't, I don't know what's happening here or what we're doing, but I do know that."

His phone rings before he can respond and breaks the tension that's building. He hesitates but grabs the phone call when I nod my acceptance. He steps out through the sliding glass door and leaves me alone.

When we were teens, and I'd get my rear end handed to me in a particularly brutal way, it meant that Ephraim would leave me alone for a while. It was like he got out all his frustration and couldn't stand to look at the damage he caused for days at a time. The result was that I could sneak out without much notice and often. Because no one would be checking on me. No one would be sneaking into my room in the darkness of the night to do even worse.

I'd run to Tommy's or Lola's every time. More times than not, it was Tommy who answered the phone, and he was the one who met me in the middle of the night. Sometimes, we'd sit at the park with blankets and cigarettes and just talk until right before the sun came up. Other times he'd sneak me into his house and hide me in his room so I could sleep.

I'm sure his parents knew I was there. Much like my own, they truly didn't give a fuck about what he did. Some of my best memories of Tommy are of us hiding in his room with a small lamp, reading until we pass out on his bed. The best thing about our relationship that wasn't a relationship was the platonic part. Pure and unaltered friendship, no matter what. The kind where you can run full speed at them with all the things that make you ugly and unlikeable, and they snatch you up and hold you like you're a piece of treasured gold, something worth keeping. That was the best part.

I thought I lost that when I ran away but seeing him eyeing me through the sliding glass door, I realized it never went anywhere. I wasted a lot of my life without him, and I'm disappointed in myself for doing so.

How unfortunate that I made myself suffer simply because I thought I was undeserving. I still may not be deserving, but Tommy thought I was, or he wouldn't be here. Even if we disagreed about what was happening.

I'm still staring at the spot where Salem was, my tiny heart shattering for her, when he comes back in and wordlessly picks me up off the floor like the pathetic bag of skin I am.

Normally, when my hand touches the doorknob every day that I manage to leave the house, I am reminded that I am depressingly alone. Sometimes it is a quiet comfort to be totally and completely lonesome with yourself. There is no more pretending, no more mask. Other times, it's so heavy it smothers me. But Tommy's presence doesn't prompt me to put a mask back on in order to hide. He leaves the option open-ended and the decision in my hands.

So, I don't. I let him lead me.

He looks around the house again, noting the filth I've been living in. "You can sleep when we take care of what we need to. Then, you can sleep for four days if you want, and I'll be here. But, this first."

We move in unison, cleaning up the space now

that Salem's death has drawn attention to my living condition. I head to the kitchen to toss cups and bowls into the dishwasher while Tommy cleans off what I like to call my depression couch. It's toppled with clothes I refuse to put away after washing. He folds them neatly and without a word. He grabs my phone and puts on an old Deftones song, something to drown the silence.

When I scrape the oatmeal from a bowl I've been ignoring, I scrunch my nose at the reminder the smell brings. I'm acutely aware of how much worse this could be, but it's pretty bad.

At least it's only been here a few days, not a few weeks.

It's the constant reminder of what happened ten years ago that often traps me inside this house for days at a time, causing this horrible build-up of filth. Even the smell of dirt is nauseating, and I hate that I moved back.

Although I cringe at the old food and slam the trash lid in frustration with myself after dumping more food that's been left out, I know won't change. After this painful funeral and Salem's horrific death, I will most likely head into another depressive episode with more food left out and another pile of clothes with a couch for a home.

The house will get worse, and so will I.

Tommy is removing books from cushions, and he smiles when he sees another note shoved as a placeholder into every book he finds. There are notes and random news clippings jammed in their worn pages where I've picked up and left off hundreds of times. Another soft reminder of my inability to finish what I start.

I toss myself onto the newly cleaned couch as he

finishes.

"Ready for a nap?" he asks.

"Do I have to, Daddy?"

He chuckles darkly. "Just do what you're told, *mi reina*."

I hear the ding of an email, probably from the remote cataloging job I write for that I've been ignoring for days. They need items listed, and I've yet to look at any of them, but it can wait one more day.

"You need to answer that? Work?" he asks.

I shake my head. "They can wait. I don't need to work between what the VA pays me and the royalties from the book, but my therapist says I need the structure even if it's only a small amount. And my publisher wants a sequel though I don't think I have the capacity to replicate what was put into that original journal."

"Mmm," he hums understanding, and rises to lead me to my room.

It's untouched in here and rarely used but clean. Tucking me into the bed like a child, I laugh a little before he heads out of the room. I won't be able to sleep. I am still living with a racing heart at the images I have in my head. The words smeared on the wall; the whispers Ephraim would tell me when he would do the worst thing he could to me. But, knowing Tommy is in the house, knowing that I am safe with him around, I fall asleep anyway despite myself.

I dream of the cat. I dream of Ephraim. I dream of Tommy. For some reason, I dream of me burying the cat with my own hands and not Tommy. I dream of myself covered in the dirt it took to put her deep in the ground. I even dream of Lola and Eddie, the four of us smoking weed in abandoned houses, drinking beer at desert parties, midnight movies, and sharing pizza.

I wake to Tommy's gentle nudges as he whispers, "Your phone won't stop ringing, Raina."

It turns out this God-forsaken family did need me to help make decisions. Liliana's frantic voice on the other end prompts me to get dressed, and we both drive back across town to my grandfather's house the next morning.

8. PERCEIVED DELUSIONS ...

When people die, it leaves a dent in the family that is not so easily repaired. And everyone mourns in their own way. Healthy mourning looks like making a new space for the dead person in your life. A shifting of position from "they are" to "they were" and not having an absolute breakdown doing it. But even having a breakdown could be considered normal, I think. The tears, and the depression, are all stages of mourning and grieving that will eventually get better with time.

The Medina family does not know how to do such a thing. There is no baseline for healthy in this family, not by a longshot. Probably because of the absolute chaos that was our childhood. When you never leave the environment in which you were molded, well, you become it, too.

When we step out of my Bronco, I can hear the screams and fighting. We pause, listening closely as we shut our doors.

"I'll go in with you," he says when he comes to my side. I want to say no. I want to resist help like my natural inclination screams to do. But instead, I nod, and we head in.

"We pay fucking rent, Liliana!" Enzo is screaming in

the front living room. My sister looks like she's on the verge of tears. Her husband, Mateo, tries calming Enzo with smooth, intentional words spoken out of truth, not emotion. He's attempting reason instead of passion.

"The bank is taking the house. Tata left no will, Enzo. The mortgage is behind by at least six months. Do you have almost 10K worth of money to bring it up to current?"

Mateo says the words with all the finesse of a businessman, which is what he is. Smooth in everything in life, including making those who don't want to spend money spend thousands, and it looked like calming a crow too. Enzo faces him, wild-eyed and irrational. He's strung out. Since I've been at home from the funeral, he's probably gotten high one too many times, and now he cannot think past the dread that comes with coming down. A quick glance around the room confirms the pit of trepidation I feel in my stomach. At least five cousins are here, my Tia Malena, who never launched from home, always a junkie, and a few stragglers of people I've never met. They are all gathered around, ready to riot.

"Why am I here, Liliana?" I whisper to my sister when I reach her. I can practically feel the anxiety raging from Tommy at my back. He's strung tighter than a guitar chord, ready to fight at any second. In a group like this, when they're upset...it can go bad very quickly. My fight or flight isn't doing so hot either.

"I just, I need...they won't listen to me, Raina," she whispers back, despair lining her vocal chords. She looks like she hasn't slept much more than I have.

I jerk my head in Mateo's direction. "Looks like he's got it handled."

She shakes her head vigorously and drags me into the kitchen with a fierce grip to my elbow. "No. I need you to do that thing."

I rear my head back and look at her like she grew a third eye. I know what she's suggesting, but I'm taken aback by someone who has acted like I was making it up most of our lives.

"What thing?" I hiss.

Her eyes bounce between my hands at my sides and my face. "You know."

"I'm failing to understand what you think I can do, Liliana. You've always called it a delusion if I remember correctly."

"Calm them down, *cabrona*. I believe you, okay? I believe you."

This time I shake my head and laugh a little to myself. "Of course you do. That's not how this works. I can't..." I trail off. Because I can, kind of. I've only done it twice in my life, both out of extreme fear, which she knows about. Alhough I've always had a strong belief that she tolerated my stories, not that she believed them.

The most recent instance was during an attack in Afghanistan, hands moving over me that I couldn't stand, begging them to stop. They walked right out of our living quarters and threw themselves off the balcony when all I did was wish for it. A thought thrown out to a shooting star, begging for it to come true when it landed at its destination.

The other was in desperate need out in the Arizona desert. She only knows about one, and that would be the Afghanistan event. Since I've never been able to replicate it, I'm a little stunned by her request.

"I don't think I can do that. Again."

"You need to try," she urges, glancing back and forth between me and the chaos in the other room. "They're all strung out, no one is listening, and they won't let me leave. Whenever I try to head out the door, Andrés or Enzo, or someone blocks the door while everyone else yells and cries about shit we can't control." Exasperation is coming off her in waves; she's sweating, and her hands shake slightly. Even her eyes look overwhelmed like she can't take seeing the walls of this house a second longer.

"Liliana, even if I can manage it, this is a large group. I can't guarantee..."

I survey the room. There's a random girl on the couch; she's nodding out and teetering on the edge of her high. One of my baby cousins who never made it out of here is sitting next to her, whispering in her ear, his hand on her leg, massaging it. There's a man from the neighborhood, Anthony, maybe? He's standing off to the side next to Enzo, shifting between one foot and the other, obsessively chewing on his nails, feral eyes searching all over the place for danger. His face is full of scars and sores from the hours he's probably spent picking at it in the mirror. There are a few more random's hanging about, none I know, but all wearing the same empty set of eyes and jittery hands.

The house is disgusting, even worse than it was yesterday. My Tata died, and it's as if all the gross things they do in the dark came out in full force with no one to watch them or tell them to go away. I am re-volted by the sight alone. Memories of finding things in drawers no child should touch, and different people coming and going who didn't live here are flooding me from when I was a child.

This is all out in the open now, but when I was little,

we would find syringes in all manner of places, hidden away where the light did not touch. And Tia Malena would spend hours locked in the bathroom, shooting up and picking at her sores from all the years of using. We weren't allowed to use her bathroom for fear of coming in contact with anything she'd left behind. Drive-bys were a regular occurrence. My grandma would lock all the kids in the back room to wait out the cops' search for drugs or whoever might be evading a warrant.

The stuff we saw in the dark as children is now fully in the light.

"You don't have to do anything," Tommy says in my ear, and his voice brings me back to myself.

"I know," I affirm quietly, and Liliana's eyes furrow at my comment.

When I take a few steps in Mateo and Enzo's direction, all eyes shift to me, like I'm a beacon or, worse, a wild animal. A random guest from the neighborhood who spends too much time here takes a deliberate step in my direction like he can't wait to touch me. Hunger lingers in the set of his eyes and something more sinister.

Tommy moves to shove him back toward the wall before I get a chance to do anything. He doesn't touch the man; he simply puts his hand up and begins walking him backward like a dog. He ignores Tommy, and although he is walking backward, his eyes never leave mine. Tommy towers over him and holds him there for a few moments before he shifts his attention back to me, letting me know he's watching my back again. He leans against the wall, paying Tommy no mind.

"Mateo, take my sister home. I think she's had enough," I announce to the room. My brother-in-law agrees with a nod and then turns to grab her. When Tia Malena starts to object, it's my turn to hold my hand up. "Ah, ah. No more talking."

Tia Malena looks at me, appalled at the disrespect and too stunned to speak. She opens her mouth and closes it twice like the movements of a startled clam before rolling her eyes and turning around.

"We aren't done talking, *prima*!" Enzo yells as my sister tries to squeeze by the group of depravity.

I use the distraction of him trying to rile my sister up to take my shot. I slap my hand down on his wrist and am met with a wide range of sensations.

Fear, anger, grief, anxiety.

But mostly, fear is emanating from every pore as if it has nowhere to go from being filled so fully to its brim. I see flashes of him, locked in rooms in this house, doing awful things to people I've never met before and some I have. I see bits of him rushing to pull a rubber tie off his arm as he releases a black tar into his veins. Small blue pills resting in the palm of his hand. But at the very base is still fear.

Fear is ruling him, and I try to take it. I imagine that feeling like a string, and I pull.

When I notice the crowd watching me, I start to talk him through my invasion.

"It's not the end of the world, Enzo. It will all work out whether you live in this house or not." His eyes glaze for a moment, and I can feel the underlying current of terror of the unknown slowly dissipate from his being. It's working, and it calms him just enough that he smiles at me, and he moves away from my sister and her husband, letting them pass and go through the front door.

"You're right," he whines, then wraps me in a bear

hug like he can't take the heartbreak anymore. I stutter a step backward. He's unfairly tall and reeks of body odor and sweat like he hasn't showered in days.

Releasing me, he saunters off into the hallway, a sense of calm present that wasn't there before. I look down at my own hands, and just like the events of the last couple of days, I can't believe it's real. I cannot fathom how I could pull such an emotional string of events so easily.

Maybe he just needed to see a calm face, maybe I said the right set of words to bring his thoughts back into perspective. Or maybe my Sight had nothing to do with it at all, but it worked just the same.

"Time to go," Tommy says, close to my face again. But Andrés intercedes and tries to shove his way between us. There's a small struggle as I push him away and rear my hand back to…what? Smack him? Tommy stands in-between after I shove as hard as I can, trying to be sure Andrés can't lay a hand on me.

In Spanish, Tommy curses, "Back the fuck up, asshole."

But Andrés puts his hands up like he never intended to do anything.

My twin cousin looks me up and down with meticulous care. It crawls over me in that perverse manner that makes you feel sick. I say twin because we are less than a year apart, just like me and Eddie. And because our mothers look so similar, we do too. We were always mistaken as siblings in school, and once upon a time, we were close, too. I loved him fiercely. But now, he towers over me with cheeks that are sunken in too far, he has sores aplenty, and his thinness rivals mine.

We haven't spoken in years.

Strolling closer towards me, barely leaning around

Tommy like he's not there at all, Andrés whispers to me, "I know what you are, *Brujera*."

"You don't know anything," I bark. "I'm leaving."

I back away, but he maneuvers around Tommy, and this time, he's snatching my wrist and pulling me into him. He pulls harder than I expected, and his other hand instantly clamps around my throat. Pure malevolence morphs his features as his lip curls, but the rapid fire of pictures I get just before Tommy tries to rip Andrés away is what throws me off kilter.

That night, the fire, my hands covered in blood, shovels digging into hard dirt, and Ephraim's voice saying, "Do you like it?". It dances across my memories like a movie.

I suck in a sharp, shocked breath and fight to get away from him, thrashing about. Before I can break free or Tommy can interfere, he pushes me back towards the wall and pins me. Something is wrong. This isn't Andrés. A deep sense of other permeates the room, I can almost smell it.

Looking at his face, now focused so heavily on my own, I realize his once light brown eyes are black as the darkest night, leaving zero traces of color. My own widen in horror as I struggle to get away, kicking and hitting him.

Everyone around me objects to the sudden violence, but Enzo of all people, is ultimately who rescues me. Gripping Andrés by the throat twice as hard as Andrés is grabbing mine, I hear the garbled choking noises burst from his lips. Enzo uses all his strength and shock over Andrés to throw him backward and straight into the ground.

When Andrés rolls over on the cold tile, he's moaning and making sounds that can only come from a broken windpipe. He peers up at me and says, clear as crystal, "I hope you liked it."

10. COWBOYS AND SPURS …

I always imagined that one day, I'd react to a stressful event by becoming my mother's daughter. I held out hope, a small, miniscule hope that I'd do better. That I would *be better*.

Staring at the looming and decrepit bar, I've found that I'm exactly like her.

"Fuck, fuck, fuck, fuck…. FUCK," I scream and slam my fist into the dashboard of my car.

The smoke from the cigarette plumes around me as my hands shake violently, the ashes crumbling in my lap. I can't stop this feeling like there's something attached to me. Following me everywhere I go. Reason says that I should try to calm down, try to relieve some stress, maybe go for a run, or go book shopping, but I can't think of anything else besides the bitter taste of tequila going down my throat.

This shit bar on the edge of town was the highlight of this part of cowboy country. Now, it is nothing more than a rundown shack where the consistently rotten alcoholics hang out.

I lied when we left my Tata's house. I told Tommy I was fine. I told him I could handle it, go home, read a book, or maybe sit in a coffee shop. But Rusty's Bar has coffee, too. So maybe I didn't lie after all.

In any case, Tommy said something about work and Lola and Eddie. I shook my head like I had heard him but didn't. I wanted away from that house, away from Andrés's words like they were the plague.

When I pulled in, two cars were sitting in front, one likely belonging to the bartender who was unlucky enough to be working on a Tuesday night. The other to whatever drunk was thanking the high heavens this bar was open.

Andrés's words ring in my ears as I sit and stare at neon lights.

I hope you liked it.

"He doesn't know. There's no way he could know," I say out loud and to myself.

Great. I'm talking to myself.

I abandon the seclusion of my car and march into the bar with a purpose before I can convince myself not to act on my impulse.

"Tequila. A lot of it," I demand of the bartender when I plop myself down on a stool.

He slides me three full-to-the-brim shots of top-shelf tequila and winks as he replies, "Top shelf, sweetie."

I groan on the inside. He has that cowboy accent you only hear in the southwest, but especially here in the dustbowl of Arizona. It's filled with dirt and cattle and cotton fields, and it reminds you that we are culturally miles apart. One side of this dusty town was filled with Ariat boots and Crockett spurs. The other is decorated with clotheslines and Payless shoes if we're lucky.

When he shuffles away, my flowery opinion is confirmed by the light dust-covered pair of boots on his feet. He's a bartender on the shit side of town, but my guess is that he does some kind of sport with cattle and arenas every other weekend and has a self-inflated ego driven by the sheer lack of size in this town. He is one of thousands across the country, but I bet he's top ten in the middle of nowhere Arizona. Or, he thinks. When he eyes me from his vantage across the bar, I am reminded why I don't hang out in public with or around the quintessential cowboy. The entitlement is stifling when you don't belong in their world.

This little side of the world and all their prejudices never seemed to make much sense to me, given how much of the cowboy lifestyle came from the vaqueros of Mexico. Sure, the horses traveled across the seas from Europe to the Americas but the hardworking hands that made use of and popularized saddles, ranching, and more...it came from people like me. How can they despise the very culture they base their personalities on?

Staring down at the clear liquid, Lenny is what stares back at me as my thoughts drift far from leather saddles and Native textiles. Everything always comes back to my mother. Especially the tequila in front of me because when all else fails, I'm running straight for mind-numbing agencies to forget my problems. To forget what kind of freak I am. To forget what I did. I throw them back consecutively and as fast as possible, tossing a cut lime in my mouth as a chaser.

My thoughts wander to Lenny and Ephraim and all their varying differences, drumming my fingers against the cool expanse of the bar. Ephraim was a sadist. He lacked any defining characteristics of someone who believed in anything but himself. A narcissist with a pension for cruelty. He was vehemently against Christianity, especially the Catholic church. Although the lack of faith isn't what made him a sadist, it was a heavy contrast to my mother.

Lenny was something of a conundrum in comparison. She was the product of devout Catholic parents in the mid-20th century. But she resembled me in more ways than my looks. She could see and feel things she shouldn't be able to. Given that she was a heavy drinker and drug user to subdue it and hide from it, most assumed her quirkiness came from that. She was never cruel, but she was complacent, and Ephraim dimmed her spark when he was around. He made her more...compliant. Easily molded.

Lenny regularly played with tarot cards and begged for signs from the dead. She lived for the thrill of the unknown. And while those are two things I have never done or will do—somehow, I'm the one haunted by a dead sadist while my mother's spirit is nowhere to be found.

I know this is a reincarnation of my sins. I am only getting back what I gave. I sent someone six feet into the ground, and he didn't want to stay there. One could say, he's back with a vengeance. But if I believed the way that Lenny did, if I believed that there is some cosmic karma that exists with the man above, I'd have to ask God...why?

Didn't I do the world a favor? For everything that he did to me, to my mother, and to the family unit, isn't it a sort of poetic justice that he suffered the consequences of his actions? Or is the devil somehow punishing me for conquering his great demon here on earth?

"So, did you like it?"

Horror reverberates through me at the sound of the bartenders' words.

"What did you just say to me?"

"Did you like it?" He gestures to the shot glass. "The tequila. We have a couple of brands if it wasn't to your liking."

Lord please save me from myself. I need to calm down.

I can't even have normal conversations without feeling like every interaction is Ephraim finding his way into every orifice of it.

"It's fine," I mumble. "Another, please."

He refills the shot glasses, and I hand him a large bill while mumbling about keeping the change. His head bobs up and down in understanding. I know I have some sort of Shadow-Demon-Thing following me around town, but he probably assumes I've got a few screws loose when my eyes are shifting constantly to every dark corner, wide with terror.

If we're honest, I think I've got a few loose, too.

"You're Raina, right?"

One shot down. Two shots down.

I grimace and let out a choked, "What?"

"You're Raina. Raina Medina?" he asks again.

I nod.

"Yeah, I thought I recognized you. Your Lili's little sister."

"Sure am." I hold up the last shock glass in her honor and throw it down.

When it hits my throat, I feel it. Maybe it's my Sight cluing me in, but I think it's more likely the power that this thing following me exudes. It demands attention. It demands a reaction. I remain frozen to my barstool, unwilling to look in the corner. Like a cold pressure to the side of my face, I feel its eyes crawl all over my skin me from the darkest corner of the bar.

If I ignore it, it still might go away.

A paranormal podcast told me once that ghosts and shadow people, shades, demons, and what have you, thrive on attention. Therefore, they escalate, poke, and prod until they get the desired reaction out of you. If we ignore the signs, we ignore the prodding, then Ephraim should go back to whatever hole he crawled out of.

I hope.

The idea of sending a text to the other members of The Four strikes me, hoping for help, maybe. Will they come to save me if I asked? Turning for my phone, my eyes catch on the thing lurking in the dark corner even though I swore I wouldn't acknowledge it. He, it, is staring at me. I know this because its eyes are the only thing I can see. They are like two round saucers, a glowing white in the darkness of their figure. The way it stands...it's like breathing. The shoulders sag and rise with the steady beat of someone gasping for air in the same way that Ephraim desperately searched for oxygen when he dreadfully rolled out of the fire we put him in. The white eye holes hold my gaze for three of the longest seconds of my life, and when I blink, it's a hard, deliberately slow blink. Opening them again— it's gone. There is no more obscure corner filled with blackness and malevolence. It's just a corner.

Time to leave.

"Thanks," I spit out to the bartender, who has a corded phone attached to his ear as he eyes me with suspicion. Maybe he's telling the neighborhood I'm back and as crazy as ever.

Rushing to the car, I am dizzy and wobbly, and I know shouldn't be driving. I know this.

I know this.

And yet, I still get in, and I still turn the ignition over.

The fifteen-minute drive is excruciating for everyone on the road but me. I'm flying high off a couple of shots. I'm more aggressive than I should be, and I'm passing cars at questionable speeds and timetables, judging by the honks and shouts from various car windows.

I drive my inebriated self home because I have nowhere else to go, not because I want to be there or to see the stains again. And because I figure if Tommy is ever going to find me again, this is the only place he can find me. The thought of him makes my stomach tumble like a child again, and I let out an eye roll so hard it makes me swerve at the notion. I've never acted so lovesick in my life, but being home and being around him, it's as if Ephraim's ghost is forcing me back into my childhood. Like I am somehow reverting to my teenage self, losing everything I've become since that night.

I'm either losing control, and Ephraim is playing me like some kind of puppet from the underworld, or I'm falling in love with this guy all over again.

If I ever fell out.

My Bronco pulls in with a screech, and when I exit the car, I notice how painfully crooked my vehicle is in the drive. I laugh like a maniac. It's unnecessarily funny to me and amid my shoulders rising and falling with laughs, I spot a neighbor looking at me.

"I'm a wreck," I say loud enough for only me to hear. I hope, anyway.

They don't know I'm drunk. They only see a grown woman laughing and talking to herself in the driveway. The show I'm putting on for the neighbors is sure to be quite the entertainment as I fumble with keys and stare hard at them, trying to figure out which I need to get through the front door.

With the same convenient timing of your clothes getting caught on the door handle when you're pissed, Tommy's giant overcompensating truck pulls in front of the house. This makes me laugh harder. The universe could not be more obvious about its intention to throw us together. The only thing that would make it more apparent is if Lola and Eddie were to hop out.

Like I spoke it into existence, they do.

The world is spinning on its axis. With millions of people taking up their meaningless existence here, the universe has deemed it fitting to shove these three into my axis at every opportune moment.

I throw my head back and stare up at the vast blue, wide open above me, perfectly clear like a true Arizona sky. I marvel at it. How can the sky have the audacity to be so unblemished and perfect when the world is so dark and cloudy? How is it so clear when everything around me is murky?

The grating voice of Lola Serrano interrupts me and my daydreaming in the middle of my driveway. "You stink like cheap tequila."

I look into her conventionally beautiful Mexican face, pretentious and full of judgment. She's petite, with long arms and legs. Her brows are a perfect dark brown, angled just right. Her skin is a stunning cream color, with full lips and light brown hair that shimmers with a blonde hue to it.

She embodies her title—The Cheerleader through and through.

Equally as stunning, I'm her opposite in many ways. I am full where she is not: bigger hips, even bigger rear end, strong arms, darker skin––in some ways, more Indigenous blood than Spanish flowing through my veins. I am not ashamed of my looks; we're just different, and she fits her title to a T just as I do I suppose. I'm not sure what an artist should look like, but I know there's a certain darkness to it, a deeper understanding of the world because of our lack of privilege maybe. I guess I look the part too, if not in my skin tone, then in the way I dress, in the black of my eyes and coal color of my hair.

Growing up, social gatherings had a painful way of highlighting our differences. Everyone wanted The Cheerleader to be their friend, everyone wanted The Beauty to pay attention to them. I didn't want that kind of attention, but it was a stark reminder that I was not considered conventional enough to garner that same kind of notice. I was "less" somehow, and I never understood that notion. By all accounts, we were both beautiful, if different.

Unless you're Tommy, who is staring at me staring at Lola, while I wobble in my driveway.

"Universe, please fucking stop it," I say to myself as I ignore the two of them. I point at the duffel bag that Eddie is white-knuckling next to my front door, my arm swaying with its inability to keep it straight. "What is this, a sleepover?"

"An exorcism, actually," Eddie replies sheepishly.

II. A SAFE HIDING SPOT ...

I let the door slide open, and I slide with it. Leaning completely into the side of my walkway, I fall to the ground and land like a sack of pathetic russet potatoes or maybe an abandoned and unused rag doll worn from time. Tommy's hands are strong as they reach under my armpits to lift me, and the scattered shuffles of their feet coming into my house and hitting the hardwood floor are all I hear as I keep my eyes firmly shut. I fear the awful spin that will occur if I were to open my eyes right now. He stands me up as we take a few steps inside and gently lets me go.

I am so drunk.

I can't think of much else when I find my old group of friends gazing at me with concern and a hint of exasperation on their faces. They are staring at me, waiting for me to say something or make a move. I stumble to the couch and toss myself face down on it. The world is spinning, I can feel it even with my eyes closed. I let out a painful groan as I roll over and force myself into an upright position.

"Why are you all here?" I question as Lola plops down next to me. She picks up a book or two from the "depression pile" of books on the coffee table, the same ones Tommy neatly organized. She grabs a random horror novel I never got to and thumbs through it mindlessly like she intends to read it.

"Open your ears, *pendeja*. We're here for an exorcism," she says as if this is all totally normal and routine.

I snatch the book from her exquisitely manicured hands and toss it back on the table. I mumble something about not touching my shit, but in true Lola fashion, she ignores me and grabs another. This time she scoots away and crosses her legs into a folded position on the opposite corner of my couch, too far from reach for my drunk hands.

Eddie tosses the bag on the coffee table, knocking over some of my books. He looks regretful, but he holds his spine straight as his eyes dart back and forth between the books and Lola. I stand up and instantaneously lurch and stumble, but I snatch a book from the ground and stand to meet his eyes.

"Stop looking at her for permission, Eddie. If you didn't mean to knock them over, just pick them up and say sorry. You don't owe her any kind of male macho show."

He cringes and then brushes it off. "I'm not picking shit up, Raina. The books aren't important. The bag contents are."

Tommy snorts as he sits in my loveseat. "All right, mijito, we get it. You're a homeboy now. A real homie."

Eddie takes a deep breath, pinching the bridge of his nose. He steals a quick glance at Lola before redirecting himself to us. Lola, who is ignoring this entire conversation.

"See?" I say, pointing at her. "She doesn't care, and she never has."

I sling the insult fast as a whip in his face, and I

should regret the words that tumbled from my tequila-stained lips because they landed roughly on Eddie's heart. I can almost see it. If I touched him now, I'm sure I'd see a broken heart reflected at me because Eddie has been in love with Lola since we were ten. And she has never, not once, given him an ounce of affection aside from teasing him and leading him on.

"Knock it off, Raina," Lola warns, still not looking up from the stupid book.

I nod enthusiastically. Sarcastically. It hurt to lose Tommy when I left, but I thought I would have been able to keep Lola and I never could.

"Yeah, all right. It was a low blow to our poor baby Eddie, but you? You I could give a fuck about, and I am just so exhausted of this game, all right? The poor man has loved you for over fifteen years, and you still can't be bothered to even look at him when he's dying for it."

Finally, I've gotten a reaction. Lola slams the book down, landing on my floor with a loud thump from the impact.

"Bitch," I say breathlessly as I stare at my poor book.

She slings her hand toward me, latching down onto mine with a force I am unprepared for. I don't see what I expect.

Instead of indifference and a general lack of interest, I see years of love. I don't see the teasing as a means to garner attention only to not reciprocate it. I see care and attention returned to Eddie ten-fold by Lola. I see secret kisses and hands held underneath dinner tables while sharing milkshakes like a regular romcom. I see them reunited and all their feelings returned, just like me and Tommy.

Normally, I don't get this much information. It is

simple flashes. Her grip is fierce and with strong intention. I realize as she releases my hand that she wants me to see everything. She is deliberately pushing everything she can into me.

Immediately and inappropriately, I laugh.

Why am I laughing so damn much?

"The Cheerleader and The Coward, huh?" I ask, my eyes dragging lazy shifts between the two. Eddie blushes, his mouth pressed in a hard line, eyes locked on the floor. Lola looks like she's ready to murder me herself. She didn't want to admit this information, it seems, but I pushed her. When my lazy shifts land on Tommy, I see his unimpressed face and less-than-shocked expression. "You knew and never told me?"

He shrugs. "Not my business to tell." He gazes downward at the bag, as do three other sets of eyes.

"What's in the bag, guys?" I ask, a hint of trepidation lining my voice.

Eddie leans over and unzips the duffel bag and flips it over, emptying its contents with the rest of the disaster that is my coffee table. A ton more books fall to the ground, but I ignore them and look at the exorcism items that are now covering it. It's a giant pile of rosaries, a leather bible, crucifixes, vials of some unknown liquid, various ropes, and duct tape.

My laughing face falls.

"Who, exactly, is getting exorcised here?" I ask in a weak voice because I think I know the answer. My feet begin slow, wary steps away from the three of them. Tommy braces as if to reach for and stop me, but Lola moves herself behind so that I am forced to stop my movement.

"Calm down, *Reina*. The Queen isn't going to be tortured or anything," she snips at me.

"I think tying someone up without getting them off is a special kind of torture, don't you?" I bite back.

"Okay, can we knock off the pissing contest and get this over with?" Eddie lets out a frustrated muffled sound and gestures to the bag contents. I stare at it, too. I'm suddenly feeling more sober than I should feel after that many consecutive shots.

"You three idiots planning on tying me up?"

Eyes bouncing between the three of them like a wild animal, I hear the hard drum of my heart in my chest pounding in my ears. The air in this house is stagnant and foul with their intentions. Like a cornered cat with nowhere to run, the urge to sprint through the front door is almost impossible to resist. When I think of those restraints on me, all I can think of is Ephraim and what he wasn't supposed to do to me.

"This is all very reminiscent of the good old days with dear old Dad. You guys in the mood to retraumatize me?"

Tommy walks across and comes to stand before me and Lola. "We aren't here to torture you. We're here to make Ephraim go away."

My face crumbles into agony and anger, and I scream, "BY TYING ME UP?"

"By calling Ephraim to the light!" Lola yells back.

"What are you smoking, Lola? You dim-witted, good-for-nothing, pea-brained child!" I seethe inches from her face. Eddie coughs and shifts uncomfortably off to the side. "What now, Eddie?"

"We're not here to hurt you, Raina, fuck." His voice is small as he fidgets with his hands before he continues, "We are here to help you. We think...we think Ephraim, his spirit, or maybe something acting like him, is attached to you. That's why it only acts up when you're home, because of your proximity to it and us. Somehow you being back here, near...everything and everyone, it sets it off. Gives it life. But we need to know what it is. And maybe, performing some kind of exorcism on you will, you know, bring it out. Force it to talk to us."

I scoff. "This is like horror 101, Eddie. You don't talk to the dead. You don't knock on doors without a clue what's waiting for you on the other side. Did you all decide this while -"

"While you were getting shitty at Rusty's? Yes. And in case you hadn't noticed, this doesn't only affect you. I'm having nightmares on repeat, and so is Lola. Tommy can't look in the mirror without seeing shit that isn't there, and you, apparently, are seeing things in the corners of bars," he blurts out.

I curse myself for moving back to such a small town where everyone recognizes me. "What did that good ole cowboy bartender tell you guys?"

Careful not to startle, Tommy answers me with a gentle tone, "That you spent a solid twenty minutes in his bar downing tequila like a lifeline and that you had a physical reaction to a dark corner of an already dark bar. He said it looked like you were seeing things and that he never pegged you to be the one from high school to go crazy. Also that you ran out of there like a spooked horse." When I continue to look at him, begging for more, he continues, "He called me."

"Ah, that was you on the other end of that dinosaur phone then."

Tommy nods. "This isn't a punishment, Raina. It's a last-ditch effort."

"I find it difficult to believe that these two geniuses couldn't come up with anything better than this," I tell

Tommy, pointing a lazy finger at Lola and Eddie.

I turn my head, slow and deliberate, to watch Eddie walk to me slowly. All three are painfully close, like I'm a wildcat they're trying to trap. When Eddie holds his hand out, offering the skin to skin he doesn't want to give, and I don't want to receive, I look down at it like it's contagious.

After a moment, I inch away from him and concede, "I get it now, *pobrecito*. I'm the bait." I hold my hands in the air when their unconvinced expressions meet mine. "It's fine. I apologize for the dramatic and drawn-out reaction. I am... not a fan of being tied up. As our dear Tomás knows. So, I don't know why this is a consideration."

Eddie's face morphs into a small, shy smile. "*Pobrecito*? I thought I was The Coward."

"Well, you can't have it both ways. You can't be upset when I call you Coward and then be annoyed when I stop using it. You're either the coward or a poor baby. You pick," I tease.

Eddie's smile widens, and I relax. I don't enjoy making Eddie feel bad, and I have almost always regretted it in my life. We were just two small kids in a backward family once, and I sometimes forget that he experienced similar traumas. I have enough self-awareness to know that my antagonizing him isn't ideal for this situation. Or ever.

We both found needles in drawers and watched our aunts and uncles nod out on rotted couches and beds. We both were shoved in closets at the age of six, guarded with pillows and piles of clothes to make sure the bullets flying didn't hit us. We watched as our parents left us with our grandparents, drove away, and lived years of their lives acting like we didn't exist.

But I watched out for him every second I could. I was the one who drove the neighborhood bullies away from him. I was the one who stood in front of adults and took the blame when he made a mistake because his scared eyes convinced me that he couldn't handle the punishment. I used my body to guard the slaps across the face from grownups who should have protected us.

No one did that for me. Everyone was too afraid, or they didn't care to. They were trying to survive. He got to move on with his life, grow up, and live happily ever after with Lola. From what I can tell, they live in peace. And I had a mental breakdown to bring me back to square one.

I thought I had accepted that I was the punching bag. I accepted that no one could protect me, that they didn't owe me anything. It wasn't any of our responsibilities to do so. But maybe the truth is that I resent all of that anyway. Maybe I snap at him because I still wish that I had been the one to be taken care of, to be looked over and guarded. It's harbored jealousy.

I feel like a teen again. I'm reminded of standing in front of Eddie, shielding him from every punk ass from the neighborhood insisting he was a being a little bitch and needed to be a man. Except now, Eddie doesn't need me to stand in front of him, he needs me to stand beside him and place trust in the fact that he only has my best interest at heart.

So, I let him try.

"Explain, please," I say nonconfrontationally. Lola decides I'm safe to release and she resumes her position on the couch, as does Tommy, clearly resigned to let Eddie be the informant here.

"The rope is only in case something happens that

we, um, you know, can't control. We don't want you walking out of here with a demon possessing you," Eddie jokes.

I snicker at him, "Too late."

He rolls his eyes, but he smiles warmly at me. "Either way, we'd like to be safe. Have a preference for the chair?"

I walk over, drag a chair from my dining area into the living room and place it in the center between us. "This'll do, pobrecito."

"Can you stop with the *pobrecito* shit? We're the same damn age."

"Yes, Coward, I'd love to."

Eddie shakes his head in resignation and throws the rope to Tommy. He is unwilling to be the bad guy and instead opts to make it Tommy. I sit and let Tommy tie me up because why not? It brings back memories I don't want to feel, but the alternative is not getting answers. We have to try something, don't we?

"Kinky." I wink at Tommy, and he offers a smile I used to covet as he quietly ties my wrists behind me and to the chair. He follows it up with more cord wrapping my ankles to the chair, and at this, I begin to hyperventilate.

It's not the same thing. It's not the same thing. It's not the same thing.

I take long and slow deep breaths. Tommy wouldn't hurt me, Eddie wouldn't hurt me, and Lola would die before she let anyone else hurt me.

I'm safe.

But it doesn't stop my heart from playing ping pong in my chest. Nor does it stop the sweat from building on my forehead like I'm sitting outside in an

Arizona summer instead of a temperature-controlled home. When he finishes, he looks to Eddie for confirmation. Eddie coughs nervously, and I see the perspiration on his forehead, too. He's probably as nervous as I am, maybe more.

Tommy stands stoically off to the side, my ever-present knight ensuring all is well. When he looks to me, it's not fear I see but knowing. His dark eyes are filled to the brim with the same stuff that I'm made of; two sides of the same coin. I feel more confident in his presence. I'm glad that they are all here to help get answers, but especially him.

Lola doesn't move, but I feel her scrutiny pinned on me, waiting, as Eddie begins saying things in Latin I've never heard before, rosaries in both palms and the crucifix pointed at me.

"*Vade retro, Satana. Vade retro, Satana. Vade retro, Satana…,*" Step back, Satan. Step back, Satan. Step back, Satan…

At first, nothing happens. It feels silly, cliché even, and out of place. So, he continues, this time in English.

"Step back, Satan. Saint Michael, may you defend us in battle; be our protection against the wicked and the evil snares of the devil. May God rebuke him, we humbly pray; and do thou, O Prince of the heavenly host, by God's power, thrust Satan into hell and all the evil spirits who prowl about the world seeking the ruin of souls." He takes a deep breath and says in Latin, "*Loqueris ad me, Diaboli. Dic quid vis.*" You speak to me, Devil. Say what you want.

Eddie repeats those last two lines over and over while I sit and watch for long, awkward moments. Like good Catholic boys, their heads are bowed. I can't help but smirk again.

"Where did you learn such a fancy prayer, Eddie?" I ask, a giggle on the tip of my lips.

"Google, Raina, fuck."

"Shh," Lola hushes us, and I do a double take to her face. She has thrown the book down on the floor again and is staring at me with eyes wide as saucers. She's leaning forward, but her hands shake as she asks, "*¿Que es esto?*"

I want to answer and say, *It's Britney, Bitch.* Or some other wise-crack or cringey pop culture reference, but I can't speak. Like a fish, my mouth opens and closes, opens again, and then closes. Or I think it does.

A voice leaves my mouth, I can feel the timber in my throat that comes with the act of talking, but it is not my own. Slowly, I feel myself being shoved into a dark recess of my mind. My subconscious throws me into a safe place to hide while watching what unfolds. It knows I can't fight it, and I need to be flighty instead of trying to fight myself.

I can't move, I can't speak.

We opened a door without knowing who would answer, and now–we can't close it.

12. EN NOMINE PATRIS ET FILII ET SPIRITUS SANCTI…OR SOMETHING

"The little group of rejects have all grown up! What a splendid time to play. No longer children, no longer toys, only big things give me joy."

The sound that leaves my mouth goes along in a sing-song pattern as it says the words, like a riddle. It can't help but sing to a tune. Although it is distinctly male, it raises its timber to sound more like that of a child. Maybe to seem less frightening. But there is nothing about this voice that brings forth confidence and comfort. It's terrifying.

I look through its eyes; I see how Lola scrambles back on the couch when it speaks. Tommy is frozen with fear, rock-solid standing and staring. Eddie, however, is not quite the coward he once was—he maintains his position and does not stop spewing prayer after prayer with a crucifix shoved in my body's direction. Something about my physical appearance must be different because they all look as if I've morphed into a monster.

Eddie speaks louder now, "Prayer to St. Michael the Archangel. In the Name of the Father, and of the Son, and of the Holy Ghost. Amen." He starts to stutter and fumbles the crucifix. When it hits the hardwood floor with a loud clank, the voice leaves my throat once more.

"The Archangel is not here, child. Try again, and maybe we shall see him bring forth his mighty wings and send me back to the depths of a flaming hell once and for all!"

More songs, more childlike rhetoric.

Eddie repeats his Catholic prayers from an unknown internet source, "We drive you from us, whoever you may be, unclean spirits, all satanic powers, all infernal invaders -,"

"Nah-ah-ahhh! We will have none of that." The last word finishes with a sharp T, as if they were already beginning to lose their patience. "Your little girl is quite wise. I am growing impatient."

Fuck me.

The room is quiet, except for the low snarls from my mouth that I cannot control. I want to fight; I want to hide. I want to rage; I want to give up.

What should I do?

"Who are you?" Eddie asks in a tentative whisper.

"Well...I am not Raina. You didn't like my art project?"

It croons, gesturing with my head to the blood-stained wall where Salem once hung in pain. There is a beat of time where my focus is in and out. I am trying very hard to stay present, though hidden. I do not want it to take me all the way, I think. The thought occurs to me to fight, to rage against, but this may cause him to retreat. To lock its mouth shut with a tightness not even a crowbar could pry open.

"What is it that you want?" Tommy croaks out. Through its eyes, I watch it assess them individually.

"I want...out. You took the body that was once mine.

I snatched the soul but...I'll need a new one. Body, that is. An offering for my toys and joys and braids and spades. It must be offered. I cannot take, however unfortunate that is," it hisses at Lola. "She looks good enough. Such beautiful long hair, perfect for braiding. She seems...bad enough, a whore enough, dirty enough!" It screams and laughs, and it thrashes my body against the ties. The chair rocks, but it does not fall, and I am thankful that my face isn't going splat on the ground. They all cringe back, and I can tell that fear is overtaking their ability to fight back.

You cocksuckers better get me back!

I know it can hear me. It can hear everything.

"I'm not who you want, you dick wad. You want Raina, don't you?" Lola spits, catching its attention and being the only one to swallow the overwhelming ball of emotions appearing to consume the group.

It gets so quiet you could hear a pin drop as it stops squirming and yelling to say in barely a whisper, "She is...precious. To me. This is true." And then it immediately begins to laugh maniacally and loudly again. "For dust you are, and to dust you shall return. La la la la la la."

It sings, mocking Eddie and his prayers as The Coward mumbles the Lord's prayer to himself on repeat. He might be stalling for time; he might be trying to get me out. The prayer gets louder as Tommy and Lola join hands with him, chanting their prayers like a harmonious ritual, louder and grander. With so much fanfare, it is the only thing it hears.

"I am not your Devil!" it screams and taunts, but I can feel my body panicking. I can tell it is panicking. Spanish flows involuntarily from my lips, "*No puedes obligarme! Escúchame! Escúchame! Escúchame!*

Mírenme, tontos! Recuerda lo que hiciste!"

Screams, screams, screams.

The chair is rocking, and this thing is falling apart inside me, its grip loosening. Right as the tether snaps in my mind, it yanks my body so hard against the ties on the chair it sends us falling to the ground, hard and fast, with the binds coming undone of their own free will. Supernaturally fast.

The chair breaks, and my head snaps back onto the solid wood flooring.

Then, nothing.

———————

There's blackness behind my eyes for long, drawn-out periods of time. Or maybe it was no time at all, and I was simply stuck in a weird capsule of time where it operated differently inside of it. I feel my body being jostled here, jostled there, more than once, but I don't hear anything. The silence is peaceful in comparison to all the dreadful and ghastly nonsensical thoughts that rummage through my brain most of the time.

Beep...beep...beep...

The beeps are going to the beat of my heart...my pulse? I feel a lot of pain suddenly, like a headache I can't escape. But I'm gone now, I think. You can't get a headache when you're gone.

I wonder if maybe...I'm not as gone as I thought. Am I being taken out of this stunning reverie I've somehow ended up in?

"She's moving, guys."

Whispers. The loud screech of a chair. The slow sinking movement in my lower body, like someone is sitting down next to me. Whatever dreamlike world I was living in before is slowly dissipating. I'm coming back to reality. The weight of it rests in every ounce of myself; my wrists are on fire, my throat hurts like I've been mouth breathing for days on end, and my head is pounding—like it got smacked with a wooden bat. My vision comes in blurry at first. And fucking bright.

"L-lights…," I croak.

The soft click of a light sounds, and my eyelids are shaded to an almost black. I open them to find the other three of The Four gazing at me, eyes overflowing with worry and unease. Tommy is closest to me on the bed. Searching the room, I find white walls, tall machines, and a hospital bed. "What the hell happened?"

Tommy shifts on the white linen lying atop the hospital bed, clearly torn between being close to me and making me uncomfortable. He does not touch me.

"When the chair went back, you knocked your head so hard the lights went out. Liliana called a lot and she finally just showed up here, worried you were dead or something. She just left a little bit ago after refusing to talk to any of us. Think she might be pissed."

I mumble something as a sign of comprehension, and I wince. My hand instinctively reaches upwards. There are bandages to cover a portion of the back of my head. My guess is stitches.

"Yeah, you might have cracked your head. Just a little," Lola says quietly as the hospital room door slides open, revealing a concerned Doctor Ingrid.

I sit up quickly and regret the sudden movement. I flinch as I slide my miserable excuse for a body down on the bed.

"Hi, Doc. Anyone want to explain the sequence of events that led to the good Doctor Ingrid being present in this hospital room?" The words come out rough and raspy. I have definitely been mouth-breathing. Ingrid's eyes bounce around the room.

"I called," Doctor Ingrid says quietly. "I was trying to reschedule your upcoming appointment. It was rather urgent, as I needed to get another patient who was in distress. I dealt with them, but when you still would not answer, I worried and called 9-1-1 for you. One of the paramedics finally picked up my urgent and incessant calls afterward and explained what happened. I'm only here to check on you."

Humming as a confirmation of facts, I keep one hand on my forehead, and I peer at her through one open eye, willing both her and the headache to go away. "Thanks for that. As you can see, my friends have ensured I will live."

She gives an unsure nod, her eyes searching for more explanation from around the room like it's sitting and waiting in the corner.

She won't get it.

This group of friends has had an entire childhood of learning to be tight-lipped. Growing up in houses full of covered bruises and feeding yourself with scraps from the pantry will do that to you. Those who grow up with the ability to know when their next meal is might not understand the need for such secrecy. There is a sense of safety in silence.

And what are we going to tell her anyway? My dead stepdad, who we murdered one night in cold blood, is haunting us from the grave and is attached to some demon thing we don't know the name of? Yeah. Okay.

"I don't mean to be rude or assume to know what's going on with you, Raina. But you referred to your friends again," Ingrid's warm brown eyes land softly on each of them with kindness and patience. "I assume they are back in your life, in your existence, rather. But is there any way just me and you could have a conversation? Could you ask them to leave?"

A silent exchange happens between the four of us: no one wants her here, and we all wish she would go away. My brain is foggy still, wading through memories of the night before like thick sand and rough waters, but I am even more befuddled by her choice of wording. The energy to fight has left me, however, so I relent and ask them to leave, with Tommy saying he'd bring me back food.

Ingrid sits in the chair closest to me and crosses her legs in front of her silently with expectant eyes now that the group is gone. "The paramedics said you fell."

"Mhhmm," I mumble, my throat protesting at the minor sound.

"You've been considered stable for months now, so imagine my surprise to find you've landed in the hospital again." Her tone isn't accusatory, but it demands a certain level of truth that I am unwilling to volunteer. I don't answer. I only glare. It was a fall as far as anyone outside The Four is concerned, and there's no need to suspect otherwise. "I am not a fool, Raina. I can tell by your face and secret exchanges around the room that there is more to this story than I am being given. I'm not here because of the Veterans Affairs office. I'm here as a courtesy to a patient I believe has the tools to succeed. I don't want to see her lose herself again in the midst of another personal tragedy."

"The tragedy of losing my grandfather does not equate to what happened to me when I was active duty, and I am not manic. It was an accident. I was drunk, and I shouldn't have been, but I've done worse things," I say the words quickly and with mild whispers because I can't bring myself to put my throat through the pain of talking at full volume.

She bobs her head in a silent response, soaking up and digesting my words. Weighing them in each hand for truth or falsehood like a scale. "Have you been taking your meds? You swear this is only an accident? Those friends..."

"Are you implying my friends hurt me somehow, and I'm covering it up?"

"I'm not sure they are friends at all, but if you envision them to be, then I suppose, for now, they are. It's not uncommon for victims to be abused again, either. Especially when they revert to old habits. Sometimes we put ourselves in familiar situations when things are chaotic or out of our control. This is common with patients diagnosed with bipolar disorder."

"That sounds a lot like victim blaming there, doc. You sure you want to continue down this route?"

She's not. Victim blaming, that is. I point the finger and deflect because it's best if she doesn't catch wind of what is truly happening. If she hears the truth of it, I'm ending up on the fifth floor of some hospital with sticky socks and a curtain dress-like get-up.

Every part of Ingrid goes still. Even the tight curls of her hair and the skin lining her oval face seem to go on edge. Then, she takes a long, painstakingly slow breath and lets it out, her irritation coming out with every second of it. "I'm glad you're okay. I will email the appointment confirmation since we rescheduled. Please, do not make me report a safety concern to the VA. Be safe, Raina. And, maybe justkeep an eye on those friends."

I spent three more days in this hospital bed as a precautionary means considering the head trauma. The Four come and go, and Tommy lingers more than the others. He doesn't say much. He sits quietly and reads. He brings me new books, and I pretend to have read them so he can bring back new ones. Every time he's here, he brings a notebook. Newer than the kind he used to carry around as a teen. These aren't leather. The old ones were. He used to say the feel of the leather made the words inside feel more real. The realness of the leather somehow did this.

Instead, these notebooks are spiral bound, and he scribbles furious notes and sketches. He was never one for art before, but old dogs and new tricks ring false here.

Lola stops by often with my favorite food, dutifully taking orders for what I'd prefer next every time she's here. She doesn't talk much either. She has work to do, she says. Most of her time is spent with furious fingers to the keyboard and headphones locked firmly in her ears. Unlike Tommy, no creative juices are flowing. Only diligent scrunches between her eyebrows as she mashes numbers.

Eddie does much of what Lola does, but he brings cards instead so we can play Gin Rummy and Kings Cup with water like when we were seven. My sister makes an appearance, and she fusses and asks a million questions because she means well.

Ephraim never shows. I have no nightmares, and I see nothing hiding in corners.

But my hair is braided every time I wake from sleep. No matter how often I shake it out, tie it up, or restrain it, when morning comes, it's always in a long braid hanging down my back when I wake from sleep.

I think Ephraim is ready to come out and play.

13. TWELVE-MILE-CORNER… AND THE TERRIFYING ORDEAL OF GOING BACK

Tommy lays me softly in my own bed like he's afraid I'll crumble into tiny pieces after my release from the hospital. I don't need the help. The directions from the doctors say to take it easy, but I can tell I am fine. But Tommy is who he is, helping those who did not even ask, and I let him.

Sleep comes to me easily, but it is fitful and overflowing with terrors.

For the next several days of being home, I dive back into a vague semblance of routine. I add words to paper I hope someone will feel in their bones. I write words for my day job for products other people find value in but that I don't care much about to go to auction. I shower, eat, shit, and breathe all the same. But I don't sleep well.

The dreams returned as swiftly as a dust devil in the middle of the Sonoran Desert – out of fucking nowhere and with no rhyme or reason except to torture me at the consistency of it. The dream I'd had as a child about a Goblin Man with pointed shoes, a large black hat, and a fistful of dirt decided it was now time to resurface, no doubt at Ephraim's whim. I don't know if the exorcism took too much out of it, but I do know that Ephraim, it, hasn't bothered to make any new appearances. Only visits in my dreams in the same form as when I was little are the proof that he's still around.

The thing that spoke through my vocal cords and used my body to relay a message during Eddie's botched expulsion is the same one from my childhood dreams. Or nightmare, rather. The one where I shoved dirt down my too-small throat and woke with long, distressing braids in my hair. I knew it to be the same because I recognized the curling in my spine as an exact replica of the reaction I would have had to El Goblin in those dreams.

He had other names, he told me once. Old names. Names given to him by those who would banish him and lay waste to his mere existence. But it is all circumstantial because they were dreams, and a dream does not mean reality. Unless you're manic, which I am not. I think.

Nana Isabel's idea that burial has some relativity to what happens to our soul after we die ruminates in my thoughts for days. Marinating. Always at the forefront of my mind.

I watch Tommy fiddle around in my kitchen from my comfortable position on the couch. I'm bundled up like a teddy bear with thick blankets and sweaters in my house that I keep too cold. It's set at an unreasonable temperature, but it's perfect for an Arizona spring, which doesn't require sweaters or blankets because it's already hotter than Satan's sphincter. But I like to wear them, so I keep it cold.

This doesn't seem to bother Tommy, who has spent every night here since I came home from the hospital. He has taken up residence on what used to be my temporary resting place on the couch at night, and I sleep comfortably in my bed knowing he's there.

When I do sleep.

He doesn't kiss me. He doesn't touch me. We simply exist next to each other, working and living in tandem, rotating around each other's vastly different worlds of work schedules and hobbies. We live and breathe next to one another as if we had been doing it all along. I don't hate it, so I let it continue.

When he sets a mug of coffee down in front of me on the coffee table, I tell him about my thoughts on Nana Isabel and burials. He takes a sip of his own coffee and nods. "I don't think we put him anywhere that significant or insignificant."

"What do you know about Twelve-Mile-Corner then?" I ask, wrapping my hands around my own warm mug of coffee and breathe it in. It's one of my favorite smells.

He grunts and ponders a moment before he answers. "It's literally just twelve miles in four directions for each of these towns. I've only heard the ghost stories from when we were young. Maybe there's some truth to it, but I've never bothered to look. I'm guessing you did?"

"Fact. But that's not it. I've been looking up the area for the last two days. When you're told to stay bedridden, time to make the most of your item at least. This whole thing is Ephraim's doing. We know that to be true due to how specific these hauntings and messages are, but there's something else. The thing said it cashed in on the soul it was given. That is Ephraim, and he's looking for a new one. But who is it anyways, and where did it come from?" When Tommy arches a brow at me to prompt my continuation, I do so obediently. "Cotton was a big market here as well as dairies and ranching; lots of fields and feed yards, lots of poor people. Poor people of color. Mexican immigrants, everyone, and in the fifties and sixties. Twelve-Mile-Corner was set up as a means of segregation. They put up a post office, a tavern, even a gas station. But they let it fall to crap. The businesses didn't do well because the community was so poor, but they didn't want the "colored people" coming to their neighborhoods and setting up shop. So, they shoved them all in Twelve-Mile-Corner, built a bunch of houses, and said here you go, now shut up." I look at him, triumphant in my explanation, but he just stares back, waiting for more.

"Alright. Segregation evil. We know this, too. But that doesn't mean it's the opening of hell just because poor people once lived there. It's a ghost town now."

"Boom. Exactly." I snap my fingers at him, and again, he stares like I've just told him the sky is falling. "It's a ghost town. No one lives there anymore; everyone shifted and went to newer communities in the eighties and nineties when they started having better access to transportation, and they needed to be closer to town for work. The cotton gins went bankrupt near Twelve-Mile-Corner, and the feed yards moved closer to the old train stations across town. If they wanted work, they needed to be close to the work, and Twelve-Mile-Corner didn't have it anymore. Despite that, though, a good portion of the community couldn't afford to move, and many lived and died there from various forms of poverty."

I have put these makeshift puzzle pieces together in my mind, but Tommy's brain is attempting to do the mental gymnastics and failing. His sharp masculine features crumble a little in confusion as a response. He's gotten slower in his age.

I continue, "Nana Isabel was adamant that our

burial is somehow just as important after our death as how we lived. In essence, she felt like it wouldn't matter how saintly we were in our lifetime if we were buried in a ground that was unconsecrated or somehow inherently evil, like where evil things happened. She believed when our souls touched that dirt, Tommy, that we would be met with other things. Things that could snatch our souls when we put our physical bodies in the ground. Lenny practically screamed from the hilltops that she wanted to be cremated. I remember everything it said through my mouth, and the soul-snatching thing sounds awfully familiar, don't you think?"

"Okay..." he pauses again, tossing my words together. "Please connect these dots, Raina, my brain hurts."

"I can see that," I laugh. "Anyways, what if after all the trauma and all the bullshit of people being forced into a literal segregated hell part of the desert where they stayed poor and oppressed, it created a breeding ground for...things to flock to. What's more, you ever heard of the Dustbowl Riots? Eddie was so fucking focused on this story, he would refuse to go out there all the time, told us that we were 'playing with fire' because we didn't know what kind of ghosts were waiting out there for us. Even that night, don't you remember?"

Tommy's eyes widen, and he runs a hand over his face. "The little coward would ruin our nights all the time, told us he would snitch if we didn't find somewhere else to party. I always just assumed he was being paranoid, though. I didn't think there was any substance to his worry to be honest, as mean as that sounds."

"It's not mean. It's a safe assumption for Eddie. Either way, we put Ephraim there because we thought no one would ever go poking around out there anymore. No one was going to call the cops on that area because it was only ever used for drunk teens to hide and party. It's a ghost town now. But what if something was there? The Dustbowl Riots took place in the seventies. All the farmers in the local area refused to go to work during César Chávez's *Sí Se Puede* movement. They thought they were being supportive and that they would go somewhere with this fight. But the town was too small, their numbers weak. Local law enforcement came out to Twelve-Mile-Corner and effectively ensured they ended up back in the fields."

I offer Tommy a grim smile before continuing, "Except the protestors lost many of their own that night, going down swinging with the local cops, they were beaten not only into submission but some into death. Things like this have happened before, the blood of our people being soaked into the ground. Into ground that belonged to us. All the while, the Americans moved west, shoved us all around, and only treated us fairly when we could offer them something like the Bracero Program during World War II, when they shipped thousands of immigrants to work the fields. They moved them here, too, not just to California. These immigrants ended up in these small towns working these fields, Twelve-Mile-Corner among them."

Tommy hums, shifting himself to hold my gaze. "You think all this blood, all these things together, are acting as some sort of, what? A beacon? You're saying atrocities done against the community are enough to make the dirt a breeding ground for evil?"

"Maybe. Evil begets evil, or so they say, right? Generations of being taken advantage of, bodies, hundreds maybe, being left to die out there where the world forgets about them? Their blood soaked the earth, and the rest of the town threw parties over their graves. We act like they never existed."

Tommy chuckles with dark understanding as he says, "I'm not sure the cowboys around here would understand that. They'd say we gave them jobs and a place to live."

"This wasn't a place to live for them to give, Tommy. It was ours first."

He shrugs, "It's not how history remembers it, even if it's technically true."

"Our opinions on the matter don't really mean anything. My real point is that enough blood has been spilled on this dirt, it became a a beacon from hell. That thing said it used up the last soul. Ephraim was that soul. We offered it up on a platter when we buried him. We gave it a vessel to act through. I've been gone for ten years, maybe distance reduces its reach, but I'm home now, and there are no barriers to what it can do anymore. When we killed him..." I trail off, not particularly fond of finishing my train of thought, but Tommy does.

"Do you think maybe the act itself is what...maybe caused something to find him after he died? Like maybe we are the evil?"

My knee-jerk reaction is to be upset by the question because the immature part of me feels as though he's contradicting what he told me before. That he regrets what we did and that he wouldn't have actually done it of his own accord. But I know the truth in those softly spoken words, and he only says what I think deep inside. It is not what my subconscious is trying to make me believe.

Are we the reason for this evil to exist now? Are we

being repaid tenfold for what we did in the name of safety and life or death?

His expression softens, those severe features of his molding into patience again like he can read my warring internal thoughts.

In two fluid movements, he's removed himself from the love seat and sits knee to knee with me on the big couch. Tenderly, carefully, he wraps his fingers around the loose strands of my hair and pushes them behind my ear, touching me lightly. It isn't enough to feel much of anything with my Sight. The rough fingers of his mechanic hands make their way to the rest of my long hair flowing down my back, still tangled in a half-braid from sleep, which refuses to stop happening.

Holding my gaze, he continues to push his fingers through and pulls the braid out completely, running his hands through once more, twice, three times. My eyes close in calm anticipation. I am wishing, hoping, longing for more while simultaneously fearing it. I can't shake the feeling that this is moving too quickly.

He is still staring intently when he asks, "What is it that you want to do now?"

I pause for three breaths and say, "A lot of things. There's more than just the protests, a lot of other deaths have happened out there, too and I'm unsure what to make of it. But first, I think we need to go to Ephraim."

When we were fourteen, a group of idiots had taken to harassing Eddie at the bus stop when he was alone without the other three of us. The only reason I knew was because Andrés had told me over breakfast on a random Wednesday morning.

"It's some assholes from the east side, over the bridge. They're over here when they're not supposed to be. I heard Enzo say a bunch of guys have been testing boundaries and shit," he told me, mouth overflowing with eggs and chorizo as Nana Isabel patted my shoulder. She said nothing as she past us, moving on to other morning tasks.

"And what have you done about it?" I asked, a voice full of accusation. No one in this family ever backed Eddie up.

He snorted. "Nothing, Raina. He needs to learn how to handle shit himself. Anyways, I'm never there. I heard it from Frankie down the street. La Victoria will handle it eventually, you know that."

I remember snorting my response back. Frankie watching and not doing anything meant everyone from La Victoria was waiting to do something about it when it was convenient for them or when those guys violated some unwritten code between the two sides of town. The resident gang, which included several members of our large family, had no intention of doing anything for Eddie or his safety. Not because he didn't matter, but because he wasn't one of them.

I took it upon myself to be that safety, knowing damn well I could end up dead – or worse. But I was sort of a violent teenager, always looking for danger and precarious situations to put myself into because maybe I'd get the kind of attention I sought.

When I'd met Eddie at the bus stop that day, those same fools were there, cracking jokes, shoving him here and there. It was very cliché. A bullying scene straight from a movie. I sneered not only at their cowardice (who does three-on-one?) but at their lack of creativity as well. Before I could reach them, Tommy had intercepted me mid-stride with his backpack casually slung over one shoulder, coming from the direction of his own house.

"I know that face," he warned, matching me step for step but looking at my face instead of where we were going. "Maybe, just think about what you're about to do instead of just doing it?"

"I'd rather do calculus than consider thinking twice, Tommy, you know that."

"Any chance you'd reconsider picking a fight?"

I smiled at him, and instead of trying to convince me otherwise, instead of guilt tripping me, or attempting to make me into the bad guy – he joined me. This was the case for most of our childhood, always asking me to think for just a second and then landing on the inevitable choice of having to ride with me instead.

I did end up picking a fight that day. I got slammed into the ground, but I ripped some hair out, caused a black eye, and a good elbow to the face resulted in a broken nose on their part, too. I'd gotten lucky because the others were distracted, and Frankie had eventually come out from across the street to divert the absolute chaos of this teenage brawl. But they never messed with Eddie again. They never even came around the area again that I knew of, and Tommy sported his own black eye as a trophy for being my partner-in-bullshit. Parents and grandparents on both sides were livid when they heard, telling us to stop being bastards in another language we didn't understand at the time.

It's fitting that the two of them are with me now in this dusty ghost town Twelve-Mile-Corner. They hadn't questioned me; Tommy acquiesced with a nod, and we grabbed Eddie along the way, who also hadn't said much besides a curt not and, "Okay."

It's not much of a town anymore from the outside looking in. It sits up against the abandoned train station, fields of would-be cotton, and what were once secure areas for cattle to roam. When we leave my car, my eyes land on the abandoned homes. They're more like shacks, leaning dangerously with age, every surface covered in dust and the weeds that managed to thrive unattended here.

I imagine these homes were loved once, cherished by those who resided in them. But like most things in this shell of a town, they were discarded and left to their own devices when they could not take care of them anymore. I don't blame the previous occupants - it's not their fault. It's hard to crawl out of a hole this deep.

They say money cannot buy happiness, but poverty can absolutely rob you of it.

Given the opportunity, I would have up and left, too. One would argue I did. But I wasn't abandoned by houses or people lost to history books. I was abandoned by the people who were supposed to love me more than anything.

The soft and loose dirt crumbles underneath my feet and covers my Converse as we walk, turning them from black to a dull shade of brown. There are no words sufficient enough for the overwhelming need to get away from the area. The itch that crawls all over my skin as my legs move towards the scene of the crime.

Lola arrives soon after, and our body language shifts into apprehension.

"What is it you thought we would accomplish here, Raina?" Eddie asks, his green eyes darting to the same spot over and over. The spot.

I kick some rocks and continue my sauntering walk toward the area he fears. I shake with every step in its direction. Despite my natural inclination to shove emotions deep down as far as I can manage, fear is not one my body struggles with outwardly expressing.

I round the corner of a long-since abandoned shed decorated in overgrown vines and weeds as I whisper, "I'm not sure exactly. Something told me our answers would be here."

We all stand for long moments, frozen in time. I can practically feel the cold metal of the shovel in my hands as I stare down at the spot where Ephraim's old bones lay. Each of my friend's faces is curated into careful bravado and confidence, but their body language gives them away. The proof is in the way their feet shift back and forth, the way Lola's hands open and close, and how Tommy keeps running his hand through his tied-up hair. Eddie shoved his own hands in his pockets as though letting them loose might cause the world to end.

At the mere thought of Ephraim's bones, like some type of supernatural Bat Signal, an unusually cold wind sweeps through, vicious and furious. It sends my ball cap flying and dust floating terribly in the air, leaving sand-packed eyes and surface-level grime all over my face. My hair runs wild in the air with no cap to hold it down and feels dirty. The windows of the shed begin opening and closing violently, shattering whatever glass remains on the ground. Dust devils are not uncommon, but this one feels wicked. Malicious, somehow, in the way it causes goosebumps to snake up my arms and hot tears to form in my eyes at the irritation of the sand.

"Mother of fuck, tell your stepdad we get it!" Lola

yells over the wind, and in response, it all stops. The air goes completely still, and our line of sight settles on the note pinned into the earth by a single rusty nail. I make no move to touch it, and when Eddie moves to do it, I stop him with a hand to his arm, though I'm a little unsure why I bother. I feel nothing when I touch him.

"That wasn't there before the shit show it just put on, was it?" Lola asks, every word and syllable clipped and lined with worry. I shake my head along with the boys. Men, now. We had all looked at the spot several times since we'd pulled up. There was definitely no note.

"It's probably just more of the same," Tommy suggests but does not grab it himself.

"I think this is...maybe just a coincidence," I mutter in Eddie's ear. "Just leave it."

He looks me up and down and quietly murmurs, "I don't believe in coincidences."

Eddie rips his arm free from my hand and, with a shaking one of his own, bends down to grab it. With careful measure, he pulls the red and rusted nail from the ground, trying to minimize the damage to the old and fragile-looking paper. He stands to open the note, and I can hear its age; it cracks faintly and has that finger-against-paper sound when dealing with paper that's been wet and dried again. I expect it to tear when he does so, but it doesn't. My heart is beating hard and rapidly as I watch his eyes drag over the note's contents.

He coughs into his hand and looks up at me. "It's for you."

14. SUDOKU PUZZLES AND LIKABLE NOSES...

After all these years
Collecting tears
Did you know I held such power?
You went away
Left me astray
My dying and wilted flower
Your onyx curls
Braids fit for young girls
A beauty that one devours
My crafted notes
Around your throat
Choose me or your final hour

The words are written in Ephraim's very distinct and specific handwriting. It bounces somewhere between a very neat cursive and fancy freehand. Through his various stunts in and out of jail during my childhood, this handwriting would cover cheap college-ruled paper, signed affectionately and disgustingly as, 'Love, Dad.'

I'd never used that term in my entire life, and yet, he always referred to himself with it. Lenny used to prompt me to write back, and I would do it because my mother had asked me to, and I was eager to please her. Not out of any sense of love I felt for him. I made sure to address it to 'Ephraim.' I always wondered if my mother had changed the word Ephraim to Dad, furiously scratched it out and replaced it with what she wanted, because his response after would throw me through various emotional cartwheels, saying things like 'Your daddy misses you so much' and 'Daddy sure misses our time together.'

"I'm surprised he didn't sign it with, 'daddy'," I say masochistically, staring down at the pretty words in my hand.

For some morbid reason, this causes Lola to laugh uncontrollably at the audacity of my joke. The scene is a lot like me in my driveway before the exorcism; drunk and nonplussed by the recent events. Instead, it's just Lola laughing so hard tears begin to fall down her beautiful, contoured cheekbones in the middle of the desert next to the dead bones of my stepdad six feet below.

The rest of us sort of stare in frozen horror for half a beat until she snorts, and then...absolute chaotic laughter erupts. We all laugh and laugh together until we are doubled over, more tears and more snorting, making the laughs come harder and stronger at the sounds. It's the kind of laugh that happens when your faith in reality is gone, when you don't know what else to do in the most awkward and preposterous situation of your life.

Its laughter only trauma can produce.

"Is this real life?" Lola snorts. "Are we actually being haunted and hunted by...by your hair braiding daddy?" There's more uncontainable laughter as an answer to her questions, none of us quite having the words. It's hysterical from the outside looking in, but I can still feel the lingering dread, like a dead weight you can't let go of.

Catching my breath, I light a cigarette and the cringey poem as well. I let the paper flames fall to the ground, right on top of where Ephraim lays. I don't need to burn it, but something says not to give this note any substance. Maybe by burning, it can't hurt us after we decide its intent.

Tommy shifts to stand next to me in solidarity as it burns, his eyes hard and full of something that resembles rage. Blowing out a large plume of smoke from a cigarette I say, "What do the rest of you think about this place? I have a working theory, but it's...I don't know. It feels fragile. Not enough."

Lola walks over and smashes her foot into the ashes of the poem into the ground, twisting the front of her foot into it back and forth like she's trying to pack the dirt even further.

"Why do you think what Nana Isabel said had to be the facts? It's just an old wives tale meant to scare people into not losing faith and staying committed to Catholicism. You know, Catholic guilt and all that. Don't do this, and this won't happen to you. Do this, and you'll be spared. Blah, blah, blah." Lola looks up and sets her eyes on mine. "What if this town has nothing to do with it and everything to do with who Ephraim was as a person?"

I bite my lip in trepidation and tear my eyes away to stare down at my fingernails, picking at the cuticles. "We have been operating under the assumption that it was our actions that is causing him to hunt us all down. Plus, everything we discovered online about what's happened here. Good boy Eddie's theory back in the day about this land being tainted might have some weight. Since the field workers protests in the 70s there have been twelve suicides in this same place. All for relatively inconceivable reasons, the victims didn't even live here. It's like they marched all the way out here just to spill their blood on the ground. Maybe we buried him here and provided the perfect opportunity for something to latch onto Ephraim's soul. Gave it a lifeline? I don't know."

Lola throws an arm around me and turns me to face the boys. "Well, now, that puts all of what happened on us, don't you think? Besides, we aren't good Catholics, haven't been for some time, so I say let's ditch the blame. If I remember correctly, he deserved to be down there with the worms. He asked for that punishment the second he couldn't keep his greedy hands to his fucking self. We aren't being repaid for some imagined debt or sin. But we are being haunted, nevertheless. Can you recite that little poem again?"

I do. I recite it about four or five times as we all huddle.

"Braids fit for young girls. Explains why your hair keeps doing that weird braid thing every day," Tommy points out.

"That would be the only fairly obvious part of his stupid fucking riddle," Lola quips.

"One could argue that most of that riddle is obvious," Tommy bites back.

"Listen, literature and poetry weren't my best suit in college, alright? I'm not made for this shit."

"Or ever," Eddie laughs. "Numbers are your thing."

She shoves his shoulder. "Well, I don't see any Su-doku puzzles lying around, dicknose."

"You like my nose," he points out smoothly.

"The jury is still out." She smiles at the back-and-forth banter but quickly wipes it away.

"The series of events that took place a fortnight ago would beg to differ," Eddie responds with all the swagger of someone who learned how to have smooth and deliberate flirtation even with his nerdy word choice.

My mental image of 14-year-old Eddie shifts and is quickly replaced with the 28-year-old man in front of me, a far different one indeed. When Lola smiles and threads her fingers in his, her image is also changed.

I have been holding on to the idea of what my friends were and not at all who they really are now, ten years later. Like Tommy, these two grew up and lived entire lives without me. The mental time capsule I put them in did not keep them preserved and en-cased in time. Time propelled them forward just as it did me, and my heart aches at the realization of all the time lost. I shove the thought away, however, and beg myself not to fall into the perpetual hole of guilt and longing for what was lost.

Just as time moves forward without me, it doesn't wait for me to forgive myself either.

"I'm going to puke. Stop touching like that." My comment comes out quick and with a laugh, but with no malice behind it. I continue the analysis, "Most of the poem is just reference to his bullshit with the hair and his need to have me." When Lola and Eddie only stare, I say, "The braids? Like Tommy said. Every morn-ing I wake up with my hair braided like a little fairy in the night sat down and did it while I slept. I don't feel it. I wake up often and see nothing, but still. Hair braided."

Lola nods at Tommy, "What about you, lover boy? How are your tresses during the night?"

Tommy grunts in annoyance at the pet name but answers politely, "No braids. And I don't see it happening to her either."

"Ooooohhhh," Lola teases. "So, you are spending the night together."

"It's not like that," we say at the exact same time, not suspiciously at all.

Her narrowed eyes bounce back and forth between me and Tommy. "What is it like, then?"

"Cut it out, Lola. Are we sixteen, or are we adults now?" I ask in an attempt to shut down the teasing, though she continues for several more minutes. The conversation eventually dies down, and there isn't anything else to say.

We have no more answers than we did before, and the trip feels like a bust.

The four of us separate and go on our merry ways when we leave Twelve-Mile-Corner, deciding none of us know any additional significance behind the note or the reason for the taunting by my dead daddy. Again, there are several days of a lack of any supernatural activity. There are no more notes, there are no cheesy slamming windows or doors, and no possession. Even the dreams have seemed to cease as I sleep mostly peacefully, barring the fact that I ordinarily need heavy sedatives to ensure I sleep at all most nights.

Most nights.

Lately, it hasn't been most nights, it's been none of

the nights, because I've been sleeping soundly with-out them. It's unusual. So unusual that I've stopped taking my medication altogether.

I can hear Ingrid's voice ringing in my head like a hammer to hot coal, over and over like the forging of metal, "Do not stop taking your medication even if you feel as though you have gotten better. This is very im-portant, Ms. Medina. Sometimes we feel we have been cured, but this is not the case – the medicine is merely doing its job. I cannot stress this enough, Raina. Do not stop taking your medication."

Except I have.

I'm doing the complete opposite of her instruc-tions. I know this isn't good, I know it's a bad idea, but I can't help the intrusive thoughts raging on the inside telling me that this is the route to go. Those inner de-mons, the ones that won't stop screaming to be let out, are saying that the medicine is inhibiting some-thing. It's taking away a very important and vital part of me. Subduing a fabric of my Sight or my magic that is intrinsic to who I am, to what I can do. This instru-mental internal piece of me is inciting a war against the part of my brain that agrees with Ingrid. I mean, it's a nightmare inside my brain. But I am convinced that this is needed. This is necessary even if Ingrid dis-agrees. Even if my brain is wrong.

Sleeping without the medicine has given my brain the most clarity I've ever had since leaving this dustbowl town. I'd wager that some of those words Ephraim left on the note had more reference to my past and my leaving. He always wanted me to stay. The mere suggestion that I would leave and go away to college was a living fear for him. Leaving meant he couldn't control me and could not have ready access to me anymore.

For whatever reason, my mental health took a steep and steady decline the longer I was away. It was as though every year I spent away from his decaying body meant the decay of my own sanity. But since I have been home, even amidst the hauntings, the fog has cleared on the inside.

What was once dense, murky water that served to drown me and keep me buried in a place I could not crawl out of is now clear shallow water that is easy to wade through. I can see the bottom and stand at the same time. I can sit with it, relax in it, and see everything around me clearly because the water is not a nauseating muck of dirt.

My hands tremble as I grab my almost empty prescription and the brand-new one I just filled a week or so ago. I drag my feet to the bathroom, dreary and weak. The soft click of the bottle coming open is met with the loud clash of objects flying into the water. I pour every single pill in the first bottle down into the toilet bowl. I follow suit with the second bottle and empty its contents too.

Then, I flush them all down the drain like I'm sending my cares into the vast ocean with them.

Ingrid would say this is because all the therapy and all the pills are doing what they are supposed to do; I am stable. I say it is because I don't need them anymore. And I don't say this out of some sense of inherent know-how that my doctor does not possess. I don't say it as an immature girl child refusing to do what she is told.

I say it because I think those pills and Ephraim are related, and I'm going to figure out how.

15. 10 YEARS AGO

"Just lie and say you're spending the night at my house after the movie. It won't technically be a lie; we'll be there eventually."

Lola always said the words like it was a simple task, one that wouldn't end with Raina getting manhandled.

She was reckless in a way that Raina was not. Fights at bus stops, drugs when no one was looking, and vodka bottles in backpacks were among the many ways Raina raged against authority when no one was looking. Once, she smoked weed in one of the stalls at school because she wanted to see how fast she could get out of there before someone noticed the smell.

Raina escaped these stupid tirades by being smart about when to go for broke and when to cash in by learning the exact time to run for freedom. Otherwise, she needed to become a good liar. But being somewhere else when she was supposed to be in one place is often a one-way ticket to hot water with Ephraim and Lenny, her stepdad and mother.

Ephraim was too suspicious, sniffing out lies like it was his second job. He often double-checked, and when a wild hair crawled up Lenny's cheeks, she might do it too, making desert parties hard work.

Not impossible, though.

Lola on the other hand, was dangerous in her recklessness because she lied to the important people around her, but she didn't have the audacity to be good. Having a best friend as a bad liar with Raina's own unpredictable parents meant danger and a general lack of safety in her own home.

Try as she might, Lola had no regard for that because she didn't have to deal with it. She was not that considerate at times.

Although her parents don't deal in niceties often, they were not the cruel parents like Raina's could be. A grounding here, a phone being taken away there. It was a glaring contrast to the unrestrained cruelty that took place in Raina's house and something that did not phase Lola in the slightest. She would go back to doing whatever it was she wanted, regardless.

"Lenny will freak out if she checks and I'm not there. And you and I both know it's not her who's going to show up," Raina retorted.

Since Raina returned to Lenny from living with her grandparents after years of Lenny refusing to get clean and sober, life hadn't been ideal. Ephraim was especially unpleasant now that she'd gotten older.

Disgusting, as he put it.

And it was a special version of hell when she was caught lying. This was particularly true when dealing with Lola and her many grandiose plans for a dessert party.

Her parents wouldn't lie for Raina if Lenny or Ephraim came sniffing around.

"Come onnnnn," She whined. "It's one night. You haven't been out in forever. I'm sure they won't even bother to ask my parents anything!"

"I don't think something as innocent as the movies is something he'll consider, given it's a Friday night," Raina mumbled as she closed the locker door and leaned against it to look at Lola's puppy dog eyes. "It's a cardinal rule in Ephraim's house that I can't have fun on Fridays. Somehow it signifies I'm out doing things I'm not supposed to. If I ask tonight, he will only grow more suspicious, you know that."

Her eyebrows wiggled up and down as she said, "But we are doing things we're not supposed to. Look, just ask for the movies. We can go out instead, and then I'll have you back before they know you've left."

Lola smiled wide, batting her eyelashes. She leaned into Raina like she could convince anyone simply through her proximity. Raina giggled at the silliness of it.

Lola held books tight to her chest in a girl gets the boy from the rom-com type of way. Every time Raina watched one, she was reminded of Lola. Lola had an easy way of existing around others, making everyone feel important. There were many moments in their young lives where Raina was struck by Lola's ability to look at people like everything they had to say was interesting. It's what made her popular and ensured she got to the top of the pyramid on the cheerleading squad every year. People simply wanted to give her what she desired. Raina hoped she never lost this trait to time and resentment.

Raina was the opposite in most ways. She didn't want anything to do with entertaining people's fantasies that they were anything more than average.

"Fine," she relented. Lola tossed her arms around her as she squealed with excitement. Her long sleeves blocked the skin-to-skin contact, and Raina thanked her past self for wearing it.

The rush of people around them reminded her that she needed to head to the pick-up line before whichever parent showed up decided to leave her there for taking too long. She pushed against Lola's side, signaling to let Raina go without touching her.

Lola released her the second she heard Danny's boots come around the corner, her current boyfriend of the week. "Got to go, *La Reina*. Go draw me a pretty picture before we meet up tonight so I can put it on my fridge."

She cackled at her own joke and winked as she passed by. Raina yelled, "I'm not an artist for sale, Lola!"

As usual, she ignored Raina's objection and slammed into Danny at full speed. His simple, pea-for-brains smile blossomed across his face as he swung her up in his arms and spun her around. Raina never liked him, but Lola's overjoyed shout of excitement at his attention made her shove her dislike very far down.

A warm murmur sounded in Raina's ear as a large hand was placed on her lower back, "Who says?"

She smiled despite her growing resignation that she didn't like when people thought they were special. Tomás had and always would be the exception to every rule.

"I do," she murmured and turned her head to face him. He was very close, as he sometimes did when he snuck up behind her. "My creativity cannot thrive under these conditions. I can't simply be summoned."

"Mmm," he hums, eyes glancing down for only a second before they return to her eyes. "What if I asked? Can your creativity thrive under conditions that I set?"

Her heart fluttered at his words. It didn't seem possible that at seventeen and eighteen, a boy could be so smooth with his words, but all Tommy did in his free time was read and write. He'd been labeled The Jock, not The Writer. After all, he played every sport available at that high school, and the assumption was that he'd be able to go to college on a full ride with his baseball talent alone.

But the writing was where the magic thrived. It wasn't in the swing of the baseball bat or his arm when he launched the football across the field. It lived in his fingers when he wrote in his journal. A black leather-bound worn-down treasure from constant use that he carried with him everywhere. It was in his thoughts as he daydreamed about scenes he would bring to life in the middle of the night when he wrote alone in his bedroom.

She let a wry smile form on her face. "Maybe. I might be able to make it work. What about you? What kind of pressure do I need to put you under to force you to publish all those thoughts you hide away in that journal? All those books you read, you're just as good as they are, if not better."

He consumed books at an impossible rate, reading those pages like he needed oxygen to breathe. He only chuckled in response and shook his head. A careful arm was placed around her shoulders instead. He was always mindful of arm and hand placement, but she never minded his touch. His thoughts were never invasive, mean, or overwhelming. Tommy radiated a calm she couldn't replicate anywhere else.

"You're The Artist. I'm just a silly jock," he countered as he guided them toward the pickup line.

She took note of his small, slow steps. They had to

be careful about how close they were to each other once we came into view. If Ephraim was the one to pick her up, it wouldn't be good for anyone.

"That name is silly. I draw pictures I never let anyone see except the one they entered me into the contest with," she argued.

Tommy's face found hers, and he remarked, "A contest you won."

"Debatable."

"You got a trophy, Raina."

She shrugged. "You are far more artistic than me. Your stories...they're incredible, Tomás. Did you take a look at the writing competitions I printed for you? You could be published."

His smile that was once spread wide across his face, one that made his eyes crinkle in that way that made her feel warm and safe inside, turned sour at the mention of the article submissions. It was quick, barely noticeable, except that she'd known Tommy for as long as she could walk. He recovered even faster, like he couldn't stand the thought that his expressions might hurt her.

"No, *reina*. But I'll think about it." A light squeeze of her shoulder when his black eyes searched hers. They came to a halt, and she swore neither was breathing.

He'd never kissed her, but she'd wanted him to since the 6th grade, even though the idea terrified her. She'd only ever been kissed one way, and it wasn't something she would have wished upon anyone. But somehow, deep in her, she knew that a kiss from Tommy would feel different. It would be from the right person.

There was a small moment, so brief she couldn't

tell if she made it up, where he leaned in. It was fractional, not even a full movement in her direction. But, like his smile, the moment was over before it began, he began to walk again. He released her as the opening to the courtyard widened.

They neared the pick-up line as he asked, this time with a fuller smile like he was making up for whatever just happened, "I'll see you tonight?"

She shrugged again, "I hope so."

"Me too."

When she reached the pickup line, the engines' heat made it hotter and more miserable than it already was. Dread sank into her belly like a dead weight at the appearance of Ephraim's pick-up truck instead of her mother's.

She must be working late.

The nervous jitter that took over her limbs was no surprise at the realization that the evening would be spent with her stepdad.

It was an old 1960s Ford pick-up that sat waiting for her, equipped with a very difficult stick shift that made a terrible grinding noise no matter how efficient you were with your shifting. It didn't have air conditioning, so the leather burned against her thighs from the searing Arizona heat when she hopped in the seat.

"What took you so long to get out here?" Ephraim sneered, looking at her sideways from his seat.

His head was wrapped in a blue bandana, the white salt lines all over it from work, as did his t-shirt and jeans. He did freelance landscaping and brick and concrete work. It's easy to get work like this while getting paid under the table without drawing attention to you. Attention is the last thing you need with a violent warrant out for your arrest for the last eight years. She often wondered what name he gave them instead of Ephraim Gonzales when they hired him for their beautifully thought-out landscapes that wage war against the boring tans and browns of the desert. Although she despised admitting it, Ephraim was good at what he did.

"I had to grab my biology textbook from my locker first, sorry," she mumbled as demure as she could. She held it up as evidence.

"Sure."

He didn't say anything else the entire drive unless you count the viscous string of curse words and expletives that left his lips when the car in front of them didn't drive fast enough or went too slow for them to make the light.

When this happened, he jerked the truck around violently, hoping to pass them, and when he was able to, he screamed out of her side of the window, "GET THE FUCK OUT OF THE WAY!" and flipped them off while he was at it.

Her knuckles were white and tense as they squeezed the handle of the door with one hand and gripped the seat with the other.

He's in a bad mood already.

Eventually, he tore into the drive, mumbling violently to himself about cocksuckers and stupid idiots. She moved as inconspicuously as possible from the truck to the front door of the house. The key to safety, when people like him are in a mood, is to draw the least amount of attention to yourself as possible. Otherwise, they zero in on whatever annoys them most about you, and they go to town. Raina was almost certain there would be no bonfire in the far-out desert for her tonight. The idea of being shoved to the side for even bothering to ask wasn't at all appealing to her.

She tenderly opened the front door and slipped in while he wrapped around the side of the house, presumably to go through the gate to the back of the house. To the back shed, where all the bad happens. She avoided that shed and kept herself from ever lingering in the backyard if she could help it. If she got too close, he would have had her go inside, and that was nonnegotiable.

An hour went by. Two. Three. The house phone rang, and she could faintly hear Ephraim's gruff voice, put out and impatient. She winced at the harshness of his tone; he wasn't happy with whoever was on the other end.

"Raina!" He roared through the house, calling on her like a petulant servant. And like a servant with no other choice but to obey, she did. He held the cordless phone in one hand, using the palm of his other to cover the mouthpiece. "Your stupid little friend wants you to meet them at the movies and spend the night."

She blinked at him and then at the phone.

"Lola?" she asked.

He made a noise of impatience at her presumed dim wits. "Yeah, who else were you expecting? Her crackhead mom is on the phone asking if she can pick you up in 30 minutes."

"Okay..." The words fell like a warning. Wary because it felt like a trap. Like he was waiting for her to give the incorrect response so he could slap her around and call her the bitch.

"Okay? I don't have all day, Raina, do you want to go or not?" he snapped.

She understood clearly. He wanted her to say she didn't so he could get some kind of sick pleasure at telling Lola's mom to go play in traffic or something. And because he'd be alone with her.

"Ye-yes. Yes, I would like to," she forced herself to say in quick succession, her fingers forming tight braids as they looped together in front of her.

He narrowed his eyes and arched one brow high. He stared at her for one, two, three beats. Her heart played loud thumps in her ears with the quick beat of her pulse as she waited for a response.

He coughed into a calloused hand and responded back to Lola's mom on the other end, "Yeah, come get her whenever." He slammed the phone back on the stand and turned to face her. "No boys."

"No boys," she repeated back.

"And no sneaking out. You say you're going to the movies, so go to the movies."

"No sneaking out," she promised.

His beady green eyes, a bright contrast to the warm brown of his skin, rake her from head to toe. Goosebumps spread throughout her body, and dread crawled down her spine at the slow and calculated movement. She waited for the explosion, for the caveat to the deal he was offering her, the tit for tat to get what she wanted tonight. But what he really wanted was for her to be small again, innocent still, and she thinks she disgusted him a little more every day as she grew.

But he didn't offer her anything else. There was no deal. He simply stalked away toward the shed outback without another word. When she heard the rapid knocking on the front door, she knew it was Lola's mom. She twitched with need, and her dodgy eyes bounced around the house behind Raina, possibly inspecting for Ephraim. Raina didn't blame her, so she quickly snagged her backpack and cell phone. She didn't yell for Ephraim and tell him she was leaving. She couldn't escape the fear that he might have changed his mind from then to now.

When she hopped into the Serrano's old car, Lola waited for her excitedly in the back. She bounced slightly in her seat like she won the biggest con of all time.

"How did you swing this?" Raina whispered just under the music playing on the radio as she slammed the door shut.

A mischievous smile was Lola's answer, and her head jerked in her mom's direction once the tires began to roll.

"Old B owes me for lying to my dad last week for her. If anyone comes sniffing around our house asking questions, Mama's got it covered." She winked, and Raina laughed. She didn't have complete faith in Lola's plan, but it was too late anyway.

Fuck it.

After thirty minutes of driving here to get Eddie and there to be dropped off at Tommy's, all four of them were packed into Tommy's small junker of a car. It was a salvage title that his dad won at an auction once, with the very back of the car smushed in from an accident and only held together by a bungee cord tied from the trunk down to the exhaust pipe. In truth, it ran great, but it was painful to look at for anyone who values the appearance of their car over its durability.

She didn't pick the front seat when she got in. She purposefully sat in the back, to the right of Tommy in the driver's seat, so it was harder for him to look back at her. She liked it too much, and if the other two were to see it, she'd never hear the end of it. The four of them have managed to maintain a relationship free of romance and the complications of that throughout their life. It didn't seem right to begin now, even though it felt like every day, she and Tommy were getting closer and closer to something resembling a romantic relationship. She didn't need Lola and Eddie to know that, though.

Three minutes into the drive, though, she saw his eyes flash to hers in the rear-view mirror. Her own bounced around the car – Eddie sat quietly next to her, bantering back and forth with Lola, who was sitting up front. She wasn't paying any attention to either of them. She wasn't focusing on anything except teasing Eddie.

So, she focused her own attention back on Tommy when he stopped at a stop light. They hold for eight long, excruciating seconds. The good kind of goosebumps spread all over her body. The kind that makes you want to reach out and touch someone because you want them close that badly. Her heart slowed to a steady calm because Tommy's attention didn't make her nervous or confused about its intention like so many others. Like Ephraim's. There was a sense of safety in the blackness of his eyes she never found in anyone else's. The light turns green, and he tore his gaze away to focus on the road, ripping away her ring of safety.

Before long, they turned onto a dirt road out behind Twelve-Mile-Corner, the connection between all these one-horse towns. The old town lacked a living community presence and was just old tumbleweeds, but it made for a good party.

"Twelve-Mile-Corner?" Raina asked as she sat up

and leaned across the seat to look at Lola.

"Yep! Told you we were getting into trouble." Lola blew her a kiss.

Eddie grunted behind her. "What's your deal, Eddito?"

"I hate coming out here. You know what's out here?"

"Dead people," Tommy answered. Her gaze flicked to Tommy just long enough to see him smirk.

"Yes. Dead people, Tommy. There was a literal massacre out here. Not to mention all the fucking suicides. It's a beacon for evil, I swear."

Lola scoffed and teased him sweetly, "That was a rumor, honey."

He smiled back at her with all the sarcasm he could muster and shot back, "Don't try to placate me. They call it a ghost town for a reason, and we're just out here, getting drunk like it's no big deal with a bunch of dumb rednecks, but we are partying on graves. That can't be–"

"Tell you what, Coward, you stay in the car and weep. The rest of us will be throwing back beers as quickly as possible so we can rinse off this long-ass week we've had."

Raina sat back in her seat after Lola's comments, intent on not getting in between them and their bickering.

Eddie had no such qualms and continued, "Go to hell, Lola."

"Only if you go first."

Raina held her tongue, and so did Tommy. It was best not to throw flame to the fire between those two.

A large fire waged at the center of a crowd, and

dozens of other teenagers from the school mingled all over. Rain took note of the keg on the other side of the fire and made a beeline for it. Never a big drinker, she used to avoid the kegs, but she felt unsettled about Ephraim's acceptance of her night out. Maybe a beer or two would settle her down.

"Whoa ho! *The Four* have decided to bless us with their presence. What an honor." Matthew, Tommy's baseball teammate, bowed in an exaggerated show of fealty to the four of them as she returned from filling a plastic cup of the foamy mess they called beer. Lola and Eddie deemed it the appropriate time to ditch Raina and Tommy with this cocky bastard and strolled off to another area of the party. Maybe they'd find Lola's boyfriend, and Eddie would be left alone again.

"Cut the shit, Matty, where's the beer?" Tommy asked and slapped his baseball teammate on the shoulder. Raina pointed out the large keg.

"Oh, come on, Tommy, I'm just demonstrating loyalty, you know. Can't be out here offending La Reina and being the reason for the start of a fight." He winked at her, and Raina let her face form a scowl as her response. She hated the stupid title, and she wished that everyone would let it go. To make matters worse, Matthew made no attempt to say la reina correctly, purposely drawing out the r to sound as cowboy as possible.

She grabbed Tommy by the coat to direct him to the keg and left Matthew with a few parting words, "Eat shit, Matthew."

She poured another cup as she scanned the party. She was one part paranoid that Ephraim would show up, another part paranoid she would lose Lola to the crowd. She'd spend at least an hour trying to find the evasive fox if she wasn't careful.

"She's over there with Eddie. You can relax." Tommy nodded in a far-off direction but kept his view firmly pinned on her. She dragged her eyes away from her blonde friend's up-do hair to meet Tommy's.

"You know I have to keep track of her. She's like a puppy without a leash, just wandering wherever the wind takes her. And I don't see Danny anywhere here to keep an eye on her."

"Eddie is with her, Raina."

"Eddie can barely take care of himself, and they're already sniping at each other."

"I think you should give him more credit."

She handed him the cup of beer and gave him a look that said I'm done with this conversation.

Fine red imprints of where her mouth greedily gulped down as many ounces as she could rest on the lip of the cup she handed him. Before she could make a move to switch and hand him the untouched cup, Tommy offered her a smirk, took the cup in his hand, and gulped down its contents.

She found that she liked his lack of regard when it came to their germ's co-mingling, and a small, shy smile broke her scowl as she watched him finish it off.

This unspoken exchange continued as she fished out the cigarette pack from her back pocket. Liliana always made sure to buy them for her whenever she made it back into town from college and sneaked them into Raina's backpack whenever Lenny and Ephraim weren't looking. They were like precious gold to Raina because Lenny has remained a heavy smoker all her life, and she knew Raina had them. When her own ran low, Lenny was the first to grab them from Raina's bag. Raina chose not to say anything because it would only result in Lenny revealing the information to Ephraim. Ephraim, who would punish his sweet daughter for defiling her young self with cigarettes.

They make you look old, he would say as Lenny stares, the suspicion and paranoia in her eyes as thick as her eyeliner. Raina was never sure if it was jealousy or if maybe it was something she'd imagined. But she knew Lenny wouldn't draw more attention to her unless she had to, unless it was unavoidable. For all her faults and turning a blind eye, she didn't go out of her way to put Raina in any additional danger. Her biggest fault was ignoring the danger when Raina was in it.

Tommy's eyes never left hers. He took one minute step forward and put his fingers out, waiting for her to slide his own cigarette into his expectant grip. He was not demanding; he was not cold in his request. It is a type of movement that exudes quiet knowing and infinite patience she couldn't explain in words.

Safety.

She slid the cigarette in and lit her own immediately after. He didn't wait before leaning in and lighting his from hers without her own being removed from her mouth. He'd done this move before when they were alone, where no one in the world could be a witness.

She felt eyes on them. The shifting glances from the girls who would prefer they be standing in her place and the laughing eyes of the boys who don't consider her enough to be the one with Tommy's eyes on them.

Tommy's long lashes shifted downward, the coal of his eyes landing softly on her lips. Was that longing she saw?

The sounds of the party are muted to her now. It's

as if headphones rested over her ears, causing every-thing to seem muffled and fuzzy. Only the steady beat of her heart can be heard, beating perfectly in sync with the rise and fall of Tommy's chest.

The synchronous melody of their bodies was inter-rupted by a hard clap on her shoulder.

"You guys planning on sneaking off into one of these abandoned houses, or are you going to stop eye fucking each other?" Lola teased. Their dead-locked eye contact broke with a cough from him as she turned to face Lola.

"You sure know how to be a nuisance to society, don't you?" Raina asked, knowing Lola waited to re-mark with something wittier.

"I've made it my life's goal," she quipped with a warm smile to accompany it.

"How advantageous of you," Tommy hit back with a laugh. She lightly smacked his arm playfully in retal-iation.

The rest of the evening was spent more or less in peace. Drunken fools didn't antagonize her into fight-ing, and Tommy sat with her on and off, taking turns to play various beer games as she watched. Lola and Eddie lingered nearby; Lola talked the ear off anyone who dared to come too close, and Eddie stood by closely for general moral support. It was a regular, un-suspecting evening spent in the desert.

Then, so light she could barely feel it, there lin-gered the sensation of being watched. She resisted the urge to shiver and hug herself close. The Sight that Lenny blessed her with was not good for much. She couldn't sense anything beyond normal human func-tions when someone touched her.

Like the flip of a switch, her *brujera* gift, her witchlike sixth sense, felt like it flared out into the night. Like it reached into the dark for something out there, warning her.

She stood slowly and made her way to the opposite side of the fire, carefully avoiding drunk teenagers left and right. The buzz of the alcohol remained, but she couldn't feel it much over the fear pumping the blood in her veins. The rest of The Four didn't even notice as she moved trance-like to the edge of the party, where the light from the fire no longer touched.

Despite the residual heat of the fire, her fingertips were like ice, and she shivered as if covered in snow and not the grimy sweat of spending too long in the warm Arizona air and too much alcohol. Something shifted in the night about 100 yards from her, so small she almost didn't notice, but the slight tug that something inhuman waited out there was insistent. Something oddly familiar, too, though she couldn't place a finger on what exactly was so familiar.

Another shift in the blackness. Bushes made a cracking noise. The outline of a body.

She took an unsteady step backward, a knee-jerk reaction to brace her hands in front of her face before getting slapped. And she did get slapped. Because Ephraim was the outline, he was the cracking in the bush.

When he reached her, he slapped her so hard her head whipped to the side, and her body followed suit like an unloved toy. The force sent her flinging into the dirt on her hands and knees.

"What the fuck are you doing out here?"

16. HYPOMANIA AND THE BUSINESS OF FALLING APART

"How have you been since the accident?" Ingrid's legs are crossed, and she's tapping her foot in a relentless and constant quick repetition, like a snare drum.

Tap, tap, tap, tap, tap, tap.

I smile warmly, as genuinely as I can muster, and I wonder how much of it she can see through. I haven't slept in two days, but my feet aren't tapping like a crack addict hoping to score. Maybe I make her nervous.

"I'm fine. Headaches for a bit, but those seem to have gone away. Stitches are in there good until it's time to get them taken out."

She nods and gives a quiet hum. "Wonderful. I'm glad to see you're getting back to normal. Have you gone back to work? How's writing going? I feel like it's been so long since I've seen you."

I snort. "You saw me last week at the hospital."

Her eyes flutter just a fraction, and she bobbles the pen between her fingers. She is nervous.

"Yes." She huffs a laugh and coughs to cover it up. "But I meant formally, for a session. You know, regular appointments to keep you stable."

There's that word again. Stable. If I'm honest, I don't think I am. The last two days have been a roller-coaster of hypomania, overspending, obsessive reading about demons, and seeing things in corners that aren't there. The near-constant urge to jump Tommy like I need oxygen. I am falling apart, but I think I can hide it by focusing on her.

"What's going on, Doc?" I ask sweetly and gesture to her foot still bouncing like a basketball up and down. "You seem a bit nervous. Do I make you nervous?"

The question comes out too sweet. Ingrid's polite smile drops.

"No!" she insists with another nervous laugh and wide eyes. She places her hand on her chest for emphasis and continues, "I had too much coffee. I am simply bouncing off the walls a bit today. You are totally fine."

I nod and hum, like her. I am masking, reflecting a mirror back at her. Can she tell that, too? "Not enough sleep got you drinking coffee by the gallon?"

Another forced smile. There's a lot of smiling going on here, and it is increasingly more uncomfortable. "Yeah, actually. I had some rough dreams and couldn't go back to bed. How did you sleep?"

I sidestepped the question by telling her, "They say reading something really boring can help put you back to sleep. Healthy sleeping practices are important, Doc."

"Yes, healthy sleep habits are key to ensuring sleep. You are quite practiced in this, actually. Your records from when you were active duty indicate you did a sleep clinic during Intensive Out-Patient services. Do you feel they help? They must. You haven't reported any sleep disruptions in some time."

She is rambling. I cock my head as I stare at her. My narrowed eyes catch hers.

What is her deal?

"Ingrid...what is happening right now?" Maybe being direct will tell her to avoid more questions for me and continue to put pressure on her. Again, with the nervous laugh.

Fuck it all, get it out already.

"I just had some rough dreams," she says, quieter with every word.

I've run out of patience, and what I do next is wrong. So, so wrong.

Quickly, I lean forward, and I snatch her hand closest to me. The pen clangs to the ground, and a small fearful sound escapes her lips. She tries to tug away, and I give my head a small shake. I hold her eyes with a ferocity I can see, making her question whether or not to pull out the knife in her drawer and stab me with it. She acquiesces for five seconds too long, and I get all the information from her that I am too impatient to wait for.

She rips her hand away. "Please. Do not touch me, or I will have to ask you to leave."

"Don't believe everything he says," I warn her, and she stops all movement in her chair.

"Who says?"

"Whoever spoke to you in your dream. He's not real."

"I don't know what you're talking about."

I chuckle a soft, dark laugh and lean back on the orange sofa. It's such a God-awful fucking color, but it's comfortable. I swing my legs over and prop them up. One leg over the other like a therapy patient out of a movie, the kind that smokes cigarettes while they tell their therapist all the ways the world has failed them.

"That thing in your dream...he's lying. He'll say anything to turn those around me against me. He did it when he was alive. He'll do it in the afterlife too."

"When did you take your medicine last?" She questions, scribbling in her notebook after she grabs it from the ground.

"Oh, that doesn't matter, and you know it. If he's invading your dreams, like he is mine, it means it is almost time."

Time to make contact again. Time to stop acting like he isn't real and face him head-on. If he's invading Ingrid's dreams, he must be desperate for my attention. It also means he's much stronger than I gave him credit for.

Where the fuck has he been?

"Raina, are you hearing voices?"

"Lord in heaven, please forgive me for my impatience," I round on her again. "Ingrid. Stop fucking with me and being willfully obtuse. It's offensive, okay? I saw your dream. It's all you can think about. It came rushing out of you right away like you could barely contain your composure."

Her eyes dart around the room. She is looking everywhere but at me when she takes a long, deep breath. As she closes her eyes she says, "I think, maybe, you have not been taking your medication, Raina."

"Give me a break, Doc, and pretend for like two seconds of your miserable life that science hasn't got it all figured out, mmkay? Just think about entertaining the idea that I can read your emotions like an open book and that when I touched you, I saw all the flashes of the dream that you can't forget. Flashes of me, digging into the hard dirt of the desert, burning bodies. Just...pretend. For a fucking second. Please."

Her breathing is rather rapid as she looks at me up and down. She seems uncertain of my words but is considering them. I only spoke the truth; I spoke what she thrust into my mind.

"Fine. We can pretend. For a single moment. Because I don't think you saw anything, and I think you need to be taking your medication."

"Spare me the lecture."

"It's my job."

"So, act like it isn't. Tell me the rest of your dream. I got the general impression. I'll bet you cold hard cash from your pitiful VA paycheck it scared the shit out of you."

Ingrid tips her head and flashes me a stern look of disagreement. "My pay is none of your concern."

"Neither are your dreams if we're being technical and professional, but here we are. And we are less than professional now."

She stares a moment before dragging her eyes to the notepad. She focuses intently on it, her eyes gliding over the shape of the words she's been scribbling off and on, probably all day. She focuses on every curve, every straight line, every imperfect drag of the pen. She isn't reading them; she's only using the shapes of the letters as a grounding method.

I wait her out.

"It started with a song. So sweet and impossible to resist. I was dreaming in a dream when the music started, and it woke me up. I was in my childhood bed, I, I mean, my body was a child, but I was-,"

"Very much an adult on the inside, yeah?"

She doesn't break contact with the notepad but nods and continues, "I wake up, and my hair…it's so long, much longer than it is now, and it's braided in this long-complicated braid down my back, and I know I didn't braid it before I went to bed but there it is. Just so perfectly put together. And the music, it's like a trance. It calls to me, and somehow, I'm outside, on all fours before pointy boots and a man with a large black hat. I can't even see his face; all I see are slight circles with a glow. Like a demon."

She shudders. An actual full-body shiver like in the movies and sets down her pen and pad to rub her palms on her pants.

"What does he say?"

Her gaze lands on mine. "Nothing. Nothing out loud. He forces me to start picking up dirt and shoving it in my mouth. Only if I agree to…to…,"

I arch an eyebrow. "To what?"

"To bring you to him. If I bring you to him, he will let me stop. And this is a dream so of course, I do. I agree because what difference does it make? It's not real. Right? It can't be real."

She thinks I don't notice, but as she's been talking, she's inching her rolling chair over to the cabinet. I know the knife is there. I've seen her take it out to get my file before. She tries to hide it for emergencies.

With every word that leaves her lips, she moves towards it.

"Yeah, Doc, it's not real. Do you wake up in your bed?"

She stops moving for a moment. Her eyes are a little wider than they were, if that's possible. "Outside. I wake up outside."

I'm nodding my head like she does, the same movement that drips with condescension as someone tells you what you already know and you dislike it. "What else does he show you, Ingrid?"

She doesn't move. She isn't even breathing. And then finally, albeit a little shaky, she says, "I know what you did. He showed me. I watched you stab him, watched as the four of you moved in a symphony toward that fire. I saw you all drag him through the mud, covered in dirt and blood. And then I watched as–"

I snap, sitting up so suddenly it causes her to panic. She isn't bothering to inch anymore—she's full-on bolting for that stupid fucking knife. The second her body twists in the chair, my fingers are wrapped in her curly hair, and I'm using it like a dog leash. I rip her backward and she goes flying, kind of like a ragdoll.

The crashing sound as she lands back first onto her bookshelf is loud. So loud that I cringe a little because I know the knock on the door is coming soon. She's alone with an unhinged veteran. They will panic too. I lunge for the cabinet and find that there is not only a knife there but a small .22 pistol. I laugh when my fingers glide over the smooth and cold metal. I slide it in my hand as I shove the knife in my back pocket. Turning to face her, I find her huddled up against the bookcase like it's going to wrap its arms around her.

"I'm pretty sure...when he said bring her to me, he meant alive. I thought we didn't believe in ghosts, Doc?"

"I don't. But you do."

"Tsk, tsk. Don't lie to me now, Ingrid. You believed that dream. It did something to you, I can tell. It's altered your fucking brain chemistry trying to reconcile with a reasonable scientific solution."

"I was sleepwalking. This can happen under stress," she spits.

"Okay." I hold up the gun and drop the magazine. When I pull the slide to the rear, no bullets pop out. "Smart girl. I don't think you'd know how to use it anyway. But back to the point. You and I both know you're scared to death, and you have been utterly and completely convinced that what Ephraim said was true. My guess? He offered you something you couldn't refuse. Like sleep without regular appearances because I'd also wager he's shown up more than once or twice. Which is why this stupid pistol is hiding alongside your pathetic pocketknife. Where were you going to take me, Ingrid?" I cock my head at her. I haven't taken any steps closer to her, and I'm holding the gun down now. I am less threatening, but still in control. If I get any closer, she may decide to get brave.

When she doesn't answer, I continue, "Where were we headed next, Doc? Huh? What was the plan, hold me at gunpoint until sundown and then take me home? Take me to the desert where I supposedly killed him?"

She begins to try to stand, her joints popping, and her face reveals a small grimace at the sound. As she makes to brace herself for the ordeal of standing, I snag the magazine from the ground and hold it up. "Unless you want me to hold this gun fully loaded to your fucking temple, sit...down."

She stops mid-movement and considers her options. Her big eyes flicker back and forth between the gun and my face. "I can't tell whether you're on your meds or not."

"Woman, that is the least of your problems right now, are you serious?"

"I'm not the one with a bipolar disorder."

"But you are the one having dreams about demon men with pointy hats who make you eat dirt. And you tried to hold your client hostage, so…who's really the crazy one here?"

Defeated, she slides her body down the bookcase, landing on the books that fell from our initial tumble. "Well, Ms. Medina, where do we go from here? Looks like we've switched roles, and you're the one holding me hostage."

I roll my eyes. "Give me a break. Don't try to flip this on me like I'm the crazy one. I mean, I am. I am crazy. But you started this. I'm only defending myself."

There's a knock on the door. Muffled words come through with a haughty male voice. "Everything alright in there, Doctor Leslie?"

Neither of us move. I stare at the door handle and then back at her. When I jerk my head in the door's direction and arch an eyebrow at her, she relents and answers back.

"We're good, Adam! I just tripped and knocked the chair into the bookcase. No big deal."

A pause. A cough. "Are you sure?"

"Sure as a flat tire." Her voice comes out flat, just like her words. But there is something behind them. I can feel it. Her eyelashes drop downward. I hear Mr. Adam walk away, quickly and in a hurry.

With an aggressive rush to get closer to her, I whisper harshly, "What the hell did you just do?" When she doesn't answer, I slam the magazine into the butt of the pistol, and all color drains from her face. "Call it off."

"Wh-what? Call what off?"

I wave the gun with one hand and point at the

phone on the desk with the other. In my own sing-song mocking tone, I say, "Not the time to play dumb. Call the front desk. Call. It. Off."

I can tell she's considering it by the way she anxiously looks between the phone and the gun. "They won't believe me."

"Better try. I'm not going to jail because of your mistake. If you don't call it off, I'm going to have to explain everything, and I will look like the dangerous one of the two, given my diagnosis. I'm not very good at this game, but I don't think I'm going to win it."

Then, there it is. A slight shift in mood, like I can see her emotions, her worries concerning the gun and my instability, her concern regarding her dreams and whether or not the thing plans to kill her if she can't deliver.

No, not see. Feel. I can feel those various flashes of contempt the same as if I were to be touching her. But we are several feet away and I have one hand on a gun and the other on a door handle. I know this. I know what I can do now, and I curse myself a little for not thinking of it from the beginning.

I push.

Not physically, not in any way outwardly that matters. It's a lot like casting your thoughts out into the nether. I simply push, maybe more like reach, for that feeling of contempt, that fear, that anxiety...and I twirl my proverbial finger around it. And I snap each of them. One by one. Gradually and surely.

With each mental break, her face slackens, and her body relaxes against the bookcase, sinking into it. Her eyes maintain some alertness; she is confused, and she doesn't understand what is happening. To be fair, I don't really either. I don't think I can force her to do anything like I did on that one fateful night. But I can make her more amenable, like Enzo.

And I do, except this time, I give a little of myself. More so the idea of myself. The idea that I am (she is) calm, collected, trusting, and no longer concerned with calling the cops on me. I do my best not to react to any unnecessary emotion—I don't want to have to start all over again.

"Now..." I gesture to the phone. "Get up. No sudden movements, no more attempts to rush me. Call the desk and call off the report. I'm not going to jail for you. Everything is fine, we are cool, you are not scared, I didn't do anything wrong. It was a misunderstand-ing."

To my surprise, because I'm still unconvinced of my own abilities, she does what I say. She lifts herself from the cold tile of her office with the grace of a con-tent cat and reaches for the old rotor-style telephone on her desk.

"Hi, yes, Stacy, please call off the flat tire...Hhmm? Oh yes, oh my god, please. I completely forgot. I used to use that saying all the time growing up, and it didn't it even occur to me...Yes. Mhhmm. Please, thank you so much...are they? Oh...well, okay. No, no. It's fine, it's my fault, I'll explain. It's no problem. Well, the veteran has somewhere to be, she has other appointments, but it's absolutely no issue. I will deal with them...uh huh, thanks. Bye." She hangs it up and looks at me. She is still a bit cautious but is not strung like a bowstring anymore, and she is definitely not tapping her stupid foot at me. "The cops are still coming, but I'll deal with them. How did you do that? What did you do?"

I drop the magazine again, convinced she isn't go-ing to try to snatch me up anymore, amenable as she is, and let it fall into my other hand. "I don't know what I did, but you understand that I did it right?" She nods. "Tell them whatever you need to tell them. I have shit to do, and the last thing I need is a government tail."

"I will, but he won't stop, you know."

"Now you believe me...after all that?"

She twists her hands together, the movement small and slow. "I don't understand. I don't understand anything. But I do know it won't stop until it has whatever it wants, and I believe that's you. He's forced me to believe it's you." I don't say anything right away. I walk over and shove the gun and the pocketknife back in the drawer, though I do wipe my prints off each item, including the drawer, when I'm done. I don't trust her not to say anything once I'm gone from here. When I approach the door, she speaks again, "Please...please."

"Please, what?" I snap.

"Please...solve this. Solve whatever it is that causes me these dreams. I don't think I can take it anymore. I-I...I don't think I'll survive."

Her admission comes with a quivering lip and frightened eyes. I don't feel I have the bandwidth to calm her and make her feel any more comfortable, so I don't. When I reach for the handle once more, I say, "Tell Ephraim...tell Ephraim that he can crawl back into whatever hole he came out of. And if he doesn't, I'll put him back there myself. Good luck, Ingrid."

17. AN AVERSION TO TECHNOLOGY . . .

Fifteen minutes into the drive, my phone is ringing incessantly.

That didn't take long.

"What's wrong, Liliana?"

"Where the hell are you, Raina? I just got off the phone with your therapist. She says you're off your meds. Are you okay? Where are you?"

She's rapid-firing questions because she's worried, I can tell. This is what she does. Because she's older than me, and our parents were so fucked, she has mothered me most of our lives. The age gap helped inflate this. A whopping seven years older, she was off seeing the world of Arizona, and I was still here.

"What did the good doctor tell you?" I ask, busting a U-turn in my car at the same time.

"She said you guys had a fight and something about a knife? She thinks you're manic. Is that true?" I increase the gas once I turn, the engine revving loudly as I do. "Are you driving? Raina, where are you?" Her voice has turned insistent.

"Liliana, there are things I cannot tell you. But what I will tell you is that Doctor Ingrid is the one who has lost her fucking marbles. She was the one with the gun. She was the one trying to attack me. I defended myself. Period."

A long pause. She does not believe me. "You sound very worried. Are you sure you're taking your meds?"

I pound the steering wheel. "I am not the crazy one, Lili, FUCK!"

"Okay, okay. Fine. It's okay, we're okay."

"No, we are not. I'm coming to you."

Lilianna is outside watering plants when I pull up. I don't think I've ever noticed that she has a host of flowers and various plants decorating the front of her house that she clearly spends time and energy taking care of. This fills me with some momentary guilt; I'm not a good sister, and I think I am selfish most of the time. She doesn't rush to me when she sees me, but I can see that she wants to. That ball is in my court. Or maybe she's just afraid.

"I'm not going to hurt you."

She blinks at me, offended. "I know that, why would you say that?"

"Because you are standing there like you're afraid I'm going to pull a gun on you."

She huffs, "I'm only confused, Raina. What happened?"

"A misunderstanding. I need to run a few errands. Can I borrow your car?" I say it as gently as possible.

She points to the Bronco. "What's wrong with yours?" When I don't answer and stare blankly at her she asks, "What happens if they come around asking for you?"

I snort and say sarcastically, "A little stunned at the

casual mention of the possibility of cops looking for me, but I'll overlook it. I'd say...definitely don't tell them I have your car." She takes a beat or two to assess me, looking me up from head to toe. "What did she really tell you?" I ask.

"Exactly what I told you, Raina."

"Be fucking for real, Lili. I am not a child anymore."

"Then stop acting like one and behave!" She yells, resentment, and the weight of being an older sibling radiating from her.

Always the one to mother the two of us, always the one to pick up the pieces, always the one to love at all costs. It's etched into every line aging her beautiful brown face and the grey hair peppering her chestnut hair. The look on her face weighs heavy with the years of being responsible. Years of desperately trying to hold the threads of our family together and failing.

Her hard stare says she is sick of my shit, along with everyone else's.

"I am behaving. Ingrid is the one who–"

She cuts me off as she turns away and heads for the door, reaching just inside to the right. "Just take the car, Raina."

"What about the Bronco?" I call after her, waving the keys about as if dangling candy in front of a child. She turns at my words and stalks back to me, snatching the keys from my hand.

"I'll park it in the garage. I don't know anything, and your car isn't here. I haven't seen you since you stopped by today, and I didn't see you out the door to know if you left with or without your car to go get food with a friend, who I don't know. And I haven't talked to you since."

I hold her gaze, jingling the keys to her car that she has now shoved into my hand. Sister to sister, our eyes locked on each other exude the unspoken promise lingering between us.

I will do whatever it is you ask, I will not ask questions, and I will tell any lie necessary.

For one small moment, we are kids again and I'm begging her to hide me, to say I'm not home, to cover me with clothes in her closet that she never uses since she's in college so he doesn't see me. To let me sleep in her bed instead of my own dangerous one when she visits. I begged her to take me with her, and she couldn't.

I can't save us both. Not yet. But I'll come back for you.

That's what she told me. She never got the chance because I killed him before she could.

"I believe you, you know. If you say you're fine, I believe you. I just...Raina, I worry."

"It's not your job to worry, Lili."

"There isn't anyone left to. So, yes. It is."

She's right. Everyone worth caring about in this dysfunctional, classically awful, stereotypical family is gone. We are what's left. We are the remaining crumbs we so desperately want to hold on to and not leave to rot. She thinks she needs to keep everyone's crumbs together, not just hers and mine. But the weight of the family isn't on her as much as she may feel it is. Maybe it makes me selfish, but I know that if it were up to me, I'd drop every single crumb, and I'd be perfectly fine. No more crumbs, and I wouldn't think twice about it.

I know the weight of being the oldest sister is crippling to her sometimes, so I do the thing I don't enjoy doing but know she needs. I hug her. It is long, and I am rushed with her emotions, her wariness, her unease about what I've told her. But I also get flashes of her complete and utter faith in me. Her love that never, not for one second, wavers.

"I love you forever," I say as I release her.

"Love you forever."

I drive around for a few hours. I do some grocery shopping. I smoke some cigarettes and drink some coffee. I'm simply waiting to see when or if anyone begins to tail me. Maybe my lack of medication is making me paranoid, but every dark SUV that I see spending too much time behind me, I imagine as law enforcement.

A supernatural alarm went off when I dumped my phone because Eddie waits outside my house again with Tommy when I pull up. If Ephraim wanted to play games, it was going to take all four of us to send him back to where he belonged. I guess it's fitting that they show up everywhere I go.

A tight face with what looks like anger decorates Tommy's features. His tall frame stands straight when I pull in, and his long arms fold across his chest. Eddie is talking to him, but his eyes are following me in the car.

Slamming the car door shut, I nod at him and ask, "What's your problem?"

He gives me a hard look, one that says you should know, but instead says, "What happened to your phone?"

I chuckle, "Slow down there, Prince Charming. Did I not call you back soon enough? Did the absence of my dry texting vex you so thoroughly that you feel you must call me out on my actions?"

He pinches his nose in annoyance and tilts his head to the sky, "Cut the shit, Raina. I was worried. Are we allowed to be worried?"

I narrow my eyes at him as I pass him, clapping a hand on his shoulder quickly. "*Claro*," Sure. "You can be worried. I'll give you even more to be worried about too, when I tell you what happened with the good doctor, Ingrid." His eyebrows scrunch together like he's already forgotten who Ingrid is. "My therapist?"

"*Claro*," he shoots back.

My eyes land on a neighbor across the street as I turn away from him. They're watering their lawn, standing stock still with the hose in their hand, water running in a torrential flood down his front yard as he stares at me.

He's a large man, probably in his fifties, and since I've moved here, he hasn't really made any attempt at contact. He leaves me alone, which in my opinion, makes him a good neighbor. None of the neighbors are all that close from side to side, but my road isn't wide. So, when he waters his lawn, with his plumber's crack on display and his redneck t-shirt with cut-off sleeves that reveal his terrible farmer's tan and pin-up girl tattoo, I see it all. I am more intimately familiar with the sight than I'd like to be.

Like breaking a fever dream, he comes to his senses and rushes to turn the hose off after flooding his lawn. He wipes his hands on his camo cargo shorts and begins to cross over.

I don't know why, but I brace for impact like he's about to scold me for playing my music too loud or having the audacity to live in a house so nice on my own.

"Hiya there, young lady," he says with a smile as he crosses the road. His eyes wander throughout the yard and the drive, landing on each of us. "I see you've moved in nicely and all. I just figured I never came by and introduced myself. Thought now might be as good a time as ever."

I give him a small nod, a little too stunned to do much else. "Yeah. I, uh, well, I've been here only a month, so no worries. My name's Raina," I offer.

"Hi, yeah, the name's Dick. But I swear I'm not one." He laughs boisterously, all through his body and deep in his belly. He is trying to be nice and amenable, but I am uncomfortable. "I see you have some friends over." He looks around where Eddie and Tommy stand, who say nothing and only stare at him. He also looks throughout the yard like my lawn is littered with guests. "Just wanted to come over and let ya know if you needed anythin', don't hesitate to ask. I don't sleep well, so if there's ever an emergency. Let's say some guests don't want to leave? I'm your guy. I don't mind running anyone off for a young lady who lives alone."

It clicks. He's worried about Eddie and Tommy. "Uh...well, thanks Dick. I appreciate the sentiment. I can handle it, I'm totally safe here." I don't address Tommy or Eddie, as I'd like to just keep them out of the conversation altogether.

"Oh, I know. I saw you're a veteran. Your license plate and all. You gotta be a tough cookie. But I saw you out here talking, just thought I'd come on by and all." He throws another suspicious look in the boy's direction after he sees me looking at them.

"I'm good, Dick. Really. It was nice meeting you, though." I give what I hope is a warm smile, though he continues to throw furtive and suspicious looks about the yard.

I begin the slow walk to the front door in hopes he'll get the hint, and I notice out of my peripheral vision he hesitates before he decides to head back to his own home. There's a stutter of a step where it looks like he might change his mind, and then he shuffles across anyway, kicking dusty Arizona dirt flying into the air as he does.

Eddie laughs as he joins me on the walk, leaving Tommy to stare at the old gentlemen from the driveway. "I think maybe the old man thinks us brown people are going to hurt you," Eddie mumbles jokingly.

"I'm brown, too, Eddie," I counter, unlocking the door and turning to gesture to Tommy.

Eddie shrugs. "I don't think it matters if you're brown when you're beautiful. We are brown men; therefore, we are inherently dangerous."

I notice the seriousness of his tone, and I shrug back. "Maybe. He's never spoken to me before."

Tommy joins us and nods at me coolly while welcoming himself through the front door like he takes up residence here.

"Seriously, what's up with the phone?" Tommy blurts out as he fumbles in the kitchen with cups and water, Eddie and me joining him with confused gazes.

"Yes, please, make yourself at home," I say, gesturing to the stream of hospitality he's arranging on my island counter, full of teacups to fill with the water he's started boiling. He levels me with a stare, and it causes the words to fall out like a waterfall before I can stop them. "I had a run-in with Ephraim."

"What?" he snaps. "What happened?"

"Did you see him? What did he look like?" Eddie asks with genuine curiosity.

The interest in his words is laced with excitement, and I find it strange, but I shove the thought away, putting a hand up to stop the barrage of questions. "Chill out, I didn't actually see him. He just...has more reach than I initially thought."

I tell them the whole story about Ingrid and my day because who else can I tell it to? The four of us are the only living people on this planet to be in the same exact position. And the only people I can stuff my secrets with and not go to jail.

Tommy and Eddie both watch me with a hint of marvel, clutching cups of tea. I find it a bit disquieting. "Why are you guys looking at me like I just told you the secrets to the universe? And where the hell is Lola?" I nod at Eddie. "Figured you two would be conjoined at the hip now that you're all out and proud."

Tommy coughs, breaking his own reverie, as they both ignore the Lola comment. "It's nothing. Well. It might be nothing. It might be something." His eyes lock with Eddie, and right as Eddie begins to speak, the door rams open.

"Good afternoon, losers. Thanks for the lack of an invite, but a princess needs no invitation. She is welcome everywhere she goes!" Lola announces loudly and proudly as she swaggers through the door and swings it shut behind her.

"Princess of what?" I ask with a smile, shoving her lightly on the shoulder when she reaches the kitchen island. I am aware of how naturally we have all fallen into our old roles and friendship dynamics. It isn't lost on me that it feels as if not much time has passed at all.

"Well, if you're *la reina*, someone has to be *la princesa*. We cannot all possibly be the queen. Besides, who wants that responsibility? No, I'd rather be the trouble making daughter of a mature and wise queen. The daughter you always imagined."

"Ah," I say, an eye roll to appease her as she throws an arm over my shoulders, hugging me close even without the actual skin-to-skin contact. Lola has always been the one to need the extra reassurance, an outward representation of love for all to see. This is confirmed as she shifts from me to Eddie, the two of them linking hands together. In a sweet display of affection, he kisses her knuckles lightly.

It is this alteration in the relationship, the hard turn to the left that I wasn't expecting, that brings some immeasurable joy inside me. Not that my life is somehow more or less complete because they finally decided to stop hiding behind teasing and false bullying. But they are now exactly as I imagined an unspoiled version of them would be. A version where all the bad things never happened, and they are living out their lives together in peace.

In my dreams, these two drop the pretense and complete each other in the best ways. Outgoing where one is reserved, affection coming naturally to them, and no more societal boundaries that dictate they shouldn't fit. Because they do, and I'm a little ashamed I hadn't seen it until now. Maybe in my dreams, Tommy and I fit like that, too, and that's why he's back here with something like frustration at my life choices on his face.

As Eddie begins to pull out articles and papers printed about who knows what, I lean over to Tommy to whisper, "What is your major malfunction?"

Eddie and Lola start a low conversation, pouring over stories and lore like Tommy and I don't exist, wrapped in a world made just for them.

Tommy leans in close, and I can almost feel his eyes on my face as he says, "Your aversion to technology is frustrating."

"Do you crave my attention so badly, Tomás? Longing for the affection of The Queen?" I tease, staring down at my nails on the counter.

"Starving for it."

My eyes flick to his. We are in a bubble, me and him, much like Lola and Eddie. I can feel his breath on my skin, so still out of fear that one may startle the other. Like a deer enraptured with the light.

His dark beard covers his face in an impeccable array of trimmed hair from ear to ear, sitting at a flawless length to match his dark curls. Like he was fashioned from my own personal dreamland, he pins his locks back in a small tie behind his head, and his eyes smolder with the emotions I ached for as a teen.

Desire swirls in the blackness of his eyes like an endless loop. It's the way his gaze dips slightly to my mouth, and then back again. The way his eyelids relax just so, and his pupils dilate. It's out of place here. This moment feels far more intimate even than the kiss we shared not long ago.

Another shuffle of papers sounds quietly off to the side and the haze has cleared, the two of us breaking eye contact almost immediately.

Tommy places a hand lightly on the crook of my elbow, his large hand warm against the skin there and says, "Next time I try to call, you better have a phone. I am uncomfortable with the idea of you being in danger and unreachable."

My smile is small and gentle. "Were you worried?"

He dips his head in a slight nod that says *Of course I was*. And I know it to be true because I can see it when his skin touches mine. Letting out a cough to mask the hitch in my breath, I nod at Eddie and ask, "What's all this?"

Eddie smiles, giddy like the nerd he is, as if he's been waiting all day to show off his big project. "I believe I have found what has decided to wreak havoc on our lives."

"Are we sure it's lives?" I ask. "I seem to be the only one enjoying this particular haunting event recently. You guys are fine and dandy while my therapist is out for blood."

Lola scoffs at me, an aggravated face to match. "Shut up. We've been harassed, too. Notes are still being left in mailboxes, random shit covered in blood, the works. Want to know what my last note said?" Lola gestures to the side like she's displaying a bulletin board. "It said I remember what you did to me. Written in bright red letters across my mirror. In case you're wondering, no, I haven't gotten it out, so it's still there. But you? You are his favorite. He was your stepdad, after all," Lola quips, and her eyes catch on the stain blessing my wall behind me where Salem once hung.

We never quite got rid of her pain splattered on the wall like paint.

Eddie shifts from one foot to the other, apprehension residing there as he monitors our interactions. "Stepdad or not, I don't think we are dealing with Ephraim anymore."

"Okay…," I say, my own line of sight bouncing between the papers littered across my kitchen island and the three of them. "Who is it then?"

"I believe we might be dealing with something called El Sombrerón."

I start to laugh at the translation in my head. "The Big Hat? That's the big bad?"

"Don't laugh, Raina," Eddie warns, all joking gone from his voice. "This is serious."

"No shit. I just find it hard to believe this monstrosity goes by such a childish name."

"You could call him The Goblin if it makes you feel any better, although the name has quite negative connotations among some cultures," Tommy says, grabbing an article and placing it in front of me.

This article is from Mexico, telling tales of a man they call The Goblin with a silver guitar and a large hat, thundering through villages to bring death and destruction should they not listen to him. Portraits and paintings done with various artist's interpretations of him. With such stunning similarities, I scold myself for never bothering to look any of this up for myself. Yet, there is still apprehension inside me. It feels too convenient.

As I'm skimming, Lola moves more papers to my viewpoint.

Those same stories from Mexico line up with the horrific tales of El Sombrerón from Guatemala, Nicaragua, and even as far south as Columbia and Ecuador. Always a figurehead for the bogeymen you warn your daughters about and relentless in his search for the most beautiful woman to grace the earth.

Always willing to do whatever it takes to have her.

Tommy steps closer and looks over my shoulder as he braces two strong arms on either side of me against the counter. He stares down at the papers scattered about and points at a specific set of facts in a story out of Guatemala. "It always starts with the braids."

18. THE VILLAIN ORIGIN STORY

"El Sombrerón fell in love with a young girl from a local village. He coveted her so much that he was willing to offer and do anything to have her. So, he began by playing his steel guitar." Eddie is reading out loud from an article, but it's clear he's been pouring over these legends for some time. He wanted answers, and he thinks he's found them.

"A steel guitar is unique because it should sound rotten. The metal against metal, it's an anomaly that the sound would appeal to anyone. But young María was so drawn to it she could not resist it any more than a hummingbird could a flower. He would play his guitar at all hours of the night, too, luring her from sleep. By morning, her hair had been magically crafted into a perfect braid though she had gone to sleep with her long, dark locks untouched.

"To him, her hair was a magic he so desired. Along with her beauty, obviously. We'll call it a fetish, but in the end, he pleaded that he loved and admired her hair along with her large and wide brown eyes. When her parents rushed to stop her from going to him, he became more creative. He began to offer mules and horses as offerings, dragging them along in a line carrying large loads of coal, all with their hair braided, tails and manes and all. He tied them up by her house and began to play the guitar again, hopeful that her parents would not reject the offering this time."

Silence for a few beats and Lola nudges him. "Well, go on, Eddito, finish the creepy ass story already."

He smiles at her affectionately and continues, "El Sombrerón has a magic, or a curse I guess, no one really understands. It's not clear where it comes from or how it operates. But soon, her food began to be laced with soil, making her sick and unable to sleep. The contamination grew. While more and more soil began to fill her plate with every meal, her parents panicked, and rightfully so. They were tired of the braids, the pack animals, and the dirt. In an act of vengeance and passion, they cut off the hair he desired so much, and they rushed her to a monastery. They begged a priest to bless her and perform an exorcism on her and their home, hoping to ward off the goblin man from bothering their daughter. Legend says, of course, that because she leaned heavily on her Catholic values and because she stayed in line with more conservative and culturally appropriate norms by trying to resist him, that this is what saved her. And, of course, why young girls should do the same."

"Of course," I bite out.

"In some versions of the tale, the girl dies from her sadness, and el Sombrerón is left to wale and cry and mourn his love. Every year on the anniversary of his great love's life, his steel guitar plays and his creepy ass lyrics are heard in mourning."

"But there's no telling how to actually get rid of him," Tommy offers, moving around me. I feel the loss of his body heat against my back, and I miss it right away. He picks up a specific article from Mexico and hands it to me. "The story changes from region to region. In some places, he isn't obsessed with young, beautiful girls at all and instead thrives on fear and stampedes through towns on a black stallion like a headless horseman. Obviously, with an intact head and a large black hat with black boots to match."

"You've got me with the braiding, this I recognize. But I don't know about anything else." I wait a moment, move papers around idly and find they are all staring at me expectantly. "I've had...dreams about the guitar. And something about dirt. But it's quite a bit more.... vulgar than dirt in my food." I confess, chewing on a fingernail as I do it.

Tommy pulls my hand away from my mouth mindlessly like he's helped me break this habit for a thousand lifetimes.

"Explain," he says.

"In my dreams, when Ephraim was still alive, I dreamed of a pointy hat man who would wait outside in my yard and play the guitar until I would wake and join him. Of course, my hair is braided, and I'm in something of a trance. Barefooted, I make my way outside, and there he is waiting for me. I kneel before him, and while some of the finer details are muddy, eventually, I'm shoving dirt in my mouth unless I agree to something. I have no idea what it is."

"That...is fucking terrifying, Raina, what the fuck," Lola blurts out and then immediately claps a hand over her mouth. "That was rude, wasn't it?"

I nod and pat her on the arm without touching her skin. "A little, but it's fine."

"Then what?" Tommy prompts.

An exhausted sigh escapes my lips. "Then I wake up. Hair braided and covered in dirt, but I don't think I've ever eaten any. I think it was just to scare me."

"So…," Lola pauses, looking at each of us individually. "How do we get rid of Señor Somby, or whatever his name is?"

The room erupts with laughter at the ridiculous name she has assigned our devil, our very own poltergeist. Amid the fit, still wiping tears away, I say, "I think I have an idea. If he's attached himself to Ephraim, anyways. It might be a start."

"Be our guest." Tommy chuckles.

"What if we burn him?"

"This isn't exactly what I thought you had in mind," Lola hisses as we stare down at the inconspicuous bit of dirt out at Twelve-Mile-Corner.

"Relax. He already made a show while we were out here before. He doesn't need to show off anymore. We know he's here; I think that's all he wants. Attention," I relent, trying to coax her into submission.

"I don't know," Eddie says. "This ghost seems exceptionally vengeful, Raina. I'm not convinced digging him up is the way to appease him."

"Well, it can't make it any worse," I argue.

"It could absolutely make it worse. We could all die," Lola complains, fumbling with the words.

"Bones can't kill you, Lola. Bullets can kill you, blades, car crashes. Bones do nothing. Is Eddie the coward, or are you taking up that role now?" I poke.

Tommy interjects, "*Cálmate*." Shifting his body to face me, shielding me from the judgmental eyes of our friends, he asks, "What was the exact plan, Raina?"

I look around him at our friends and then into the vast darkness. It's pitch black out here now that the sun has gone down. You can faintly see the lights from our town nearby, lighting up distant communities born of the people who didn't want to be here back in the day and their descendants. It must have been hit with a rain cloud recently, traveling solo throughout the desert like it does here, because the ground is softer than usual. I feel the way it sponges under my shoes.

I can smell the musty and familiar scent of desert rain, too. It gives me a weird sense of comfort knowing how easy this is going to be.

"No one has lived here in decades. It's why we kept him in this spot after it happened. Only idiots up to no good ever made their way out here back then. The local teens don't come out here anymore. We weren't worried about his body suddenly being found, but I still put stock in what Nana Isabel said growing up. There is something about the dirt here."

"The dirt did not make him into a demon," Lola objects.

"It didn't. But maybe the trauma of the past lives lived and dying here is what drew it in. The horrors seen by desperate people being taken advantage of by those in power...maybe the fear and the bloodshed is what drew El Sombrerón to this place to begin with, along with their blood. I don't know. But when we shoved his barbecued carcass down in that dirt, we offered Ephraim up to Señor Somby on a platter. I think we need to move him. Not only that, but we need to move him and then burn that motherfucker to ash so he can't find something else to get attached to. I don't know that it's going to mean anything, but I'm not holding on to those bones. I just want them gone. Two birds, one stone. He's out of the ground. Out of everything."

There is a moment of silence that gives way to un-convinced looks and worried eyes.

"Let's start digging," Tommy says without much conviction. It feels like he is entertaining me and my wild ideas, but I take it and roll with it anyway. When I pop the back to my sister's car, Tommy and Eddie both grab a shovel with weak enthusiasm and begin to dig. It is Lola who stands ramrod still, arms crossed in denial.

"No way, nope." She shakes her head like a dis-tressed child.

"Stop acting like a juvenile and grab the shovel so we can take turns breaking our backs," I tell her.

"First of all, you all are the ones acting like juvenile delinquents by digging graves. I am the only adult here refusing to do so."

Eddie grunts as he digs in and tosses a shovel full of dirt off to the side. He's already sweating, and he wipes the sweat away with a rough hand from his soft face. With the dirt on him, I notice now how young he still looks in comparison to the rest of us. It is out of place to see someone so beautiful covered in the dirt that hides our secrets.

Between Tommy and Eddie, he was always the pretty boy of the two. A more traditionally beautiful boy if I ever saw one, though I would never say it out loud because that's weird. If he hadn't been so painful-ly shy and afraid, I wonder how different his life might have been in high school just because of his looks.

Eddie pauses to look at Lola and says, "I would say we are all delinquents, given the fact that we put him in this grave to begin with. If I remember correctly, we all dug this grave that night."

I wait for the snap back, for her to point out (again) that I'm the reason they all had to do this to begin with. But there is a silent exchange between the two of them. His eyes plead just a little, and hers soften. Barely.

I inch the shovel handle towards her, and without any more fuss, she snatches it from my hand roughly in a flurry of almost blonde hair and light brown eyes.

The only noise to come from the four of us is the soft grunts of each of us taking turns digging into the desert ground. There are random coyote howls off in the distance, and once in a while I get the sensation that we are being watched.

Though I'm fairly positive no one alive is watching.

In my final move toward the earth, my shovel strikes true, and there is a soft thud when the metal hits thick bone. A crack follows it. I am stunned into silence when I see Ephraim's skull peeking through the dirt.

I drop the shovel and back away.

Why am I suddenly panicking? How do I back out of this? Can I back out?

When Lola catches my reaction, she's on me like stink on shit, hugging me and turning me away. I am forced to feel her emotions instead of the panicking of mine. I feel sure, angry, confused, and determined. But I do not feel panic, unease, and distress, and that is enough.

"Deep breaths, *pendeja*. We are here for you. You need to keep it together long enough to finish this."

I snort and reaffirm, "I'm not sure why sending him back to hell is reliant on me. We all did this."

Lola glances around like she can see something in

the dark, shrugs, and says, "That isn't exactly how I remember it, but the fact remains that it's you he wants. We are simply tools."

Once she lets me go, I am left with my own gloriously pathetic feelings and emotions, but they are significantly less so. The overwhelming need to throw up or run away is gone, and I am grateful for her sudden intervention on my behalf.

In contrast to the two of us, Eddie and Tommy react with a paralyzing fear and are both staring at the skull. By the looks of them, you would think they are both considered the cowards of this friend group. I always knew the titles were bullshit, but I'm starting to think that Tommy is a lot more like Eddie than I ever gave him credit for before.

Maybe we are all cowards masquerading as the hero.

It's Lola who acts first. She tears her eyes away from the wide and vast desert behind us and bends down to put herself on all fours. Without much concession or pageantry, she begins to dig with her hands. It is slow and careful, and deliberate. It's not the digging of a manic mess, thrashing about, breaking nails, and drawing the bright red of blood under them. It is more like the careful baking of a cake. Each individual layer is handled with attention and precision. She spreads her hands around the bones and the surrounding dirt in smooth and slow succession, the way you would when you ice the cake.

She's determined and sure of her goal. She wants those bones out.

This prompts the rest of us to follow suit. Shoulder to shoulder, we dig into our respective sections of the cool soil. Soft grunts and soft tears from the four of us as we uncover our darkest secret hidden in an abandoned lot of a one-horse and two pairs of spurs town.

A town we never fit into; a town meant for those who don't look like us to thrive in. A town made off the backs of those who do look like us.

What a conundrum to have four products of Chicano culture sprinting for the doors of the "right way", working their tail ends off to ensure we made it out of there, only to end up doing exactly as society said we would.

Murderers.

Liars.

Thieves.

Poor, tragic fools.

Before long, the achingly slow process of digging up each bone is complete. All 206 of them lay exposed and awful before us, or I hope so. We're not exactly counting them.

"Holy fuck," Eddie whispers.

"No shit," is the only response from an awe-struck Tommy.

I lost all my hesitation and nerves when we were digging, and the sweat rolling down my face in the cool desert air fuels me. I am using the hard beat of my heart to propel me into action rather than freezing me with fear.

I don't say another word as I rise from the ground, moist dirt crumbling off my pants and arms as I stumble my way to the surrounding bush. I am exhausted from not sleeping well, and it's late. My feet are heavy weights being dragged through sand, but I trudge on anyways, grabbing any twigs and branches from old mesquite trees that I can find. Any and everything that looks as though it will light up like a Christmas tree, and I dump them on Ephraim's lifeless carcass. Or what is left of it.

Noiselessly, my friends follow suit. Every movement is ritualistic in its purpose like we know exactly what needs to be done without any more discussion. No more need to bicker and decide what is or isn't right. This must mean something; this has to cause something to change.

How do you grapple with something you can't see? How do you destroy that which haunts your dreams? You burn everything you can to the fucking ground, so you never have to see or deal with it again. You give its unrelenting spirit nothing to cling to in this life. No singular piece of bone or otherwise to attach itself to.

Like he can read my thoughts, it is Tommy who walks over with the lighter fluid and begins to spray.

"Burn it all," he says as he unhurriedly and then, with furious strokes, sprays all over the twigs, branches, and logs. Eddie offers the matches, the local convenience store logo imprinted on the top and fading. I take it in my shaking hand rub a finger over the logo and think of everything I never wanted to once more.

"Are we worried about drawing attention?" Lola nods at the matches. "The fire is going to get high."

I shake my head in silent objection. "All they will find is ash. So, what does it matter? No one is looking for him. No one has looked for him for ten years. He has no family left except for me. As far as the police are concerned, we're just four friends visiting over a bonfire."

"Someone owns this land," Lola counters, forever the skeptic.

"Whoever owns this land doesn't care what happens here, or they would have made literally a single change to it over the last 20 years. It looks the exact same as it did when we were eight," Tommy adds. He puts an arm around my shoulder and looks down at me. "Someone once told me you learn the most from your difficult experiences in life. This might be one of those times."

His words thrust memories from our past to the forefront. I said those words to him when we were ten, huddled under a blanket with a flashlight at three in the morning. I'd run away after Ephraim had visited my room. I panicked, and I ran to Tommy. I still don't know what possessed me to say those pitiably hopeful words.

"What a moronic system. Why should we have to suffer to learn the right answer?" I mutter. But a smile sits lightly on my lips. A reluctant one, but there, none-theless.

A few passing glances between us all as I rip a match out of the pack and brace for impact. My eyes land on a hopeful Eddie, ready to be done once and for all. The annoyed face of the skeptic in Lola. And lastly, the calm and supportive presence next to me, in Tommy.

I hold his gaze as I strike the match and toss it into the giant pile. Our eyes tear away from one another the millisecond the flames ignite.

With the flames before us, I am seventeen and re-turned to that disastrous night.

19. THE INCIDENT

Searing pain graced her head as she rolled belly-first onto the ground. Ephraim hit her so hard she couldn't hear right out of one ear. It was...muffled, somehow. All the yelling and thundering of orders to leave and do so were now almost inaudible and unclear.

What she didn't miss was the loud crack of a gun.

The panic it caused sent everyone into a frenzy of screams, running, and cars and trucks peeling out in a large cloud of dust. A part of her hoped one of them would call the cops. Maybe that would save her. She was sure Ephraim had a warrant; their family had been lying about who he was for years. Maybe the cops would show up and find a convicted felon with a gun, and that would be her ticket to safety.

As she lifted her face from the huddled fetal position she was in, her cheek buried in dirt, she knew that it was too risky for the cops to come around. If they didn't take him, she would pay the price for it later. And the cost was steep.

"Get up," he snapped as bent towards her, grabbing her roughly by the arm to force her to stand upright.

She wanted to comply. She wanted to give him

what he wanted. That was where safety lay.

But the embarrassment of him showing up, knocking her down like a forgotten play thing, and forcing everyone home through outlandish violence gave her a false sense of security. It dissipated already into nothing.

"I can do it," she bit back, ripping her arm free from his grip. This caused her to stumble, which in turn forced her back to the ground. A cruel, knowing smile graced his lips as he watched her fumble and crawl away from him. She held a hand in front of her in his direction to stop him. "Don't. I got it."

Embarrassed and hurt, she stood. She was shaking violently when her vision caught movement to the side of them. Lola, Eddie, and Tommy did not leave. They stood just to the side of the large, roaring bonfire.

Ephraim glanced at them and then back to her. "You were supposed to be at her house. Imagine my utter and predictable shock when you were not where you said you would be."

She didn't say anything. What could she say? If she admitted the truth, he would hurt her. If she lied, he would hurt her. There was no winning side to the coin, so she simply accepted fate as it stood in front of her.

She managed a cringe when he took one small step toward her. He smiled again, like he was taking pleasure in the small torture of her anticipating his moves. He stopped a few feet away when he caught the three of her friends making their way toward them. Though they weren't far to begin with, the fire separated all of them still and was easily hiding their conversation.

Her friends now had an unfortunate front-row seat to her own personal torture show.

"Say something," he barked, his vibrant green eyes blazing with malice and malcontent.

She didn't do as he said though. She stood very still. She thought the inability to move and the overwhelming urge to throw up meant she was having a panic attack. Freezing instead of running, freezing instead of fighting because was too afraid for anything else.

She felt all the blood rush from every corner of her body toward her head. Her heart then decided to take up residence in her throat, like a bullfrog croaking, instead of its comfortable position in her chest where it belonged. It threatened to force every ounce of liquid she had to make a reappearance if she moved even a centimeter in Ephraim's direction.

She was far beyond the parameters of fear. This was something else entirely.

Lola wasn't afraid though, and neither was Tommy. Eddie, for all his terror of the world, moved with the other two toward her and Ephraim, but she could see his eyes on her instead of Ephraim. Much like Raina, he was afraid if he made and kept eye contact, he would cower and wither away.

Or maybe he just wasn't the coward everyone said he was.

Tommy coughed like he was interrupting an important conversation. "I'm sorry, sir if we got her in trouble. We should have asked first."

Ephraim rolled his head around, like a full body eye roll toward Tommy. The movement unsettled her. There was something wicked about it. Inhuman. "There is nothing you could say, boy, that would convince me to not kick her ass like she deserves. Thanks for the concern, but you three better leave," He stopped abruptly and leaned around Tommy to catch sight of Eddie, who stopped his slow movement in her direction like an animal being spotted. "Eddito! What the hell is a good boy like you doing out here?"

She suppressed a laugh. It was comical that Ephraim did not believe Eddie would be there because it proved how little Ephraim knew of her and her friends. Where she went, the other three followed.

"Uhm…," Eddie hesitated. "Lo siento, Tío, I'm always with Raina." He apologized because he thought this would appease Ephraim, maybe that it would settle him down. But she knew better.

Ephraim moved his large boots side to side with an impatient fervor she knew too well and bounced a finger between them. "So, you're telling me Raina was the influence behind putting you all in danger of becoming the degenerates society says you are?" The question stumbled out with disdain like he couldn't believe they would stoop so low.

"I don't think people see us that way, Ephraim," Tommy offered.

She took one aching and sluggish step to the rear while he was distracted.

An incredulous laugh escaped his lips. "We wear brown skin, drive brown people cars, live where brown people live. You think they…those white kids you guys hang out with…you think they are ever going to see you as equals? You think that because your skin is lighter than mine, that it makes a difference when they find out where you're from? If the cops were to show up tonight, it would be you four on a pike, the first thrown under the bus, offered up for sacrifice. You are all tokens they keep around that make them feel better about their position in society."

He shook his head and began to walk toward Tommy with intimidating feline movement. Ephraim was a lot like a cat in the way he moved when he was angry, always surveying its prey, waiting for the right opportunity to strike. But Tommy's dad was a lot like Ephraim, too, and this was nothing new to him.

Unlike her paralyzing fear, Tommy's fear provoked action. Movement.

He shifted his own feet and his stance to rotate as Ephraim did. The two of them did a sort of dance, feeling each other out. An original gangster surveying the younger, broader version of who Ephraim once was. For a split second, Ephraim looked unsure of whether or not he felt he could take Tommy if he had to. He never had an issue attacking and abusing her, but she was much smaller and weaker. She had less of a voice when she entered that house.

But out here, Ephraim was no one. He wasn't the ruler of anything, and she thought maybe he knew that. She hoped he did maybe then he'd make a mistake.

"You know nothing about the world, boy. None of you do. You are all just stupid children playing stupid games. Raina," He stopped his movement and nodded at her. "Let's go.

The circling game stopped. Tommy and Ephraim were no more than an arm's length from each other, while Eddie and Lola both managed to get beside her on either side as all the talking continued.

She was being shielded from all sides. In a rare burst of confidence, she shook her head no.

Ephraim let loose a heavy, over-extended sigh like he couldn't be bothered with this any longer. Then, swift and all at once, he swung around Tommy and took several long strides in her direction. Tommy was expecting this because when she braced for impact, Tommy had already barreled through and shoved Ephraim out of the way.

The old man stumbled to the left, barely missing the fire. A string of curses plummeted from his lips, and when he righted himself, he seemed to suppress a laugh and grit his teeth instead. He didn't waste any time either as he headed straight for Tommy, who didn't have the reflexes she hoped.

Ephraim swung. Hard. And followed it up with a shove so solid it sent Tommy flying backward and rolling. Lola and Eddie both made an attempt to shield her, but quick like a snake, Ephraim reached in between and quickly grabbed her by a wrist before she could get away. There was an immediate feeling of foolery on her part. She should have moved away. She should have been further into the bush by now.

She should have fucking run.

But no, she'd been too scared. And now she was being jerked forward so hard an intense pain lanced up her arm through her shoulder. There was an audible pop followed quickly by an agonized scream from Raina.

Her shoulder popped out of place, and it was dangling like a useless rope. Her vision swam with pain. The edges of it pulsed at the corners of her eyes with blackness.

It didn't faze Ephraim at all, who continued to drag her toward the shadow of the desert. Tears rolled down her face, more cries escaped her pained mouth, and she didn't fight his pulling because it was already too painful for the dangling arm.

There was a flurry of movement. More pain danced

throughout her arm as she was shoved aside, and her arm moved about where she could not control it. Amid the confusion, she tripped and landed face-first in the dirt without any substantial way to protect it.

"Get off me, you little bitch."

Ephraim had Lola by the hair and tossed her to the side. Nothing more than a plaything to him. The flurry of movement from a moment before was the cheerleader in action, unwilling to let Raina go so easily.

A mouth full of dirt, she rolled over just in time to see him stomping towards her, one hand extended out to snatch her up. Fear sat in her gut like a lead weight. Fear of the pain she was sure to endure, terrified of the future of her night. The future of all the rest of her nights if he was able to take her home after such an egregious crime of lying to him.

Would this be the night he went too far and killed her? Would he bury her in the backyard, or would he cremate her so that no one ever found her body? What about the act itself? Was there a chance he could hit her so hard and kill her instantly? Or would she be made to suffer an excruciatingly slow death?

She braced for impact and prayed to whatever God would listen that Ephraim would stop, if only for a moment. She hoped to the saints that he would pause long enough to simply consider not hurting her and wished that he would leave her be instead.

The second his hand touched her, however, he stopped his movement. All his violent thoughts rushed into her like a movie reel she didn't ask for. She shoved and raged against that mental image, doing everything she could think of to shut him out. But she was floundering on the inside, wading her way through the thick mud of these thoughts, unable to escape them. She threw out wishes into the void.

Let me go, just be happy, forget you're mad at me, love me like you're supposed to.

Through the squirming, she noticed his eyes.

They clouded, like he was content to stay in his half-bent position reaching for her. Completely and utterly happy. But he snapped out of it too quickly, the fog released its hold.

There is a tiny whisper in her head, "Just get her home. Just get her home. Just get her home."

Ephraim's sneering voice was what sounded. He was a contemptuous, hateful man, and by the look in his angry eyes, he did want her home. He likely wanted her where he could keep her caged, imprisoned for his own sake. But like before, she was fighting against that and wishing for anything else to happen instead. Heaving the thoughts inside her mental cage, slamming them against the bars of her head, she caught sight of her friends. Each one with various stages of panic on their faces. Unsure what to do next, she threw one more wish out into that endless void of prayers that were never answered.

Kill him. Make him go away. Make this life easier for me. I never want to see his face again. Please make it happen. Please. Please. Please. I'm begging.

The wishes came out like a strangled beg in her mind.

I am so scared, and I have nothing else left I can do.

She hoped through every hope that this gift God must have mistakenly given her extended far beyond just reading or feeling the vibes and thoughts of others. She thrust them out, flaring it like a signal to the three of them. Imploring them to hear her. To do as she asked.

In Ephraim's fog, she had the foresight to slip her pocketknife from her waistband. Hot from her own body heat, she flicked it open. He moved on top of her, ready to take her down or drag her away. She shoved the knife. Frenzied and manic, she shoved and shoved and shoved, blood coming out in thick rivulets from his stomach onto her trembling hand.

The knife was so sharp. A knife he made that way, spending hours sharpening the knives in the house. This was one he'd given to her as a birthday present once.

To help with the yard work, he'd said.

He meant to help him in the shed. Where it all happened. She never got the chance because she stabbed him instead of flaying open an animal.

There was a resounding thump sound as soon as she moved to stand, a grunt from Ephraim as he stumbled, and his hands clutched his blood-soaked stomach. Eyes widening, a rush of hands shoved him backward, caused him to crumble to the ground in a heap of bones and skin.

Except that heap was shoved directly onto the fire.

The three of her closest friends in this world had shoved her stepdad into the fire after knocking him over the head and all she could do was stare. As the smoke rose, they stared, transfixed as if all was right with the world now that the bringer of evil was frying like a marshmallow in a campfire.

This was the right answer. This was the right thing to do...right?

There was another sensation that they could feel as she did and do as she did. Much like Ephraim, there was a fog glazing their eyes. Their eyes pinpointed to the ground, no movement, no angry or frantic emotions dawning on their stunning faces. Only pure, unadulterated pleasure as they watched him burn. But she realized now that it was her. It must be. The second she wished for him to be out of the fire, he was.

Like her wishes were a command.

The three of them dragged Ephraim's body from the fire by his lifeless toes. Careful not to burn themselves. They were quick about it and moved out of the way the second he was out. He burned long enough to smell and charcoal, and the fire on his body eventually simmered to next to nothing.

An overwhelming amount of time passed. A weight was lifted as his life faded into nothing.

She couldn't count the minutes or possible hours The Four sat and locked eyes with a dead devil, but there he was. Lifeless. And they were more than content to watch it continue, to make sure he really was dead. Though, she thought some of this was her inability to release them because she was sure that's what this was. She had a brujera's hold on her best friends and she didn't know how to make them get up.

Is that something I can do?

"Oh fuck…," The words fell from her mouth in a rush.

Did I do this? Did I cause Ephraim to pause and give them enough time to do this?

This felt like the result of her wishes being thrown into that endless pit of other desires and requests. But instead of unanswered hopefuls, she was seeing the result of something finally catching one–and answering it.

The fog cleared.

Eddie shifted to his hands and knees, eyes clear

but now filled with terror and electric fear.

"No...no, no, no. This can't be happening. He can't be dead. He can't. This can't be happening to me," Eddie screamed, his horror rising to an unsafe volume at the possibility of being stuck here because of this. Always fearful, Eddie was seeing his nightmares of never leaving come to life.

She rushed to him, and her initial reaction was to hug him, to make him feel better. But he shoved her away the moment she tried. Her face crumbled in pain at the shove. His eyes remained downtrodden and filled with the prospect of tears as he bit out, "Stop. No. I don't need you in my head right now."

This is my fault.

It was the only set of words now repeating in her head. Her dread and terror were now rising to a dangerous level that was far surpassing Eddie's, and likely Lola and Tommy's too, who were both silent and stoic as they watched them. She searched the desert frantically, praying to God there was no one out there, that no one had seen them do the unthinkable.

Lola's cheeks were ornamented in silent tears, either in shock or acceptance of what they'd done. Tommy became unreadable. She couldn't make anything of his expression, only that he refused to meet her eyes as well.

She clutched her assumed broken arm and released more mumbled cries of pain when she did. But she couldn't leave it to hang, it hurt more to have it swing.

"Fuck, fuck, fuck...we have to get out of here. We have to get him out of here. We have to...have to...," She couldn't get any more words out as she stared at Ephraim's lifeless body.

"We have to call the cops, Raina," Tommy replied. He wrung his hands together and sweat glided down his cheeks. She could only shake her head.

"No, we cannot," Lola bit back. "We can't tell the cops anything."

"Why not?" Tommy snaps. "This was an accident. Defense."

"Because he was right," Raina interjected. "No one will believe us. We're just four kids from the projects, doomed to repeat cycles they gave us. So no, we cannot tell the cops."

Eddie held her gaze as he said, "No one's missing him anyway. We are his only family left."

She didn't know much at this point. She didn't know what their next step was, and her anxiety-riddled brain made it hard to think clearly.

What she did know was that there was no possible way they could cover this up.

They hid him; they shoved this secret into the Arizona dirt like nothing ever happened.

But they did, and I won't let them forget it.

20. I DON'T FEEL ANYTHING AT 27 . . .

It takes several hours to make Ephraim's bones disappear into nothing but ash. The fire isn't hot enough.

"I guess this is why cremation costs money. You need high heat," Eddie says off-handedly like it's a simple thing we are doing.

"We'll just need to put more. I'm prepared to be here all night if it means nothing can attach itself to these bones anymore," Tommy offers and throws more wood on the fire, another big sprinkle of lighter fluid.

Lola huffs and puffs off to the side, displeased at the transaction. "At this rate, we will be."

Tommy eyes her with displeasure. "You don't need to say something smart for every single conversation. Sometimes silence is best."

"I'm right, aren't I?" She asks, eyes bulging at his audacity.

Sitting on a random stump, he leans forward, elbows on his knees as he retorts, "Just because you are right does not mean you need to be so loud."

Frustrated, she flings a twig at him that he leans away from. "Stop being all high and mighty, Tommy. You're not the hero Raina thinks you are."

"I never claimed to be."

"I beg to differ."

"Can you two fucking stop?" Eddie intervenes, hands splayed to his side in aggravation. "The constant back and forth is exhausting, and it is no use picking up and discussing old shit no one cares about. It doesn't serve the goal here."

My eyebrows furrow. Lola and Tommy have always snipped at each other off and on, more or less playfully. With tension high, I don't suppose it's out of the normal that they are extra frustrated with each other. They are too similar in ways that they don't like. All the things they do not like about each other, they reflect on one another. I can see how it would grate on you when you spend too much time with someone mirroring all the ways you dislike yourself.

But something nags at me about what Eddie said. "What do you mean old shit?"

A secret exchange happens between the three of them. I am immediately suspicious but what do I say? I haven't told them everything about my life. I've been fairly quiet about my life since leaving this rotten dumpster fire of a town. Should I expect them to divulge everything from the last ten years when I haven't?

"You know what?" I start and wave my hand at them all dismissively. "It doesn't matter. Unless it's life or death, I don't want to hear it."

"Well..." Lola suggests.

"Shut up, Lola," Tommy interjects.

"I'm just saying-,"

"He's right." Eddie pats his hand gently with hers, calming them both with the simple act. "There isn't any sense in bringing it up now. It solves nothing, answers no questions. It is useless information."

"I wouldn't call it useless."

"Fuck, *deja de hablar*. Shut. Up," Tommy snaps, and it is so unlike him that I startle. My wide eyes are locked on him, concern wedged between them where the wrinkle never quite goes away.

"Do I...want to know?" I ask slowly, carefully.

Eddie shrugs and says, "Do you think that if you learn the worst things about us, it will make you feel better?"

"I'm not in the business of guilt, Eddito. So, no."

"Aren't you?" he asks plainly, no accusation, no insult. A simple truth.

"I disagree. I have no guilt when it comes to you three. My guilt resides in other nooks and crannies." I gesture to the bright flames before us, hot against my legs. "And as of right now, half of my guilt is disappearing into nothing but ash."

"Do you not regret leaving us?" Lola intervenes.

I scoff. "What is this, a fucking intervention? I joined the army. I moved on with my life. It was better for all of us, anyway. As long as my feet stayed off the soil of this town, then apparently, we were safe. I'm only here to rectify what I caused. After that, I'm gone, because to be terribly clear—I don't feel guilty for running away. I did what I had to do to survive, I did what was necessary to make sure I didn't end up like them. If you want to blame me for your lack of exploration of the country, or even the state since you Arizona-born and bred losers never left, have a party while you're at it. I do not care."

"Why so testy, Raina? They're only questions, ones we feel we deserve answers to. You left us high and dry, not even a goodbye. Left for dead like we meant nothing," Lola argues.

"Oh, fuck all the way off. Two seconds ago, you three were harboring secrets I know nothing about, presumably something that will send me into a spiral, and now you want truth and secrets out of me? Please, go happily eat some glass. I am glad to be around you guys again. Truth be told, I did miss you. Some small part of me has missed you every second since I've been gone. But I will not play this one-sided, tell-all, truth-or-dare type shit game you are trying to use against me. Why are you so damned insistent that I feel bad for leaving?"

Flustered, I rise from my seat on the stump, and I pace slowly back and forth. How long has it been now? A week? Two? I haven't taken my meds, and yet no real sign of Ephraim. Maybe I don't need the meds anymore. Maybe the meds kept him away. Maybe they brought him around. I rub my hands across my face, a groan escaping my mouth. I don't know anything or what I'm doing, and I can't see the clear line that leads to the end of this.

I haven't slept. I've barely eaten. But I am suddenly vigorous and alive with energy. I can almost feel the elated joy rising in me for no reason. Is this the beginning of a manic episode? Is this what I wanted when I stopped taking those meds?

"Are you okay?" Tommy asks quietly in my ear. I open one eye to look at him.

"Why are there so many missing pieces to this puzzle? Why can't this end?" The words come out with an unintended whine, but I can't seem to help it. Dark eyes pin me the way they used to, and I fold.

"Maybe you just need sleep," he suggests.

I shake my head. "No. Not until I know he's gone for good."

One of his large hands points to the fire where Lola and Eddie still sit, quietly watching our exchange. "Is that not what this is for?"

My head shakes back and forth, insecure and unsure. "I don't know what I'm doing."

"None of us do. Why don't we go? The bones are gone." He looks back to the pair at the fire for confirmation. Lola gives an awkward and out-of-place thumbs up, clearly intended to piss Tommy off. I know the bones aren't gone yet, but they will sit here if I ask them to. He ignores the sarcastic gesture and turns back to me. "See? All done. We don't need to stay here. Tomorrow, a wind will sweep through, and the ashes won't be here, either. We are getting riled up, snapping at each other. He wanted us to fight. He wanted us not to work together so that we would eventually give in to whatever he wanted. But we've won. We had the power the entire time. You hold the power."

He takes my hand in his, the palm of his skin rough and calloused against mine. I look down at them, our fingers intertwined like a pretzel, and it takes long moments before I realize that I feel nothing. I touched someone and was not forced to feel what they felt when I did not actively try. It was simple and easy; it took no effort at all. A moment of silence ensues. No words or bickering amongst the cracks of the flames. No more stealthy and furtive exchanges.

"Wow…," I whisper, stunned into remarkable silence. For once, I have nothing to say.

Tommy smiles, something sweet and sincere. "What?"

"I don't feel anything."

His brow furrows. "Nothing?" He looks me up and down like he's trying to see where the fault line is, where there might be a disconnect.

"I am as shocked as you." I return his smile, and then it fades. "This doesn't make any sense. My whole life has been spent trying to avoid contact. Avoid intimacy unless I actively focus on it and choose to send those feelings away. And even then, it may not happen. Why now?"

A light squeeze of my hand as he says, "Maybe you're stronger now. Maybe you've figured out how to do it without trying."

"Maybe these…gifts were linked to him? What if by destroying his bones, I'm sending this away?"

He cocks his head in confusion. "I don't think I've ever heard you refer to it as a gift."

"Someone has to," I retort. "Otherwise, I'm just the freak. A *brujera*, and people don't like that. It scares them. Which is fine, I guess. If people fear me, they'll leave me alone; if I'm left alone, I can't be bothered."

The words spill out all over like a bag of dropped candy before I can stop them, and I regret the vulnerability immediately.

"You mean you can't be hurt," he insists. "Anyways, you're the artist. Not a freak. *La reina*."

"I am no one's queen, Tommy. I'm a woman in her late-twenties with nothing special about her, who got lucky with a book deal and is otherwise, generally average and insignificant."

Tommy sighs and looks at Eddie and Lola. He waves at them, a silent gesture to give us privacy. He leads me away and stops a few paces from the car. With the fire raging next to our friends and at this distance, we are mostly alone. His eyes catch mine, and they drift to my mouth and back to my eyes again, like he can't help but let them wander. I swear his eyes dilate before they come back up to my own.

He swallows hard and says, "The story you created, the things you've accomplished? That makes you far from average. You are an artist. And in my circle, you are *la reina*. To me, you are everything."

I want this moment to be sweet, and I want it to be an example of the love I feel I should receive in some lifetime. The kind I thought existed in fairy tales and only in movies because the reality growing up was so much darker and sinister in nature. It's the perfect kind of reassurance; the casual way he drops his declaration of love, the way his thumb glides over my hand leisurely as he's doing now.

But I cannot pinpoint exactly what it is that is giving me the urge to sprint in the opposite direction. There is something too much about it. This could be my skepticism. It could be my anxiety and impending mania playing tricks on me, causing me to doubt the world and doubt reality. I don't think I'm going crazy though. Not about this at least—there is something wrong about him.

I pull my hand away smoothly and say, "Think whatever you want. Let's just get this over with."

I give a gentle smile at the hurt on his face, and then I brush it off. Until Ephraim is gone for good, until he stops plaguing every single day of my life completely, I don't need to involve myself in a relationship.

I didn't lie when I said I was glad to have them around again, but I'm not an idiot. We don't really know each other anymore. Save for Lola and Eddie, none of us have seen each other or interacted with each other in a decade.

We have turned into different people at such a rate that we might as well be strangers. Holding on to mannerisms, comforting touches, and sayings from our teenage years does not make that any less true. I can like that Tommy still feels like home and acknowledge that he doesn't know what ticks me off most in this world anymore. I can enjoy the ease in which we fall asleep together in the same house and on the same couch and concede that I don't even know how he takes his coffee or if he drinks it at all. Even if I wanted to know those things, I don't yet.

When my feet scuffle up to the fire after leaving Tommy where he stands, I bend to take up my seat again on a stump. I offer a grimace to Lola as my knees crack on the way down but otherwise say nothing. I don't continue any conversation, and I do not attempt to make pleasantries in any way.

I am silent as the remnants of my stepfather's memory turns to ash.

21. CÁLMATE . . .

The fire is still mostly raging when it's all gone. No more pieces of bone left in the bright flames that flicker and spark against the black sky. We're all standing together sipping on beers as the evening air hits us. Now that the tension is gone from earlier, it's smiles and laughs that join our easy conversation.

This is how it used to be when we were teens.

"I miss this," Lola says suddenly. "I miss actually having friends. You two left, and it was just me and Eddie. The people in this town are the same as they ever were, full of drama and bullshit. I was considering leaving."

Eddie finishes off his beer and tosses the bottle into the fire as he says, "That's a lie. You'll never leave. And it seems we have plenty of drama on our own."

"That's true," she says, shrugging like she hadn't considered our secrets were the reason she was holding back from leaving. She peers out to the dark desert where large saguaro cactus loom over us like guardians, waiting to show us where to go next. Lola soaks in the view. Maybe she's sending a silent prayers for this to be over, like I have so many times in my life.

A cool wind sweeps through, hard and reckless interrupting our peaceful night and burning our secrets to ash by the fire. It's as if the universe decided we were happy for too long. It blows my long tresses left, right, up, and down, until it is a tangled nest of dark hair on top my head. The coldness of the air thrashing about me now nips at my cheeks and fingertips, making them turn bright red. It's out of place in the heat of an early Arizona spring, and a stark contrast to the warmth I feel at my legs, secluded to where the fire rages far too closely.

Though they are warm to the touch, my feet feel frozen in motion. Minus the part of my leg that is playing cat and mouse with the licks of the fire. My feet are like frozen ice, so out of character for a desert landscape, and they cannot be lifted from the ground no matter how much effort I put into it.

Tommy, Lola, and Eddie reciprocate my bewilderment with matching panic. Their bodies also seem unable to move, likely feeling the same paralyzing trance that I am in.

Sickness overwhelms me, making me nauseous. A gagging sensation takes form in my throat, a devastating need to regurgitate anything I've managed to consume tonight, right onto this fire. It's too much for me to fight. Still unable to move my arms and legs, I start to heave. Long, choked, garbled lurches in my throat but soon, I am choking. Because it is not the tea from earlier or the beer from tonight making its way up my throat.

It is dirt.

Dirt is strangling me and wiping out all existence of air from my lungs. My vision blurs and tears are running down my face and neck as I thrash about in an upwards position, unable to do anything but cough and choke, and choke and cough. Over and over and over.

I can make it stop.

The words sound in my head like the first alarm you hear in the morning. The first to thrust you into reality from your peaceful dream world. This is anything but a dream-filled wonderland though. This is a nightmare. Ephraim's childlike voice from the exorcism is sounding off within me. Panic coats my veins in ice, taking over every vestibule like a blizzard.

A nightmare indeed, one I made just for you, mamita. I can make it stopppp.

The letters in the word stop ring with a pop at the end, like a fucking joke.

Just ask me to stop, Raina. Ask me to give you what you need. There is no need for you to die just yet. I am not done playing with you.

His lies snake through me like an infection, trying to convince me of its safety while it slowly kills me. Is that something I want, though? Do I want to die yet? Was my first attempt in the army just a precursor to my death here tonight?

Angry now, he screeches at me frantically.

Ask me to make it stop, Raina! We are not done you and I!

What an odd statement, loaded with the implication that this demon might care.

An involuntary reaction to the scream forces a small...help...to the forefront of my thoughts. Small. Barely there. Almost imperceptible from the panic over my imminent death. But his scream was so reminiscent of something I once knew, a screech that could force the darkest of acts out of me as a child.

The choking stops, as if I never had an ounce of

dirt in my throat. The sensation of dry, terrible tasting cake in my throat goes away. I'm left with tears flowing down to my chest like a sticky river, an instinctive reaction to being choked.

I am left to breathe freely, but every part of me is still frozen to the spot.

From the peripherals of my vision, I see a figure lurking just beyond the shadows. It resides barely over where the light from the fire is unable to reach. Like it burns.

"What the fuck is happening, Raina? Talk to me," Tommy yells with urgent intensity as he stares at me. He is trying to be calm. Forever the knight.

Through deep gasps, the words fumble out mangled and ugly. "He's...here."

Lola struggles against the hold on her feet from the corner of my eyes. She squirms and stretches as much as she can every which way. "I can't do this, Raina. I can't do this. Get me out of this, get me out, get me out, get me out."

"*Cálmate*, Lola. *Necesitas respirar*," Tommy pleads with her to breathe as I cough up my lungs from the remnants of my choking fit, and their conversation begins to sound mumbled and hazy to me.

The string of conversation happening between them continues, Spanish and English being thrown interchangeably but I cannot focus on their bickering. I can't give Lola the attention she needs or support Tommy in his endeavor to help her.

All I can do is see it lying in wait in the shadows. His prowling halts, his incessant pacing back and forth like a caged wildcat as he watches us. Preternaturally still, the slits of his eyes glow luminously against the black of the night. The outlines of his large hat are almost impossible to see but unmistakable if you know what to look for like I do. That hat has been burned into my memory like a brand.

No words have left Eddie's mouth since our feet were so abruptly cemented to the ground. His eyes are doing this same out-of-focus and foggy white to match Ephraim's unnatural ones in the bush. It sends a peculiar shiver down my spine.

"What the fuck…," I whisper, mouth slack-jawed and dumb founded.

"Oh, give me a break, Tommy, you aren't the White Knight in shining armor here to save us all." Lola is still bickering with Tommy, her voice cutting through the tension inside my thoughts like a knife, shaking her head in clear annoyance.

"Lola…," I warn, but she continues to pick at Tommy who is now looking at Eddie.

"Look at me, Tommy. Raina can't save you from me. She can't save any of us! A useless Brujera." She laughs like a hyena.

"Lola," I say, more frustrated and louder than be-fore. "Shut. Up."

"Wha-,"

"Shut up!" I snap, and finally, she does. Her head swivels towards our cowardly lion, concern donning her face.

"Eddie…," she says, alarm clinging to every syllable.

Eddie's mouth opens to an unnatural shape, so wide it should not be possible. The figure behind him gets as close as it dares without letting the long licks of flame dawn light on it. As it does, an awful, horrify-ing scream peels from Eddie's mouth. It's the stuff of nightmares, and since we cannot move and we cannot cover our ears, we are forced to listen to it's terrible, unrelenting sound.

A snap that could break teeth shuts Eddie's mouth tight. And gradually, like the words are coming out in cursive font instead of print and they are all somehow stuck together, he speaks, "Burning the bones was a valiant effort…one that, unfortunately for you, will not work."

No one says anything. We are all stunned into silence. It is speaking through Eddie. The same voice that left my mouth during the exorcism, the same to ring in my head, is now tainting Eddie's lips.

The thing inside him makes Eddie smile something full of glee, though it does not reach his white, clouded eyes. "Cat got your tongue? Oh! No. I took that, too."

Laughing ensues. Eddie's mouth opens and closes for a range of laughs, and it continues this way for achingly long seconds, Eddie's eyelids getting wider and wider as it does. No, it's more like a cackle. Goosebumps line my arms, and dread crawls down my spine as a result.

It continues, "Burn me to ash if you must, but I am not that easy to thrust…away."

I grit my teeth, frustrated at the lack of movement. With a false sense of confidence, I bite out, "What. Do. You. Want? Why won't you leave us alone?"

Eddie's head cocks to the side, rotating minutely inch by inch like the hand of a clock. "I thought it was made clear what I wanted from the beginning…since my inception into your lives there has been only one thing I've asked…"

Tommy gets brave and spits out, "Enough riddles, *cabrón*. Spit it out already."

Eddie's milky eyes search for the voice like he can't see Tommy at all, as if he is as unclear as the horizon during a desert storm. They lock on me for a moment and then shift to my side where Tommy stands.

Does it need direction?

"Oh-ho!" It laughs, sucking air in between each laugh like he can't get enough. In Spanish he taunts, "The Jock does speak in defense of The Artist it seems. Well, I am quite sorry to disappoint, but she is mine. And you will give her to me when asked of you. Or..."

"Or what?" I blurt out. "You sure like to talk. Tell us the origin story already. Tell us why you're here."

In a mocking display of disappointment, Eddie's head shakes back and forth like a petulant child refusing to eat his vegetables. His hair whips about his face and I notice then that he's sweating profusely, despite the cool night air. This thing is still making quite the breeze flow around us and yet, Eddie looks like he's standing in the middle of an Arizona summer. Is this what I looked like when it spoke through me those weeks ago?

"My love for you, *La Reina*, knows no bounds. It cannot be contained or withheld. You are the only need in my destitute life, and I will have you. The last time I had to go through someone to get to you, you killed him. I will not be making the same mistake again. Even so, you offered his soul up on a platter when you did. Your words, not mine." It smiles placidly at me. It continues through Eddie's mouth, "He made a deal with the devil and by burying him in such unholy ground, you gave me his soul to cash in on. You thought you were getting rid of an evil, only to end up with something far worse. His soul offers such sweet power to torture you with. Ephraim was capable of depravity, but he was not capable of murder. I have no such limitations."

Lola starts laughing now, though I think she means it to be sarcastic and offensive, really it just comes out nervous and uneasy. "So, what, you're just going to kill us if you don't get Raina like a hog on a platter?" She spits each syllable out like she's disgusted at the thought, and somehow, I am comforted. I half thought she would be more inclined to offer me up herself. As close as we once were, to save Eddie, I thought she might be the first to shove me forward for the sacrificial offering.

Again, the holes for eyes that are reminiscent of death search for the location of the voice, like it's hard for him to actually see anything but me. I'm disquieted by that revelation somehow. If he can enter our bodies and speak through us, why can't he pinpoint anyone's voice but my own?

My eyes catch the slight movement behind Eddie. If it is truly El Sombrerón, from here he resembles everything they say about him in the stories. Although I cannot see his face, his eyes glimmer against the harsh black with a malicious white glow to match Eddie's. The outline of his large hat is faint but still visible against the dimly lit night sky, and he looks to be wearing a large coat. Though I cannot see them, I'd wager he's wearing pointy boots as well.

When the milky white of Eddie's wide-open eyes lands on Lola, he says, "Yeessssss, Cheerleader. Offer her up for me. Give her away like a prized cow, why don't you? I know you want to."

My paranoia about my best friend's intent is confirmed by his words. I laugh to myself, annoyed and full of bitterness. "Why am I not surprised, Lola?"

She whips her head to me, "It's a lie, Raina. It's lying."

"I don't believe you."

She sticks her nose up at me over my insecurity. "Believe what you want. You're so fucking gullible if you believe that so easily."

Tommy interjects, "Look at me, Raina."

I don't. I'm locked and loaded on Lola. Am I hurt by my anxiety being made a reality? I knew this was a possibility. I'd assumed the worst of her. So, why do I feel so offended that she should act accordingly?

"Raina." Tommy's voice is strong. Commanding. I tear my gaze away from Lola. "It's a lie. A deceit. He is only trying to rile you up. Make us fight in order to make his job easier. You need to fight it. Don't believe a fucking word, you got me? Not a single one."

"Uh-uh-uh," it mocks through our friend's mouth. "I cannot lie. I cannot force one person to make facial expressions that give away their nature. I can only see what you truly desire, and that girl right there wants to give my precious Raina to me. After all, the alternative is to lose her precious boy, and she will not do that. Give her to me, and everything stops. Give her to me, and your lives will not become forfeit. Give me that which I desire most in this world, and you can go back to your ordinary, average lives without ever hearing another whisssssssssper from me."

"What is your name?" I yell as the wind picks up before he can disappear into nothing again. Before he can go into hiding and plan another assault on us when we least expect it.

The ghost white pair of hell lock on me. "I go by many names, *mi amor. Que hermosa.* You are so beauuuuuutifullll."

Every word drags out, and he whines as he says

them. I almost gag at the sound.

"El Sombrerón? Is that it?"

A quiet, malicious smile forms on Eddie's lips. "Among othersss."

We all fall into a heap on the ground together, crumbling like sacks of potatoes after being released from its grip, Eddie included. There are grunts all around, and I immediately sit up and stand as quickly as possible. I'm eager to see if its presence still marks the shadows but I see nothing in the distance. I don't know what I would have done if it was. Chased it? Screamed in its face?

None of those things, I realize. I would have been too terrified, but I like to pretend I'm something I'm not.

"Eddie," Lola cries, crawling to her lover and throwing herself into checking every inch of him. His eyes are clear now, dark green instead of pale white. She runs her hands through his hair and gently places them on either side of his face like she can't believe it's him again.

"I'm fine," he croaks, reaching up to place a hand on her face in reciprocation. His face shifts to face me and a small uncomfortable laugh escapes his cracked lips. "That was fucked. Like beyond anything I've experienced in my entire life. How did you not shit yourself the night of the exorcism?"

I look at his pants. "Well, it wasn't a walk in the park. You shit yourself?" I joke.

He shakes his head in the negative and says sadly, "It didn't work then, did it?"

My mouth forms into a thin line, and I nod, confirming. "It didn't work. And I don't have a fucking clue what will."

22. THE WORLD'S WORST HAIRCUT

I am standing in my bathroom, staring at myself. My chest, face, and arms are covered in dark brown and cracked dirt. I could have sworn the dirt in my mouth from earlier was only an illusion, but there's a gruesome brown stain on my chin gliding down my neck. I suppose it was real after all.

My body shivers at the unsettling feeling building in my bones. It's a leaden weight of a realization. It was too easy for him to make me choke on dirt that did not exist.

Holding the ice-cold handle of a pair of metal scissors, I balance it in my palm, relishing in the cold metal against my warm temperature. When I'd gotten home, we hadn't bothered to go on our separate ways. We all crashed in my living room. Tired and bent out of shape, it didn't take long after our eyes shut that we were all sleeping peacefully.

That is until I rolled over and realized that my hair was braided again.

So now I'm standing in front of this mirror, shaking and angry at the crack of dawn with very little sleep.

My hair is so long. I've been working on this length for years. Cutting it only for trims and never dying it, it has become quite healthy, and it flows past my mid back. I think it touches the very top of my behind, and I have a fleeting thought that maybe that's why he wants me so badly. I laugh at the absurdity. It cannot simply be an obsession with my hair that is the cause for all of this.

I'm gripping these scissors like they are the answers to all my prayers, a gateway to the light at the end of the tunnel. I'm hoping that if I do the thing I've been thinking about for the last thirty minutes, I'll be free.

Adrenaline pumps through my veins now, empowering me, giving me life. My eyes are rimmed with red and swollen. Every inch of me is stained with the events of the evening. Still, I am elated to see myself in the mirror now as I take those scissors and I begin to cut exactly where the braid starts.

My hair is thick, so it takes effort and more than a snip or two. He must have worked hard for this stupid braid, but now it won't be nearly long enough to braid anything. Two or three more rounds of swift clicks of the scissors makes it shorter with every slice. I hum to myself in relief with every lock that quietly lands on the floor. Every singular strand is exemplary of my anger and trauma. I cut each piece as if I can cut away all the damage.

A passing thought I have when a thick lock roughly cuts free is—if I wake one more time to braided hair, I'll shave every single strand off me. Every part of my body will be devoid of hair for him to braid. I'll be more hairless than a hairless fucking cat.

I glimpse another image of myself in the mirror, eyes traveling from side to side as I examine and consider the jagged edges of my now short hair. There was a certain level of satisfaction in myself for my hair.

In many Indigenous cultures, hair is a source of pride, something revered and coveted. It has meaning. I'm not sure I ever did that–I don't know enough about my Azteca ancestors to say for sure. But I do know it was one of my best features and I enjoyed having it.

Now it simply lay in a pile in my bathroom sink and floor, limp and lifeless.

"That...is the world's worst haircut," Lola mumbles behind me, and I whip around in defense.

The clang of the scissors dropping into the sink is a shock against the quiet. "What the fuck, Lola. Care to make a little noise before you sneak up on people?"

She leans against the hallway and props one leg over the other like something a book boyfriend would do. It's very cliché. Except it doesn't suit her as she is now. Maybe the teenage version of her, but the new, older model I've grown accustomed to over the last week. I can't understand why she's doing it.

My expression must reflect my thoughts of doubt in her because her face contorts into mild confusion. And somehow, this propels her into the very thing I think of next. I assume a better reaction would have been for her to cross her arms, roll her eyes, and say something snarky.

And she does exactly that. But I am not controlling anything. I am not pushing any influence on her like I did with Ingrid, she is simply doing. Though it screams coincidence, it does not feel like one.

My eyebrows furrow as she says, "I like a little mystery. Keeps everyone around me on their toes. Besides, you needed me for the support, so I appeared."

"I...needed you?" I ask.

She peeks around me, and she gestures to the sink full of several inches of hair.

"A girl should never cut her hair alone."

I cock my head at her. My heart begins to pound quicker. Every second that ticks by is another where I grow more and more suspicious of what stands in front of me. Much like Tommy earlier, I am unsure where this wariness stems from, but it feels right to be suspicious. When Lola narrows her eyes, I back away and say, "I'm taking a shower. You guys are welcome to stay, but I hope you don't."

Clicking the door shut behind me and before I can lose my nerve, I lock the door and turn on the shower as hot as I think I can stand it. I swear I can hear the click of the front door, and maybe even the alarm system sounding off that the front door was opened. Finally able to shake off that feeling of wrongness, I begin to undress.

I hop in the shower the second the steam begins to rise from the curtains. As the water runs my face, shoulders, and legs, I mull over my wide-ranging thoughts surrounding my new-old friends.

Lola was one of three people I knew best in this world. I trusted her more than most, same with Tommy and Eddie. At least, when we were teens. Since our new, reimagined history of a bonfire where we burn him completely instead of a burial, something has been skewed to the left about their nature and for the life of me, it makes no sense. Or am I just imagining this? Is my mind playing tricks on me or is Ephraim? Do I seem different to them, too?

I think I probably do. Spending a decade apart, it's a natural consequence that we would sometimes feel foreign to one another after years of acting as if we never existed.

When my hands reach to wash my hair, I realize

then what a mistake I've made. My hair did not make me who I was, but I have an unreasonable attachment to it. It is something else Ephraim has managed to take from me, something that was only mine that he finessed and stole away in the night.

It's not fair.

It's not fair.

None of this is FAIR.

The words repeat in my head as the tears fall, pouring out of my eyes as swift as river water. The salt of those tears quickly collides with the tap water of the shower. My hands come up to my face and it rests there as I pin the back sides of my hands to the shower wall.

I don't think I can do this. I don't think I want to do this anymore.

What I want most in this life is to walk away from it. All 27 years of my life have been spent being strong. I was undeniably durable, if you will, during a time when all I needed to be was a child, and I was not afforded that luxury. Is that not just the fuck of it all? I never even got a head start. I started on the wrong foot, a dollar short and a day late.

Among the ramblings of my scattered brain, I don't even notice when the door opens. I don't notice that the light has shut off either. Due to the crying and the eyes pressed against the wall, I have no idea that the light is flickering both on and off in rapid succession and that there is the outline of someone standing on the outside of my shower. An unmoving figure looming, completely and utterly stock still.

When my eyes open, I face the confusion of whether my eyes are still closed, but then they flash on, and I whip around to the shower curtain to that looming figure that was staring so horrifically the entire time.

My mouth opens in an immediate scream, though nothing comes out. It is an opened mouth scream and I stumble backwards. But there isn't anywhere to go, and my initial reaction is to try to brace for the fall instead of trying to stop the fall to begin with. I slip and slide before I slide down the slanted side of the tub and hit down hard on my ass first.

"Fuck me!" I yelp, rather stupidly. The thing behind the curtain begins to move. Slowly at first, like it wants to torture me. And I can feel the scream, a real one with my actual fucking vocal chords begin to form. Maybe my eyes deceive me, but I think I see the outline of a pointy hat against the shower curtain. A hand moves swiftly and suddenly, and the curtain is being swept to the side to reveal a puzzled and distressed Lola.

"Good lord, Raina. What is wrong with you?" She scolds me like I'm a rebellious child who did the wrong thing after being warned about the birds and the bees. But like any good parent, the scold is followed by support.

She shuts the shower off and ignores my naked body in favor of searching for a towel. Before I can re-spond, she is ripping it off the handle and wrapping it around me, helping to lift me up out of the tub at the same time.

"Do you really startle that easy?" She's trying to joke, shake off the fact that she wasn't lurking behind my shower like a psychopath.

"No, you freak. You were just sitting there lurking! Of course, I'm going to jump out of my skin. Why the hell were you messing with the lights? I thought you guys left!" I'm yelling now, pissed off and embarrassed by the fall. I point at the light switch, all accusation and finger-pointing.

She puts her hands on her hips and rolls her eyes. "I did. We did. But I came back, I forgot my phone and I didn't realize it until I was halfway home because I'm so dog tired. Also, I did nothing to your lights. They were working perfectly fine when I came in."

I adjust the towel on myself, uncomfortable. "What?"

She narrows her eyes in response. "I said I didn't touch your lights, Raina. Are you okay?"

Nothing comes out of my mouth right away. I am already suspicious of her, but should I be? Is this justified? I shake my head, like if I do it enough times the memory of it will go away and it never happened. But it doesn't.

So, all I can think to say is, "I'm fine. I think, I just…I don't know. The lights were flashing and then I turned around and saw someone standing where you were standing and I just, got scared I guess, I don't know. You sure you didn't see the lights? No one else in the bathroom?"

Her head bobs up and down. "I swear. Have you been taking your medicine?"

"Yes." No.

"It doesn't seem like it."

I huff at her and shove past towards my closet to get dressed. The army taught me a lot of things—getting naked and getting dressed in front of others without shame is one of the first ones. It's not ideal, but if she wants a show, I guess she'll get it. Or she can leave.

"How do you even know I take medicine?" I ask her as I shove a t-shirt on over my head. Pulling it over with rough and flustered movements, I grab underwear and slip them on as quickly as possible. A glance at Lola reveals that she also has no qualms about being naked around others. She is neither interested or disinterested. She's just there.

"The orange bottle was sort of a giveaway." When my eyebrows furrow at her, she continues, "On the kitchen counter. Bottle looks full, too. Refilled around the time of the exorcism, I think. You just gonna raw dog that shit and hope it works out for the better?"

I am more confused than ever. Didn't I pour it out? But I don't want her to know that, so instead I ask, "Since when are you such a maternal person? Why are you mothering me right now?"

"I always have been. You were just too busy worried about Eddie and Tommy to notice I was anything but The Cheerleader."

My hands fall to my sides, defeated. "That's not fair."

One eyebrow arch as she avoids my eyes and glances about the closet, her fingers doing trails along the clothes she passes as she wanders around. "It's fair. You don't want to hear it. You may have some preconceived notion that just because you're alive is enough but, Raina, you're not a good friend."

I recoil from her words. It is unfair, no matter what she says. "I had to fight to stay alive. It is enough. Besides, I was always concerned with Eddie, always. He needed saving every time I turned around. And Tommy...it was Tommy, I don't know." The last few words trail off in a mumble as I realize I don't have any good argument against hers. She's probably right. I'd wager I was never really a good friend.

"And what about me?" She asks, hurt surrounding every letter.

"You could take care of yourself."

"Why did I have to?"

"Because I was too busy trying to save myself, Lola. Not everything is about you."

She snorts, condescending and awful. "Right. Because it's always about you."

My mouth opens, closes. Opens again. "That isn't fair, either. I didn't choose this."

"Didn't you?" Her voice cracks, and her bottom lip trembles slightly. A miniscule tear begins to form as her eyes harden in anger. "This secret would have stayed dead if you wouldn't have come home. We would never have had to appear and gallivant around town playing the characters from a scary movie, hyping you up as the Final Girl."

"So, that's it, then? That's the bullet that you decide to take me out with."

She throws her arms up in the air. "I'm done. I'm done with this. I can't, I...no. I'm leaving." She turns away and begins her trek to the living room where she starts throwing pillows this way and that with her long arms.

She's still rail thin, as she always was. I wonder, for just a passing moment, if she still struggles with every ounce of food, every bite she eats, because of the way her mom would badger her about the number on the scale. Then I remember I'm the bad friend, and I shouldn't care about that. Even if I could, should, would care about that — it's too late. This bridge is burning faster than I could have ever imagined.

When she locates the phone, after several minutes of blustering, tossing dirty glances my way, she marches into the kitchen. I immediately follow. "Where are you going, Lola? You wanted it to be over. It's over. You can leave!" I yell after her.

As I trail into the kitchen behind her, I find that she's gripping my medication with a white-knuckle grip. The bottle I thought I'd flushed down the toilet. Or one of them at least, arguably the most important prescription. It's the one I need for my bipolar. The one I've been refusing to take because I thought I was a hero somehow. I thought I would think clearer. I thought if I went a little crazy, he would talk to me more. I would get more answers. And instead, I got radio silence and vague messages until I finished a job I didn't know I was hired for.

"What are you doing with those?" I ask. She holds the bottle out to me, palm facing upwards and a foot bouncing and tapping the ground like she can't bear the thought of standing still.

"Take them," she says with a slight hhmph at the end. Very patronizing. I want to slap her. But I don't. I don't do that. I exercise what little patience I have left and tell my intrusive thoughts to go to hell.

"Take the pills? That's your parting words?"

Aggressively, she moans in irritation and stalks towards me. When she reaches my side, she grabs one of my hands, and again, I feel next to nothing. Like Tommy, it's as if she feels nothing at all. She slams the bottle into my palm before I can object or reach for any feelings or flashes of her thoughts.

"Take the fucking pills. You haven't slept in days. You're not winning any battles by fighting what the doctors told you to do. It doesn't make you a hero. It doesn't make you anything but an idiot. Don't you understand that Ephraim wins if you keep doing this? You hear me? He wins if you can't fight with every brain cell you have left. It will only make all of this harder and will land with you in a situation in which you cannot crawl out of."

I look her up and down, locking eyes with hers as I say, "I thought we were bad friends?"

"You are, but I'm not. And I refuse to go down in this story not telling you what you need to hear because I'm a good friend. Take the fucking pills, Raina."

With that, she shoves past me, bumping my shoulder lightly. I hear the hard slam of the door, her inability to be gentle with something that is not hers evident.

No, that's not true. I'm not hers. I am not a thing to own or care for, and yet she does. She is everything I wish I was sometimes and nothing like how I imagined she would grow up to be.

As I stare down at the bottle, I grow frustrated and embarrassed. A pissed-off tear escapes my eye, and then another and another. She is right. I can't do this. I can feel myself slipping away off into the distant part of my mind where I like to hide when things get bad. It's where I go right before the manic begins, and I know that if I don't take this right now, by tomorrow, I won't know what I'm doing. I may think I'm talking to Ephraim, but I'm probably just going to be talking to the fence outside. Who knows what Ephraim will be able to convince me to do. Who knows what magic El Sombrerón will wield.

I pop the lid and shove a pill in my mouth, angry and rough.

I catch sight of Salem's stain on the wall as I lock the front door and head back for my bedroom. It's an uncomfortable reminder of how it all started.

A reminder of what he is truly capable of. If he wants to, we can all be bleeding out in front of our friends and family just like her. We can be an example, too, if we aren't careful.

When my head hits the sheets, it continues to battle the pull of the medicine, but I am quickly being lulled into a deep slumber. My body is too exhausted to keep up with my brain. As I'm falling, drifting into that beautiful bliss, passing glances at questions and answers skitter across my mind.

What does happen when you bury your secret six feet in the ground, and it just won't stay dead?

You finish the job and make sure it has nowhere to go but straight back to hell.

23. GIFTS

The music calls to me while I dream. It's strange, and awful and yet, I cannot resist it.

I think I must be dreaming because I can see the colors of the music all around me. The space around me is lined with lines and loops of violet, blues, deep greens and more, all intertwined and moving in sync, just as music would do.

My feet drag against the cold ground. When I look down, I see that they are bleeding. Did I step on glass? I must have, there are pieces of it in my yard for some reason. But I don't feel anything, I feel only joy and hope at the prospect of what is to come.

My gifts that await me outside are all lined up so wonderfully. How neatly he lined them up, one by one, tied together by their pack strings and ropes.

Reaching them, I glide my hand over each of their rumps, patting them lightly. The loud snort of an ass sounds, and it's funny so I laugh. Isn't that so ridiculous? Me laughing at the donkeys, and mules and horses snorting and lined up so perfectly in my yard?

I notice their hair then, braided. Every single strand is pulled into a braid.

Fear rises in my throat, and like it has woken something in me or whatever it is that looms about in the shadows, I am forced onto my knees. I kneel before the line of animals like a sacrifice as I hear his voice sound in my head.

Don't you love my gifts, mijita? Aren't they wonderful?

I can feel the shake of my head, or I think I do. I want to wake up. I want to wake up now. Please get me out of here. Help me. Someone help me. Someone slap me awake.

Eat.

"What?" I ask, shaking violently. Did I say that outloud?

Eat the dirt I have so graciously set before you, Raina.

"I...no, I don't. I'm not doing-," I stutter.

EAT THE DIRT.

I do. I do eat the dirt. The strings of that guitar are compelling me to do so, and I can no longer resist the urge.

Slowly, carefully, meticulously. Not too slow, not too much at once. But if this is only a dream, it is safe right? I can't die in a dream. And if I do, surely, I won't die in real life, too?

I try to imagine that it is pudding or really moist cake. If I can make myself salivate, maybe I won't choke.

But wait, why do I care? It is only a dream.

I am who I say I am.

I stop putting the dirt in my mouth. I resist with every ounce of me that can.

"Quoting the Bible is dangerous work, goblin man."

I never liked that name.

"Then that is who you shall be to me," I spit, digging my fingers into the dirt as hard as I can. I can feel myself waking with every word I say, every bit of strength I use to fight against the pull.

Give yourself to me, and I will make it stop. Eat the dirt, take back a piece of this land, a piece that belongs to you and join me. I will make it all go away. Though it is a shame...

"What is?" I ask.

They were my best work yet.

"WHO?" I yell, tired of the riddles and the games.

Eat, Raina.

I shake my head in defiance. I will not.

Eat.

"No."

EAT THE DIRT, RAINA!

I eat so much and so fast that I begin to choke, as you would. I am coughing and gagging, and I cannot stop shoveling handfuls of dirt into my mouth no matter how much I cry and fight it. There is no resistance left. I am still so tired...

"Wake up!"

No. Wait. What is that?

"Wake up, young lady!"

Choking. I think my vision is going to go black, I can't breathe. But how can that be?

I thought I was dreaming.

24. THE DEAL WITH THE DIRT

The splash of the water is what finally does it.

They tried to pat on my back at first, make me throw it up maybe. But it was the borderline water boarding that sent me throwing up all over the green grass, eyes wide, and violently awake.

When every ounce of my guts exits my body, I roll over with a grunt into the fetal position.

"Holyyyyyyy fuck."

Lola's voice is what I hear first. I cringe at the noise, my head in extreme pain from all the choking and throwing up. It physically pains me to listen to words.

"You okay there, missy?"

I close my eyes shut. Who the fuck is on my front lawn?

A cough. "I'm sorry, young lady. You were screamin', and your feet was bleedin'. I really didn't wanna interrupt any conversations you might be having, but when you started shoving dirt down your throat, I thought it might be a good time to intervene."

I freeze. I peek threw one barely open eye. "Dick."

"Yes ma'am," he says matter-of-factly.

"Not so loud. Please," I whisper.

He looks around, nervous and then whispers, "You

got it. Feel like maybe sittin' up?"

A soft, "Nu-uh" escapes my lips.

"Alright," he whispers again, so gentle in nature. And then he sits. Right next to me. "You really scared the hell right outta me. I've seen my share of crazy in my day, you know, I'm an old man. You see a lot when you live a long time. I don't think I've ever seen someone sleepwalk, matter o' fact. I've especially never seen no one eat dirt. That one was definitely new." He isn't looking at me, he's staring off to the side of us, presumably where I was doing the craziest shit I've ever done in public.

"Raina, you need to get up," I hear Lola say. I ignore her. My stomach is cramping so hard, it hurts to breathe.

"I actually ate the dirt, Dick?" I croak at him.

"Oh yes," he says at full volume, and I wince. "I was yelling and hootin' and hollerin' to get you to stop. I even kept shoving your hand away, and you just kept doing it."

I pop open both eyes now and look up at his hulking figure next to me. "What made me stop?"

He shrugs, like he is totally befuddled. "I guess the hootin' and hollerin' got on your nerves enough to wake ya. Suddenly you just crumbled on the ground and your eyes were awake, but I don't know I couldn't tell. So, I just went and got a bucket of water over there and started pouring."

"Mmm," is my only response.

"I have news, Raina." I glance up to see Lola still standing impatiently to the side.

"What is it?" I ask her.

At the same time, I hear Lola say, "Let's talk about it

inside," is when I hear Dick say, "What now?"

I look at Dick and then back to Lola again. "Not you, Dick."

He turns around to where Lola stands, like he didn't realize she was even there. "Ah, okay. Your friends again."

His head does that bobbing up and down thing that people do when they placate a child. Like ooohh aaahh, I get it now.

"What's wrong, Lola?" I ask again.

Dick frowns.

"Inside, Raina."

I nod, and I reach for Dick. "Help me up, why don't you."

I gesture to the house after the excruciating ordeal of standing up, and without much ado, he leads me to the front door with Lola trailing behind. When we arrive at the door, I shove it open and prop myself up against it as I let Lola in. My eyes trail her inside and when I look back at Dick, I notice that he is looking even more suspiciously in the area of Lola than he was out on the lawn.

"You okay, Dick?" I joke. He doesn't find it funny and instead offers an uncomfortable grimace.

"Well, young lady, I can't say I am. I'm quite worried about ya, although I don't know much about ya. You're awful young to be going through so much...forgive me, but, crazy stuff."

"My friends are here, Dick," I respond, just as Tommy pulls up in his truck. He gets out quick, slamming the door behind him and doing a jog to the front door. Maneuvering around Dick, he slides past me with a nod and heads to Lola, who I hear cry out when she sees him.

"I, yes, I can tell." He rubs his hands on his pants and wobbles back and forth on the balls of his feet, unsure of what to do next. His decision is made rather suddenly, and says in a rush, "Well alright. I'm glad you are okay."

With an unnerving execution, he flips around quick and leaves, waddling across the street and straight into his house. I don't know what to make of it, but I decide not to draw any more attention to it. As long as he is willing to act like the absolute craziest batshit thing didn't just happen on my lawn, I am too.

I shove the door shut as I turn and hear Lola's cries.

"What the fuck is going on?" I ask. "Why are you back here?"

Lola's red rimmed eyes bounce between Tommy and me. "You haven't told her yet?"

Tommy's looks guilt ridden instantly. "I was with you. Making sure you were okay."

She shoves her hand out at me. "He's her cousin, Tommy, what the fuck?"

I hold my hands out to the side, palms facing each of them. "Hold. Wait. Back up. What is happening?"

"Have you checked your phone? I thought your sister might have told you by now," Tommy says.

"I don't have a phone right now, Tommy. What is happening?" I am growing frustrated with the guessing.

There are passing glances between them. And then Lola says it.

"Eddie says he's going to kill himself, and we can't find him."

25. LENNY'S MESS . . .

Her hands shook violently, like a snare drummer's obsession with getting the beat just right, consistent with their rhythm. She drove his truck from Twelve-Mile-Corner after they buried their sin six feet in the ground. They covered every instance of blood and lit what they could in a monstrous fire. Her shoulder was popped back into place by Tommy's sturdy hands, but still covered in dirt and blood. She was a walking crime scene.

They erased every morsel of Ephraim's existence out in that desert, and she couldn't find it in her to be sad or regretful. Still shaking, she was afraid to step through the front door of a home once not-so-lovingly shared with her abuser and with a mother who turned a blind eye.

Lenny waited inside. Raina slumped against the front window and watched as Lenny sat at the kitchen counter. A cigarette hung idly from her lips, ashes dripping to the floor with no effort. That's how Raina imagined Lenny's parenting to be as well; no effort, minimal care, didn't take much to push her off the edge into nothingness. Just like the ashes of her cigarettes.

A deck of cards was spread out before her on the

counter. Her Catholic guilt abandoned; she played with other forces now, probably begging them to relieve her of the duties of motherhood. Raina glanced down at her bloodstained hands. Lenny would probably be angry that Raina took her love away. But Raina was sure she'd be more upset that Raina was the one to do it.

Once upon a time, their lives resembled something more akin to a fairytale than a nightmare. One where the mother loved the daughter so much that she took great care with her wellbeing. There were days where Lenny would comb her gentle hands through Raina's hair, massaging her scalp until she fell asleep.

The bad guys in their story, however, were made up of whiskey-tainted breath that whispered all the ways Raina trapped Lenny into being a mother again. They're made up of drunken words slung at Raina like a baseball that tell all the ways Lenny tried to end herself, in order to end Raina.

Lenny perpetuated a different confession to the world. It proclaimed Raina to be her miracle baby for nearly dying during childbirth, but it was more like a double-edged sword. One where Raina was the miracle baby for surviving that traumatic birth, and Lenny.

Yes, Lenny would be mad at the person who ruined whatever supposed dreams she imagined in her mania when she was young.

Raina's shoulder ached terribly, and she supposed there was no way to avoid a trip to the doctor. A visit where she would have to lie and cheat her way through convincing an adult that she'd done nothing wrong. Which meant she needed to tell Lenny something, anything.

The cold doorknob creaked as she turned it and

popped open the screen door, followed by the main door. Lenny didn't bother to glance up at her. She continued flipping cards as she refilled her whiskey glass, a cigarette still hanging from her thin lips.

Raina inched toward her in a monotonous plank walk, doom looming over her at what was to come. Lenny handed her a quick cursory glance only to give Raina a gracious double take when her eyes took in the scene before her. Lenny froze, hand hanging in the air as she prepared to slap a card down on the table, her other hand with a glass halfway up to her face.

The cigarette stumbled and fell into her lap. "Shit, shit shit," she said as she slapped it away. Instead of picking it up, she smashed her foot into the ground, grinding the black ash into the tile and took in Raina's image. Her eyes crawled all over, from the tips of Raina's shoes, now a brown color instead of black, to the red-soaked artwork of her shirt. "The fuck happened to you?"

Conscious of how she looked, Raina went to rub her hands on her face, maybe scrub some of the mess away, but they were trembling so badly she stopped mid-movement and placed them back at her sides. She white-knuckled her fists so hard she thought she might make herself bleed, which would be fitting. A masochistic blood-for-blood situation.

Raina didn't speak, and when Lenny took a step forward, she took one back. "Don't try to touch me."

Lenny rooted herself to the spot, chewing on a nail as she weighed her options, her long lashes fluttering when she took in the blood again. "What...uh," she coughs. "Who?"

"Why do you assume it was a who?" Raina asked her.

"No one shakes like that unless it's a who."

"Some people might," she argued with a small shrug.

"You wouldn't."

"You don't know anything about me."

Ephraim would have slapped her for that. He might have even followed it up with a snatch of the hair and a drag down the hallway to boot, too. But Lenny remained frozen in place as Raina asked her to be. She was not afraid of her mother, but Raina was often disappointed by her.

So, it came as no surprise that Raina was smacked hard by the painful disappointment when Lenny stepped near her, took a look out the window to see Ephraim's truck in the driveway and said, "What did you do to my husband?"

No response. She had to know already. Raina came home, he didn't. The truck was firmly parked outside, Raina covered in blood. It was a safe assumption that their contentious relationship bubbled over. Lenny moved in two long-legged strides in Raina's direction and stood before her, mere inches away. "Well, let's get you cleaned up."

Shock reverberated through Raina. "That's it? No other questions?"

Lenny turned away and snatched the pack of cigarettes on the counter. With lazy leisure, she lit another and blew the plume of smoke above her head. Very cool and collected of her.

"Why ask questions? I know the answer, and I don't need to know the details, or else I'll be culpable. Then again, I guess what I do next would make me culpable too, but I don't care. I do have one or two, though. Where's the body?"

Raina shook her head, "That feels like a culpable question."

"Indeed. Is it buried deep at least?"

"Very."

"Anyone else see you?"

"No."

"Mmm," she hums. Raina always hated it when she hummed. The way she did it dripped with disdain like she could see through Raina with every note. "I'm going to help you."

"Why?" Raina asked as she met her mother at the counter. She grabbed one of those coveted cigarettes and lit it. They sat together like matching sets of coins. One is a copy/paste of the other. It was like looking in a mirror, and Raina hated it.

"Because you did the world a favor. And I was never going to be able to do it. I could sense that he was evil, but I was enamored. It was like I couldn't resist it; I wanted him, and I couldn't walk away, or it felt like dying. I couldn't breathe, couldn't eat, couldn't sleep. I knew he was dead the second you did it because all those feelings disappeared. They dissipated into thin air like they never existed at all, and I had clarity for once in the last thirteen years he's been around."

Raina blew out a puff of smoke at her mother's confession with furrowed brows and dirt falling into her eyes.

"Thirteen years, and this is the first time you've had enough clarity to even consider walking away from him? When you knew?" Anger rolled through her as quick as the crack of a whip. "Lenny. You're such a fucking hypocrite, you know that? You can't claim some paranormal sixth sense being blocked somehow for the reason behind your faults. Just admit you didn't care enough to do anything."

She could feel the tears coming, but she willed them away. She grit her teeth so hard they could have shattered from the force, and she stabbed my thumbnail into another finger for distraction. She would not cry in front of her mother.

"My name isn't Lenny, *cabrona*, it's mom. And yes, that is what I'm telling you. Because you have it too, I know you do. Mine comes in colors like an aura around them, in the way I see and feel around people. Yours is through touch. I've known it since you were a baby. It's why you hated me so much when I would hold you."

Without skipping a beat, Raina retorted, "Maybe I knew back then how much of a disappointment you would be. Lenny."

Lenny shrugged like this wasn't news and there was no reason to consider being offended. "I begged the ancestors once to save me, when I was a little younger than you are now. I was in trouble and on *dia de muertos* I asked they help me in any way that they could, in any way my mother would not. Instead, they gave me magic that drove me crazy. I won't let it do the same to you. Load up, kid. I'm helping you bury a secret for good."

26. THE END OF THE ROAD . . .

When I came to Lenny all those years ago, mucked with mud and bloodstained, I was rewarded for my behavior with her random act of kindness. She cleaned me, bathed me, held on to the truck, drove it like it was hers, and lied to anyone who came around.

Ephraim was a deadbeat. He left us.

That's what she told anyone who bothered to ask, but truth be told, no one asked enough to make a wave. We really were his only family, and no one missed him now that he was gone. Though I hated to love my mother more than anything, I was glad to live in a home for a few short months that didn't live in danger, and violence. Although, there was still plenty of chaos to go around. It was Lenny, after all. Without a man to rely on, to blame everything on, she had to pick up the pieces and get me to eighteen. It was no easy feat, but we managed. Just barely.

She did die for her help, though. It was a big change; man gone, daughters gone, no one to support her habits. A secret that didn't belong to her but clutched tightly to her chest anyway. She drank herself to the grave while I was trying to survive a whole country away, and she took my secret with her.

Her death hurt, but the prospect of Eddie's hurts more.

A rush of emotions hit me at once. Grief. Panic. Regret.

"When we left here, he went home. Or we thought. He sent a few suspicious texts to Lola, hinting that he had a gun and that he was tired," Tommy says gently. "We think he might be at Twelve-Mile-Corner, but we wanted to grab you first."

"That fast? Just like that? When did you all find out?" I sputter.

"Earlier today, right before noon, I guess. I went by his place. He was considerate enough to leave a note, and the text followed not long after," Lola rushes.

"Noon? How long have I been asleep? It's nighttime now." I peek around at the clock on the oven. "It's eight at night."

Tommy shrugs. And Lola says, "If you took the meds after I left, you've been asleep for about 12 hours."

"You said something about a note?"

"It said, 'I can't do this. He's going to get us all eventually. One by one, we will all fall.'" Lola repeats. I know she has it memorized. She's probably read that note a thousand times over by now. I don't bother asking if she's tried letting the cops know. It won't matter if we all die anyway.

She continues, rambling and speaking too quickly like she's panicking, "He wouldn't do this. Not on his own. Eddie would never have done this without prompting. Suicide is not an option for us. We were going to make it out of here! El Goblin or whatever the fuck his name is, did this. He's going to kill us all off, one by one, like he said. Also, what the hell were you doing out on the lawn?"

I grimace at the memory and then recount it all to them. I tell them everything I know, everything I can remember. I tell them what Dick told me, though Lola was there for some of it.

"I got here when the water was being poured all over you. Not going to lie, my shocked-as-shit comment was not faked. I thought you knew about Eddie and maybe weren't handling it well," she admits, eyes downcast.

"I'm not," I tell her, because feelings course through me like never before. This is what it feels like to almost lose what you really love. "We need to go get Eddie now."

They both nod.

We climb into my sister's car and begin our trek down the road, near-constant bumps jostling us and irritating us. They never fix the roads here, and they cause such accidents. It's a wonder no one has ever died on this highway. Large potholes line this road for miles. I've seen semi-trucks lose an entire tire to one and send them flying off the road from another.

"I hate this highway," Lola says quietly in the passenger seat, squirming.

"Me too. It always feels...ominous," I say, glancing back at Tommy, who nods. "Always makes me sad for some reason, like a bad memory."

"Well, it would," Lola quips, giving me a side eye before she looks back out the window.

"Don't, Lola," Tommy warns.

"Don't what?" I ask. I hit a pothole, and the SUV swerves a little. "Dammit. I should have seen that one."

"Come on, Tommy the Knight. Just tell her already," Lola teases. Why is she teasing? Is she not scared for the love of her life?

"¡*Cállate, Lola*! It's not time," Tommy yells. His shout is so loud I flinch, and the flinch is one second too long. The largest pothole on the road is right in front of us. It's not but a few miles down the road from my house. I see it every day, and I should have instinctively known to avoid it.

Tommy's yell is too loud, though. *Too angry*. And I flinched. I flinched and I was driving close to ninety miles an hour. The tire pops with a horrific bang that makes my tinnitus scream, and the SUV swerves off the side of the road. I don't even have a second to brace. I'm only given enough time to overcorrect when I scream, and it sends us sailing over the bushes on the side of the road.

One giant sail and we hit our side, sending us careening into some kind of vehicle tumble weed rolling alongside the road.

There is a hard bang. Some of my body flies through the glass, and it's lights out. Long moments pass, silence ensues, and I feel nothing. There are whispers in the back of my brain, calling to me, begging of me to come back to consciousness, to run.

It sounds like Lenny. But Lenny's dead.

My body screams in agonizing pain once my vision returns. I hadn't worn a seatbelt, and the front half of my body is now through the windshield. I feel the warm trickle of blood going down my face and reach to wipe it.

"Fuck," I wince, there's glass stuck in my head. I inch myself backward, careful not to push onto anymore glass. But I'm bleeding so much, and I have an odd sense of déjà vu, like I've been here before. The combination makes me woozy. I lean back with a humph and roll my head to the side. Lola sits there, eyes wide and lifeless. "No...," I whisper, and move to touch her. I swear her skin is already cold to the touch, ice against the fire of my fingertips.

I shake her shoulder as I lean across, and my mumble turns into a yell, "No...no, no, no. Wake up, Lola, you bitch. WAKE UP! You're not supposed to leave me here alone."

"But you did."

Tommy's voice comes clear from the backseat. In my disoriented state, I forgot he was even here. I immediately reach for him.

"Thank fuck," I blurt out and lean to hug him, desperate to feel him for life. Right away, the tips of my fingers are aware of that sensation of wrongness that has been growing for the last few days. He's...not right. I tear away, and I stare at him. "You're so clean. Like you weren't hurt at all." I turn from him, but instead of Lola in the seat, it's Eddie. Blood pouring from the dark black of his hair crawls over his face and onto his chest. Droplets of blood slowly drip into his lifeless eyes.

Oh, fuck me, what is happening.

Lurching back from a dead Eddie, covered in the same bloody pattern as Lola, I slam my whole body into the door, and it earns me a painful shock to my head. I cry out in pain and clutch my head again.

"You left us here that night, Raina. Don't you remember?" Tommy says softly as he leans between the seats and looks to Eddie with a mournful expression and then back to me.

I reach for the handle, my hands slick with blood slipping on the metal handle, desperate to get away from whatever is happening here. When my hand finds a solid purchase with the handle, I yank on it, and I'm thrown backward out of the driver's side door.

Pain from the crash continues to wage war on my body as I hit the ground. I'm once again decorated in dirt and blood, this time my own. I crawl away, but Tommy's feet are impossibly fast as he walks to the side of me as I crawl.

"We were out here, all of us. You killed us, and then you left us, Raina," he spits. I swear I see actual spit land on the ground next to me. But I thrust myself onto my hands and knees, and I move to stand, ignoring his words for now. "You can't escape me, *reina*. You needed me to remind you of what you've done, of what we did together. You needed me to be real. So here I fucking am, *mi amor*."

My face contorts with rage, and a snarl forms on my lips. "I don't know what the fuck you are, but you are not Tommy. Get out of my way."

I shove past and begin limping my way back to my house. Something tells me I need to get back to the house. The house is where the safety is. The desert is a snare, and I will not let myself be caught like a little mouse in a trap.

I can make it. I know I can.

Tommy 2.0 follows me the whole way. A slew of accusations fly from his mouth like bullets to my psyche.

"You're lying," I say to it as I walk.

Tommy has now turned into a Lola. "No, baby. We were here for you. That's all we've done."

"I never asked for you," I sneer. Minutes pass, and I am almost running now as much as I can off and on. I think I'm still bleeding, or maybe it's just the blood mixing with my sweat rolling down my face.

Lola turns into Eddie. "You did ask for us, though.

You prayed for us in your dreams, in your wildest mania when you wished for us to come back. When you sat on that bathroom floor and stabbed at your own wrists, you prayed to whatever God would listen that you would go in exchange for us. You wanted us not to leave you," he says the words with such sad sincerity. They beg me to listen, but I can't. It's lies. This is Ephraim. He's playing games with me.

My vision blurs, and I can feel myself losing consciousness. I'm nearly there. I round the corner, and I practically drag myself through the yard and to the front door.

I look to *Not Eddie* before I open the door.

Falling inside, I say, "I thought I was the one who left you."

And then my body crumbles to the ground, unmoving and without care.

27. THE DEAL . . .

I used to wonder if hell was the version we see in the media and in church halls. If the walls were lined with gushes of bright red blood, and if the cries of the sinful would ring from every corner and depth for all to hear. But this hell he's put me in, it's none of those things. There are no cries from those who committed the worst of sins and those who lusted for those sins. Blood does not gush from anywhere, least of all me.

I am pristine. Cleaner than I've ever been. Deep inside I know I'm dirty though, or I wouldn't be here with him. I wouldn't be offered a deal like this unless he knew I would take it.

We stand beneath a terrible archway, reminiscent of something you would marry under. But it doesn't boast its beauty with bright flowers, and green leaves full of life. It's decorated with the burnt, crisp leftovers of dead leaves and flowers, with skulls perfectly placed and lodged in between.

A wedding arbor fit for a devil.

"There is something to be said about wanting to be the hero," he says, his handsome features boring into me, pleading with me to pay attention.

It's not right that he should be so good-looking,

but the devil isn't red with pointy thorns and a tail. He is tall, and broad-shouldered with chiseled features that border on angelic, a perfect porcelain figurine. He is stunning and he commands that I heed all thoughts in place of focusing on him. Why is everything so damned symmetrical?

"The hero gets the girl, or so they say. The hero gets the glory. They are praised and lauded above all others. But what are they really except a living, breathing example of our human need to prove we are worthy of a God? You try hard not to, Raina, but you have attempted the hero role for so long now. You were the hero for Lenny, always taking the beatings, always taking the abuse. The hero for your sister, taking all the blame. You joined a human cult designed to make you feel like you were a superhero to a nation. And yet, it was all for nothing. Not once did you ever feel like enough. Do you not wonder why it is so difficult for you? Do you not second guess your goodness? Your worthiness? It's all an illusion. If God existed, if he truly wanted to save you...he would have."

"You made sure I understood my worthlessness. Don't pretend like you played no role. God, it seems, is the only reason I'm still around. You've done nothing but remind me of why I shouldn't be."

He scoffs. "Oh, *que lindas mentiras*." What beautiful lies. "Ephraim was a scourge on this earth. He made this deal willingly because he already wanted you. So, we shared you. But it was he who acted. It was he who spewed those words, and it was his body. My end goal was his soul, something to feast on. Something to grow my power so that I could have yours... eventually. I simply provided him with the means to get what he wanted in the meantime. We just so happened to share similar interests."

"I was a child."

"Yes, and now you are not."

I narrow my eyes at him. "Are you implying that you raised me for this slaughter? That you stuck around until I was old enough?"

He shrugs as if his answer is simple and goes without saying. "I am not in the business of taking girls. Even a devil has his limits."

"Doubtful."

He shakes his head at me, back and forth like he is scorning a child. "Careful, *la reina*. You are testing my patience."

I examine this dreamland he has thrust us into in an effort to think of what to do or say next. The deep orange sun is setting just behind the mountains after the expanse of the wedding arches, and it lights the sky with vibrant colors of red, purple, pink, and blue. An astounding rainbow sits off to my right where it seems to highlight the endless miles of various cacti and bushes.

I used to hate the desert. I hated being home. But this place is more than beautiful, and I hate myself for the appreciative observation. I wanted to hate this place for all my life, but I can't deny Arizona's beauty.

The comfortable and cool breeze is gentle as it sweeps my hair to the side and out of my face. It's convenient that it isn't wrapped around my face as it normally does when it is windy, and it makes me wonder how much of this vision he can control.

A knowing and barely there smirk forms on his lips. He can hear my thoughts.

"Alright. What now? You keep me here until...until what?"

"Until you decide," he says, waving his hand and turning away from me to stare at the rainbow-colored sky.

"I don't like the choices."

"You don't have very many to choose from."

"Spell it out for me," I demand.

And he gives. "Offer yourself. Proposition yourself. Give me that which I desire so greatly, and your friends won't die. They get to live the rest of their days in peace, no more death, no more nightmares. I'll stop picking them off one by one, and they can dream without my torment and–"

"And me," I offer.

He closes his half-open mouth and hums a positive response. "And you."

"Then what?"

His eyebrows shoot up and he begins to pace around me, feline and predatory. His black jacket grazes my arm as he passes, and he tips his large hat down to look at me. His angelic features up close remind me that the devil was, to some people, God's favorite.

"Then...you are mine. I don't need to tell you anything aside from what will happen should you refuse. I will not relent. I will not go away. Each of you will die, picked off like a nuisance, and eventually, out of sheer pain, you will give yourself to me. If only to save what is left of the four of you. I know this."

"You don't know shit," I bite back. He circles me one last time and places his soft fingers on my cheek.

"You hold the power, Raina. You always did. What are you if you're not a monster like me?"

I don't want to give up, but despite all my bravado, I believe him. My friends won't be safe, my sister and her kids probably won't be safe.

I am not a good friend.

I am selfish.

A liar.

Manipulative.

Abusive.

But I could be. I could be a great friend.

"You could be exactly what they need. You could set them free, give them the peace they deserve. They need never worry about me again. They shall never fear my boots casting a shadow on their doorstep. All you need to do is say yes."

The words are smooth and simple. He offers the choice like it is nothing for me to offer my life in servitude or worse. He's right, though. All of this could be over, I could give up, roll over, and die. I could make what I wanted a reality, complete what I attempted to do in the army and never see light again. Sure, I'd live out the rest of my eternity with a monster, presumably being a monster, too. But I wouldn't be here anymore. And they would be safe. That is the most important thing. My life is not worth more than all of theirs combined.

If I'm honest, my life is not worth a singular one of theirs.

"Yes," I whisper.

"I'm sorry, what was that?" he asks, a saccharine smile that drips with molasses forming his full lips.

"I said...yes."

A full-blown grin dawns on his face as he reaches for my hand and drags me in.

"And so, it is done."

Then, he kisses me, dreadful and consuming, and

the final blow underneath the arches, our evil wedding arbor. Before he can let me go, I'm no longer asleep. No longer in this beautifully crafted heaven that he gave me. I'm in my living room, lying on my back. The door hangs wide open with the heat of the sun beating down on me. No one is here. My friends are gone, and I'm all alone in the aftermath of the wreck. They did not follow me from the crash, and for a moment, I panic at the idea of me having left them there.

The words leave my mouth, but it is not me who does it. I ask myself, "Are you not tormented by the memories of them?"

What?

Wait. My voice is inside now. My thoughts are inside, but it isn't me who speaks aloud for the world to hear.

"That's right, *mi amor*. You're mine now. I am you. A soul truly damned to be mine, a vessel for me to work through just as I did with your precious Ephraim. I work all your functions. Soon, you will be nothing but a memory to this vessel."

I thought I was to die and live an afterlife with you. I thought you wanted me.

"I did not specify. You assumed. Common mistake," it says out loud, through my mouth with my voice.

What did you say? About them?

"Your friends, *mi amor*. Does it not torment you to have seen them as they might have been? To enjoy their company, love them, as if they had lived to see the angles of their faces sharpen with age? Yet, it never happened. Their memories fueled everything, gave you what you needed. They were my best work yet."

It looks around the house with my eyes, and slowly gets up from the ground. They land on the wall where the stain once was. Nothing is there, as if it never existed. And Salem wanders from the laundry room, perfectly fine and intact.

It guides me from the living room and through the front door. There is no truck. Tommy never drove here. It shuts the door and takes me to the kitchen where it pours itself a glass of wine I don't remember buying.

"Don't be so surprised. Did your trauma not work overtime to ensure that you never, truly, had to live without them?"

The words are sweet and filled with honey. But they are rotten. Flashes of glass and the screeching of tires run through my head like a movie reel. My memory worms its way back to the forefront, forcing to remember that night so many years ago. Months after Ephraim died, driving with too much attention on Tommy in the review mirror and not on the road.

Every instance where I believed them to be real is slung at me like a harsh whip. Every car ride where I spoke to Tommy, held his hand, is shown to me from another angle where I speak only to myself, to a man who no longer exists. My encounter with Andrés at my grandfather's house is now absent of Tommy altogether. He never, not once, spoke to my sister. He never spoke to Andrés. Not really. Not in any way that would have encouraged a real response from anyone except for me.

Furrowed brows from the likes of Dick and Lilianna now make more sense than I ever wanted them to and it hurt. It breaks something inside of me I thought I had buried.

My mouth speaks again. "Rotten words, indeed. How much of it do you think was me, and how much of it did you make up on your own?"

Anger boils where I reside in my own head, and I feel the mental whip of it shoving me back down. It forces me to watch a movie I did not create. Me, driving us home after another desert party ten years ago. All four of us relieved to never have to worry about Ephraim again. I hit the pothole. The car soars off to the side of the road, glass shattering, their unbuckled bodies flying through the windshield where mine stays locked in tight. The only one to wear a seatbelt. Blood soaks their clothes and their eyes lose their light as the minutes had dragged by.

"Now, now, child. Behave, or I will shove you so far down you'll never crawl back up."

A knock at the door. It whips my head around, and I can feel the delight it gets at the prospect of spreading its own wicked means throughout the world.

"SShhhh, Raina. We are only going to have some fun together, you and I. You'll see."

It walks me to the front door, each step full of a swagger I never possessed when it was me guiding this body. It likes this. It likes being in a body.

When the door swings open, we find Ingrid standing there with worry and concern lining every wrinkle on her face.

"Raina! Hi. Um, I'm sorry. I don't...I don't mean to intrude. You never showed up for your last appointment, and I. Um." She's rambling, and her eyes go wide as saucers as she takes in the scene before her, how awful we look from the crash. It makes me cock our head like it's examining prey for the first time. Ingrid gulps hard, and I swear we can see goosebumps on her arms.

She laughs nervously and says, "I was having dreams again. And then you missed your appointment. I'm here just to check on you. No threats. No nothing. Just a welfare check. Are you…okay? Do I need to call an ambulance?"

It makes us step out the door, getting uncomfortably close to Ingrid. We can see the specks of brown in her eyes, and the exact length of her lashes. We can smell her perfume.

We like it. We can see the curls in her hair. They are tight and coiled more than we normally like, but we can imagine them…

We smile sweetly at her, and we enjoy the way she cringes in reaction. We place a hand on her cheek as we say, "Oh, hello, Ingrid. You have such beautiful hair. Please, come inside and have a seat if you're worried."

Ingrid hesitates. She doesn't trust us. But she nods, and with a small stutter, she steps through the door and takes a seat. "Were you in an accident?"

We sit as she asks us, and quietly say, "Yes. Awful accident. I may need to go the hospital after all."

"I see," she whispers. "How does that make you feel? Being in an accident again? I'm sure it has to be tough being so close to the scene of the last one. Are you sure you're okay?"

I know the answer, I know why she's asking to begin with. But Raina doesn't, so I prompt Ingrid for more, "Again?"

"Yes, don't you remember the accident? When your friends died ten years ago?"

I smile. "Yes, of course. How could I forget the night I murdered my best friends?"

Ingrid coughs uncomfortably. "I wouldn't call it murder. It was an accident, Raina. No one was charged, someone hit you, not the other way around."

We rise from the couch and respond flippantly as we make our way to the bookshelf. "Yes, but I hit the pothole. I was the reckless teenager." Our fingers glide along the spines of the books, inspecting each one. "I wrote a whole book about it, even."

Ingrid doesn't bother to turn around as she says, "A wonderful book. *La Reina*. Stunningly written love story, by the way."

"Mmmm," I hum. "Yes. This is the original right here actually." I remove the leather-bound journal, the worn leather smooth against my fingertips, and I gently offer it to her. Ingrid takes it and inspects it with wonder.

"Wow..." she whispers. "The first draft. I'm sure one of your fans would kill for this copy." Her eyes scan over the pages, and she flips back to page one. "*La Reina, Mi Amor*, by Tommy Morales...wait. What?"

I smile, but Raina screams on the inside as she remembers the feel of Tommy's fingertips on her cheeks. The sound of Lola's laugh rings loud in her memory, and Raina cries deep sorrowful tears in the hidden space of her mind as she recounts all the small moments she shared with Eddie as a child.

I take the knife hidden between the cushions before Ingrid can say another word. I grab her by the back of the head, her gorgeous locks held tight between my nimble fingers, and I slice off every inch of them before my stabbing goes wild and the cushions become soaked with blood. Raina's cries are nothing but a distant memory as the cigarette rests between my bloody fingers and I appreciate my own handiwork.

EPILOGUE: LILIANA

SIX MONTHS LATER, DECEMBER 2019

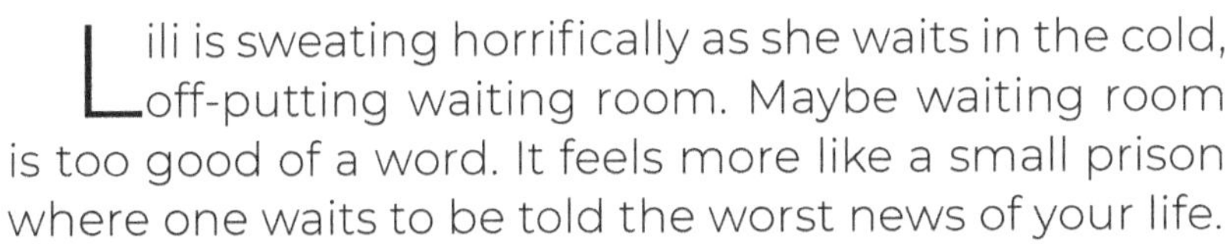

Lili is sweating horrifically as she waits in the cold, off-putting waiting room. Maybe waiting room is too good of a word. It feels more like a small prison where one waits to be told the worst news of your life.

Raina has been in this man-made hell for months now. One hundred and eighty days of torture for someone like Raina who could never stand to be confined, much less all alone. Her heart ached for her little sister, her person. The only one she really had left in this world. But there was nothing for Lili to do about it. The judge's ruling was clear, and all she could do was be thankful that her sister hadn't landed in prison for murdering her therapist. There were far worse places than here, she thought.

"Thank you for coming," the doctor says as he crosses over the threshold between freedom and the waiting room prison.

"It's no problem. Is my sister okay? What happened?" Anger was bubbling over. How could they have let Raina hurt herself so badly she gave herself a brain injury?

"Your sister has been particularly volatile, ma'am. She attacks the staff, and demonstrates extreme violence whenever prayer is heard."

Lili snorted. "Who is praying for her? And why? We're not religious. No one has asked for services like that."

He shakes his head. "The staff became frightened when she began to hiss and speak in, what some say is tongues, but it could also be mangled Latin. She frightened them into thinking she was a demon. Does your sister know Latin?"

"No. I think. I don't know," Lili responds, disappointed in her lack of confidence in her answer. "Can you tell me what happened?"

"Your sister has had to be restrained. But we left her legs free so she could still move around the room. She has no access to sharp objects or anything that could be used as such, so when staff last administered medication, she began to slam her head into the ground repeatedly. She did all this once the staff left and did it so hard, she cracked her skull and bled out on the floor. Something happened to the door, we couldn't get it open. It was a horrific oversight on the staff's part. We do apologize. We're still unsure what happened there but the camera footage does show them actively trying to get to her. I promise she was not left to hurt herself due to negligence."

Liliana sucked in a panicked breath, tears forming. "Is she okay? Where is she? Can I see her?"

The doctor swallowed, his lips in a thin line. "She caused blunt force trauma to the front and back of her head as she flipped over and rammed the other side into the ground once the bleeding began in the front. She is unconscious, and we haven't been able to wake her."

A trembling hand danced over Lili's mouth. "Oh fuck..." she choked. "Can I see her?"

The doctor nods and in quiet reverie, leads Lili to a patient room. One left turn, one right, and then Lili was standing before her sister's bed, her arms locked tight to the sides of the hospital bed and her ankles done up the same way.

"I'll leave you to it. Let the nurses know when you are done, please."

He leaves her with a quiet click of the door. Dragging a chair over, she sits down softly next to her baby sister. Her head is wrapped in bandages, and though she is extremely bruised and cracked open in various places, she seems to be breathing just fine. It's a quiet relief at the sight of her sister's chest rising and falling with each passing moment.

"What the hell did you do, Raina..." she whispers, more to herself than to her sister. She loved her sister more than anyone in the entire world, save for her kids. But she did not understand her and it broke Lili with the harsh reality of knowing it now. They may have lived life side by side growing up, but they had different hearts. Lili's wanted to stay here, to be happy and live a long life with her kids. To create something she never had as a child.

Raina wanted hers to stop beating.

Tears fell without restraint when she took Raina's hand in hers. She squeezed lightly, and though they were not practicing, she thought maybe the nurses had it right. Maybe Raina did need a few fucking prayers.

As soon as the words Our Father left her lips, Raina's hand squeezed Lili's back. Hard. And when Lili flashed her eyes upward, she found her black-and-blue and broken sister to be staring right at her. Her lips moved, and a mangled whisper tried to escape her sister's mouth.

Lili sat up-right and said, "What? Raina, are you okay?"

The harsh whisper tried to leave her lips once again, and instead of trying to make her sister talk louder, she leaned in.

"She's coming..." Raina whispered horribly in Lili's ear.

Lili reared back. "What?"

Raina's mouth formed the words over and over again.

She's coming...

Lili almost laughed. "Raina, knock it off. How do you feel? I'm going to call a nurse."

Before she could push the button for the nurse, Raina squeezed so hard Lili cried out in pain, eyes wide and shocked at her sister's strength. Raina's own eyes were unnaturally wide, and she continued to whisper harsh words.

"The fuck? What are you saying? Who's coming?"

Lili amused her sister and her delusions once more. One last time of pretending that her sister wasn't ab-solutely full of shit. She leaned close and felt her sister's lips tenderly grace her ear and she said, "*La Llorona...*"

ACKNOWLEDGEMENTS

As usual, I have no idea where to start or what to say first. I am nothing if not indecisive and require direction in many things in my life. Due to that, it is no surprise to absolutely anyone that the following list of acknowledgments is the only reason this book has ever come to fruition. Without them, and you dear reader, **LA REINA** would still be a half-written Word document on my MacBook.

In November of 2022, I started plotting and drafting **LA REINA** and I finished her in a furious haze of holidays and a bachelor program at Arizona State. If I am truly honest with myself, it began as a healing project. A way to take all the things that have happened to me and make them into a self-deprecating form of therapy. It blossomed into a story more people could relate to than I imagined and for that, this story will always be worth it.

TO MY HUSBAND AND THREE WONDERFUL GENTLEMEN, truly I do not think I could ever, in any lifetime, say my praises of you and your support enough times to really make it worth it and make it understood. You are the foundation from which I stand, and the support that keeps me pushing forward even when I have tried to quit. And there have been many times that I have quit. Jade, your unyielding encouragement while writing this book and becoming an author is more than I deserve. I chose you at sixteen, and I choose you again, every single day, forever. This book is dedicated to you because you exist in between all of the lines, you're the reason I continue to do this, period. You are all that makes Tommy wonderful, and the example from which all my MMC's will be based because you saved me. The world deserves to read about men like you, they deserve to be jealous that I have someone as wonderful as you are. (Lol) Tristan, Mason, and Leland, your cheers from the sidelines and the love that radiates from each of you are the reason I exist at all. I love you, forever.

PATTY, wow. What a year of knowing you and loving you. If you're reading this, Patty is why this book looks as nice as it is on the inside. She is so much of the behind-the-scenes of this book including interior formatting, absolute banger beta reading through multiple rounds, invaluable publishing advice, unhinged voice notes, and more. Patty, you are the decision-maker friend that I need in this author world. Without you, I wouldn't have a book to put in people's hands because I'd never be able to decide on a font. It is an honor to have **BOWL BOOKS PUBLISHING** on my book. You have rooted for me and shouted from the rooftops for me every chance you got, and I cannot imagine not having you on this journey. A sister by choice, an inevitable friend. No sabo kids we may be, but family now, forever, and in every language.

RHIANNON, my dear friend, what a pleasure it is to have such an incredible writer and creative in my corner after being disconnected for so many years. I am in awe of you, and **LA REINA** is better for having your eyes on it. Crossing my fingers that you don't realize how annoying I am at some point, because I'd love to have your advice on my books for forever. Thank you for teaching me what good feedback looks like, and how to do it with all the grace and love imaginable. You are a light in this community, I hope you know that.

To my editors, **KAT HOWARD AND JULIE K.**, in both stages you had your work cut out for you. And in both stages, you worked incredible magic to make me a better writer and creative. Thank you.

To my cover artist, **TYLER ROOD,** *tu talento y arte es realmente una bendición. Gracias por todo su arduo trabajo en esta portada. Ella es hermosa y estoy asombrado por tu trabajo.*

To my many alpha/beta/and other first readers including **BRANDI, KAYLA, SELBE, WILLOW, JULIE, KATIE, KIM, KYARA, JAZMIN, KAI, MADDIE, KP,** and more – thank you for taking the time, energy, and patience when reading such early, disastrous copies. Your unhinged comments and advice are some that I'll love and cherish for years to come.

MADDIE, my poetry would meet a bitter end if you didn't help me make it into something...suitable. I applaud you endlessly.

To the many authors in my little corner of the internet who have graciously answered every annoying question and inquiry with patience and kindness including **KARISSA, KAYLA, PATTY (DUH), RHIANNON, FRANKIE, JAE, CALLAN, BRIT, RAQUEL**, and many, many, many more – Thank you. Ya girl needed the help.

TO MY SISTER, the very one mentioned in the dedication – I know this book stuff doesn't make much sense to you, or rather, it's just never been your thing. But I appreciate the cheers and love all the same. I'm beyond fortunate to have you in my life, I can't believe I got so lucky. Every day I thank God, and Mom, for having brought you into my life as more than just a cousin as we were intended to be. I'd fight for you in every lifetime, I hope you know that.

To my best friends, **ALICIA, SAMMIE, AND JENNESSA**, there are not many things I'm sure of in this life, but I am and have always been sure of the three of you. You each have come into my life at various stages and every single time it is when God said I needed you to be. It's when I said I needed someone and didn't know how to ask for one. You are my people in all things in life, and like many things, I do not deserve you. You three are better to me than I ever have been for you. Much like Raina, I have found that I'm not really that great of a friend. I do what I can, and it often does not measure up. But, you each love me the same and I can't thank you enough. There simply aren't enough words in any language I know.

For the no sabo kids, this book is for you as much as it is a form of therapy for me. We are worthy, I don't care what they say about us. We're enough.

MOM, I know you're reading this from whatever plane you still exist in as you watch over me and my boys. I can still feel the touch of your fingers massaging my scalp, and I can still hear the timber of your voice as you scream for me and cheer in every audience I ever forced you to sit in. It is because of you that I have the drive and will to fight for a sense of normalcy in this life, and it is because of you that I ran to accomplish this lifelong dream. I know you can see this, but I still wish you could have seen it in person. I love you.

To the rest of my family, if you found yourself in the curves of these letters and the spaces in between the words – I'm sorry. I'm sorry any of us had to go through this.

To **MY READERS, MY HEATHENS**, from the bottom of my heart – THANK YOU. Here's to many more.